HUMBLE

HEROES

An Epic Family Saga Of Bravery And Humility

P.J. Lowry

For my wife, with love.

CONTENTS

ACKNOWLEDGEMENTS

I am enormously proud and grateful to my family who have helped and encouraged, and all played a part in getting this book published. Thanks also to Kathie for deciphering my handwritten pages.

CHAPTER 1

First Meeting

The year is 1985 and Peter Johnson is celebrating his 16th birthday. It is also the end of his school days, he has been at the local comprehensive, Grangethorpe Secondary School in Byker, Newcastle, for the last five years. Peter's family are not very well off so there is no question of him being able to go to university. His priority now is to find a job and to earn some money.

Peter is a smart-looking lad with good manners and has always got on well with his teachers and his fellow pupils. His job options are quite limited as he is only sixteen and Grangethorpe did not provide a good academic education. He feels he is qualified for not much other than manual work. However, on Monday morning Peter presented himself at the local job centre. He had with him a reference from the headmaster at Grangethorpe, stating that Peter was a very upstanding and honest young man who was very popular with both the teaching staff and everybody connected with the school.

At the job centre he was told to take a seat and wait to be called, which was not very long as he was one of the first ones there that morning. This was a very daunting experience for a sixteen-year-old.

He had no idea what to expect and, when his name was called, he looked and acted very nervously. The chap who had called his name recognised how Peter was feeling and made great efforts to make him relax somewhat. He said, "Peter, my name is Edward Parry, but everybody calls me Ted so that is what you can call me." Ted then went on to explain to Peter how the job centre worked and said he hoped that he would be able to get Peter fixed up in what could be his future livelihood.

Ted then went through the whole list of his current vacancies. He said, "I have here the names of three companies who are looking for somebody such as yourself, two of these I don't know much about but the other one is a very large company, a very good company to work for, with lots of opportunities for promotion. It is British Rail, which of course you know runs the whole railway system in the country.

"Now I am going to give you the names and addresses of all three organisations, but I would suggest that you apply to British Rail first. You should go to the main railway station in town and ask for the Station Master, his name is Frank Sharpe and he is a friend of mine, tell him that Ted sent you and see how you get on. You can try the other two companies if you wish but I don't know anybody in either of them I'm afraid." Ted then stood up and shook hands with Peter and wished him luck.

Peter phoned his mother Valerie to tell her that he was going to Newcastle Railway Station to enquire about a job and would not be home until the afternoon, but not to worry about him and that he would be fine.

On arriving at the railway station, he made contact with Frank Sharpe, the Station Master, and told him that Ted from the job centre had recommended him. Frank looked pleased and took Peter into his office and asked him to sit down, even offering him refreshments. Peter opted for a cold drink which came with a plate of very nice biscuits.

Frank took all of Peter's details, his name, address, and the school he attended. Peter then showed him the reference which his headmaster had given him. Frank was quite impressed when he read it and then went on to explain to Peter that there was a job for him, as a station 'Gofer' and explained what his duties would be and what his salary was likely to be, though that was not for Frank to decide.

He asked Peter what his thoughts were, did he think that this sort of job was right for him and, if so, when could he start. Peter said he was happy to take on the job and that he would do his best to carry out his duties to the best of his abilities, and could start on Monday next. He added, "Thank you, Mr Sharpe, I will not let you down."

Peter's mother, Valerie, was very pleased with his success on his first day out of school and gave her son a great big hug.

So, on the Monday morning Peter presented himself in good time at Newcastle station where he was met by a man who was dressed in British Rail uniform, he said his name was Noel and that he would be working with Peter for some time and would show him what his responsibilities would be. "You will have to wear a uniform similar to mine, we will get you measured up today and you should have it for tomorrow. Now come with me and we will get to work."

Peter showed great interest in his job and was very pleasant with both staff and the passengers that he came into contact with. This was something that was not missed by Frank who soon called Peter by his first name instead of 'Johnson'. This made Peter very happy and he thought, 'Well, I must be doing something right!'

Peter's ambition was to be a train driver but, as yet, he was only sixteen. He realised people of his age often change their minds as they get older. In any case he knew that he would have to be twenty-one before he would be considered for driver training so he would put all thought of that to the back of his mind.

He liked the idea of working for British Rail. It was not hard work and it paid reasonably well, also there were quite a few perks such as good holidays and sick pay after he had been there for two years.

The time soon passed, and he was now a guard on the trains which he liked very much and felt very proud that he had worked himself up to this responsible position which included checking the tickets of all the passengers. Also, his pay had now increased considerably so Peter was by now a very happy young man approaching twenty-one.

He now started to think of his original ambition of being a train driver. He made enquiries to British Rail as to what the procedure might be now that he had been with the company for four years and would like to make his career with British Rail. Peter was quite surprised and delighted with the response that he received and was asked to make an appointment with the chief instructor to discuss the next steps.

*

Helen Lawson is the first born of parents Andrea and Andrew. They are a working-class family who live in a nice home in Longbenton, Newcastle, which they were both very proud of. Helen is their pride and joy as they watched her grow from being a tiny seven-pound baby. At five she started school at the local school St John's CoE primary school. She now shares her home and parents with her two-year-old sibling whose name is Carol.

Andrew is an engineer with a gas company where he is responsible for checking all new gas installations, both domestic and commercial, to ensure that they are correctly installed. He is very proud of his new position with the company as he had worked himself up from being a labourer when he first started at the age of sixteen. Andrea is a receptionist at the local doctor's surgery; for the most part she enjoyed her work but occasionally would get frustrated at the attitudes of some patients who seemed to take it out on her because they were not feeling well.

Both she and Andrew are a very caring and happy couple and were very popular in the neighbourhood where they had many friends. Helen is now eleven years old and Carol is eight. They are both at the local primary school St John's which was not famed for its academic excellence. They are hoping that Helen would succeed in getting to grammar school when she did her eleven plus this year, but they were not very confident and were really disappointed when the results finally came out. So, for Helen, it was the local comprehensive, Manor Secondary School, to which she would be going for the next five years. Time moves on.

Helen settled quickly into her new school and soon felt very happy there. She made lots of new friends and got on well with her new teachers, all of whom treated the girls as if they were young women, so different from the primary school.

Helen was a popular girl and had many close friends. In her final year at Manor Comp a new girl, Marian, joined and Helen instantly bonded with her. She and Helen became inseparable. Over the years this bond between them never waned as they headed out in the great big world of work to seek employment in whatever may come their way.

Helen's first employment was as a cleaner at the Freeman City Hospital. She was not very happy there, but she was desperate to get some money and buy herself some new clothes as all of her clothing was very much school-girly type and she wanted to get away from that image. She had no intention of staying on as a cleaner, especially as the supervisor seemed to have taken a dislike to her from the beginning and gave her all the hardest and menial jobs to do. After she had been there for a few weeks, and feeling so unhappy, Helen thought, 'I must get away from here, but where shall I get another job?'

On her way home that evening, and walking past the paper shop (as it was called then), she saw a hand-written note on the window which said that a junior sales assistant was required and to apply within. 'Well,' Helen thought, 'should I give it a try? I have nothing to lose.'

The man behind the counter, Mr Miller, looked like he may be the manager or even the owner so she approached him and said that she would like to apply for the job. He seemed like a pleasant enough man and looked to be about fifty years of age. He asked lots of questions, "What is your full name and what age are you? What school did you go to and where do you live?" Helen answered all of these questions very pleasantly. He then asked her if she was working at the moment. Helen said she was, but not very happy with what she was doing which was cleaning at the Freeman. He then said, "If I was to offer you the job when could you start?" She said that she thought she should give a week's notice, even though she had only been there a few weeks. The man thought that was good of this young girl to think like that. So, he looked at her and said, "I am going to offer you this job on a three months' probation basis. If in that time we have got on well together it will then be made permanent." He then told her what hours she would have to work and what her pay would be, which was more than she was getting at the hospital. She thanked this man and assured him that she would do her best to carry out her duties.

Helen got on very well with Mr Miller and was very happy at her work and had made quite a few improvements to the shop over the three years that she had worked there.

One evening, after finishing his day at his home station, Peter was on his way home. It was a 15-minute tram ride, although at rush hour it could take considerably more. He got on the tram which was almost full and just managed to get a seat. There was a girl at the tram stop that also got on and sat across the aisle, right opposite Peter. She was dressed in a raincoat and woolly hat and did not draw much attention from Peter. Peter had his fare ready as the conductress came around and collected his 75p. She then turned to the girl opposite who appeared to be in a panic and told the conductress that she had no money, as she had left her handbag at work. The conductress was not very helpful and told her she would have to get off. The girl then said that she would not be able to get her bag as the workplace would be locked up and there would be nobody there. The conductress was adamant that if she could not pay her fare, she would have to leave the tram. When Peter heard this, he stood up and said, "How much is the girl's fare?" He paid the fare and asked the girl if this was the only tram she had to take to get home. The girl said it was not as she also had to catch a bus in city square to get home. Peter looked in his pockets to see what he could find. The least he could find was a £5 note.

The girl, whose name was Helen, said, "Thank you but I cannot take that."

Peter insisted and said, "Take it, and if we ever meet again you can give it back to me. My name is Peter and I am delighted to be able to help. I will give you my phone number if you give me yours."

This was the first meeting of Helen and Peter.

CHAPTER 2

First Date

Helen arrived home safely with the change from a £5 note in her pocket. She was completely over-awed by the kindness and generosity of the chap on the tram whom she had never seen before. Next morning, she dug out the slip of paper with his phone number with the intention of calling him later that day to thank him.

She made her way to work, spending more of the five pounds for her two fares. She found her handbag exactly where she had left it the previous evening. Once morning rush hour was over and the shop was quieter, she was having her morning break and decided that early evening would be a good time to ring the heaven-sent young man, who had rescued her from an embarrassing situation the previous evening.

By the time Helen had made contact with Peter he was just home from a busy day on the trains and he was exhausted. However, when he heard it was Helen, his mood instantly lifted. Helen burst into tears, explaining how grateful she was to Peter for being so generous and thoughtful. Peter did not want to hear any of this and was glad that she had got home safely. Helen then wanted to know when and where she could meet him to pay him back his money or if she could post it to him. Peter said, "Neither of those. The only way is if we could meet at the weekend somewhere and I can buy you dinner. So, think about that, and I'll ring you tomorrow."

Well Helen was now in a quandary and began to wonder about Peter. Was he as nice as he seemed to be, because, up to now, she had never met anybody like him? He was quite handsome; tall with thick dark hair, he was young and certainly very generous. But more importantly, did he fancy her?

Helen pondered over all those things and thought, 'I am not in any romantic liaison at the moment, so why not?' She then spent hours giving thought to her wardrobe, trying to sort out something to wear. If she was going to some fancy venue for dinner she would need to be appropriately dressed.

Peter wondered what Helen's preference in food might be. Would she like Chinese, Indian, Italian, or something English? To make sure he realised it would be better to find out. He himself did not care as he would eat most foods. After a further phone chat with Helen she opted for Chinese, which was fine with him. He knew a very good Chinese in Newcastle, The Lucky Dragon, and said he would book a table for 7 p.m. on Saturday and that he would pick her up at 6 o'clock. She was rather surprised about him picking her up. She wondered if he had his own car. Peter had not got a car and was in fact picking her up in a taxi and would also take her home in a taxi. He was determined to give Helen a great night out and to make a good impression on her and on any of her family whom he suspected might be curious.

Helen, with the help of her mother and younger sister, spent most of Saturday trying on outfits and taking off everything she could find in her wardrobe before she decided on what to wear. A long black pencil skirt with sheer black tights and stilettos, a white silk, frilly blouse, and gold jewellery. Having sorted out what she would wear, she washed and dried her long brown hair which was naturally wavy and glossy. It was now five o'clock and Helen was feeling a little nervous, so poured herself a glass of Baileys and waited for her date to arrive. When he did arrive, Helen was in a much more relaxed state of mind. The Baileys had done its job!

Peter was undecided whether he should go to the door or wait for Helen to come out. He decided on the former. He rang the bell and the door was opened by a young girl who resembled Helen but was much younger. Helen was not far away and introduced her sister whose name was Carol. Helen then said, "Come and meet my mum and dad." Peter was delighted to have met the family but not as delighted as Helen's mother and father at meeting this man who had rescued their daughter from her stressful journey.

After this ordeal Helen and Peter taxied off to The Lucky Dragon. Peter insisted on the full Chinese banquet, which Helen had never had before. With plenty of flowing wine the meal certainly hit the spot.

Up to now Peter had not commented on Helen's appearance, not that he had not noticed. After they had finished the banquet and were just sitting and still having some wine, Peter looked at Helen and said, "Helen I can hardly believe that you are the same girl that I met on the tram only a few days ago when we were coming home from work. You are so beautiful; I am so glad that you had forgotten your bag!"

Helen said, "Well thank you, Peter. I am also very glad that I was forgetful that evening!"

Peter reached over and held Helen's hand for a few moments, which she seemed to enjoy. They then began to discuss their backgrounds and what schools they went to and all sorts of things about themselves. After all, they had only met a few days before and knew very little about one another. However, they felt very comfortable with one another and chatted away as if they had known each other for ages.

Helen told Peter about the school which she went to. The local primary school was St John's CoE which was just around the corner. It was ok but not the very best academically, so she did not do very well in her eleven plus exam, certainly not good enough to get into the local grammar school. So, it was to Manor Comp, where she spent the next five years. This also was not a very good academic school so she did not do very well in her O levels and left at sixteen to start work before moving to the job that she was in now.

She then mentioned her family which she said she loved very much. Her parents, she said, were very kind and caring, as was her sister Carol who she got on very well with. On the whole they were quite a happy family. Her father, Andrew Leslie Lawson, worked for British Gas as a safety officer where he was responsible for inspecting all the gas installations. Her mother, Andrea, was a receptionist and worked at the local doctor's surgery. Carol, who was seventeen, was a very bright young lady and had done very well in her GCSEs and was now at Jesmond Grammar School and hoped to get into university.

Helen was beginning to wonder if Peter was going to divulge anything of his background. He had listened to her tell everything she could remember about her home and family without saying a word and with great interest. Then, when he thought that she was finished, he said, "Helen, I think that I envy you after what you have just told me. You have had a much better home life than what I have had. Even in the few minutes that I was in your home this evening, I could feel the warmth and the camaraderie that was present in your home. So very different from my home life. I cannot remember one happy day in my whole childhood. My father Roger was a lazy, drunken, and violent man who gave my mother Valerie such a horrible life. He was out of work most of the time as he would get the sack after a few weeks in every job he ever had. He could not bear to be told what to do and would always complain and moan to the boss why he should have to do any particular job when somebody else could have done. So, of course, he always got the sack. Then after he had spent the few pounds which he got when he was laid off on drink he would come to our mam and demand money to go and get drunk again. It did not matter to him if it was the last few pounds she had to buy food with. Then he would come back drunk at any time of the night and demand his dinner. How we used to hate to hear him come in, as there was always a row, with our mam always ending up crying, probably when he would have punched her, somewhere it would not be seen. My mother was such a hard-working lady. She worked as a seamstress in a clothing factory. Her hours were from 8.30 a.m. to 5.30 p.m., Monday to Friday. She was not well paid, but she was happy enough if her home life was right and if her husband had not been such a monster. Why did she never get rid of him or even get the police involved because of his violent behaviour?"

Peter continued his early life story while Helen listened with sadness. When Peter was about sixteen, he began to talk to his mother about going to the police, but Valerie would not hear of it as she did not want people to know what he was like. She just put up with it. On one occasion Peter tried to have a chat with his dad when he was sober about how he was treating his mother. Even when he was sober, he would not be spoken to by a young cheeky brat and told Peter if he ever spoke to him again like that, he would get what was coming to him. So that was that. However, Peter vowed to himself that when he was a bit older, he would stop the abuse that this monster of a father was inflicting on his mother. Also, now that he was almost sixteen, he would soon be starting work and would be able to help his mother out financially and in whatever way he could.

Peter's school had been Grangethorpe Comprehensive School. While not great academically, it was very good for sports, especially for rugby and karate, which Peter became very good at. Peter had kept up both sports after he had left school and was now a very strong and fit young man. His home life had not got any better, with his father still coming home drunk and fighting with his mother.

On one particular night he came home in a very bad state and became especially violent towards Valerie. Peter was not in the house at the time but when he came home he found his mother on the floor, covered with blood and all black and bruised and unable to stand up. Roger was asleep in bed. Peter managed to pick his mother up and got her on to a chair and cleaned her up as best he could, after which he got her a cup of tea and sat down beside her. "Mam," he said, "this will never happen to you again. I can assure you. You now have to go to the police and have this monster locked up and also get a restraining order on him which will forbid him ever coming into this house again. I know that you do not want to do that but I don't think that you can afford not to, as the next time he may well kill you as he has no control over his actions when he is in that state."

Valerie thought about what Peter had said, she knew that she had to do something because her life was certainly in danger. Also, she made her mind up that she would never share a bed with him ever again. Peter insisted that his mother should go into his bed tonight and then decide in the morning what they should do. Peter got himself a spare blanket and, after he had got his mam in his bed, he settled down on the sofa where he managed to get a few hours' sleep. In the morning, he heard his father calling for his mother, so he dashed up and made sure that she did not go into his room. He went into his father's room and said, "What do you want as mam is not very well this morning after what you did to her last night, so she will not be coming into your room ever again." Roger jumped out of bed and made a grab at Peter who just sidestepped him and had him in an arm lock and on the floor in a matter of seconds. "Now," Peter said, "after what you did to mam last night, you have forfeited all rights of being a member of this family. She has sworn never to sleep in the same bed as you again and, in fact, she never wants to see you again. So now what I would like to do, but mam won't let me, is to get the police here and have you locked up and charged with grievous bodily harm over a period of years. You would get years in prison, plus she would request that there would be a restraining order imposed upon you, preventing you from ever contacting the family again. Do you understand?"

Roger let out a scream and shouted, "Who do you think you are to be talking to me like that?" and struggled to hit out at Peter who merely tightened his grip on him.

"The other option is that you gather up whatever few items that are yours and get out of this house now and never return. Now, do you understand? You are not spending another night in this house, you are not safe to be left with mam. So, what do you want, as it is going to be one or the other – the police, or you leave right now and never come back here again."

Roger, the bully and tough guy that he was, now began to sob and plead with Peter not to do this to him and that he would change. Just then Valerie walked into the room. To Peter she looked worse than she did last night; her face was all swollen, her eyes were both black and almost closed, and her shoulders and arms all bruised. Peter grabbed hold of his father by his hair and pulled him to standing and screamed at him, "Do you know who did this? Look at her, this is what you did to her last night. You are a monster and do not deserve the sympathy you are begging for now. This is my mother to whom you have caused so much pain and suffering for so many years. What have you got to say for yourself?"

Suddenly Roger clutched his chest, let out a terrible groan, and collapsed on the floor. He never moved again.

When the paramedics came and examined him, they pronounced him dead. The post-mortem confirmed that death was caused by a massive heart attack. After he had been cremated, Valerie's life settled down to what it should have been and there was no great period of mourning for Roger.

Helen, having listened to the saga of Peter's childhood life, was now sobbing uncontrollably. Peter took Helen's hand and said, "Helen, I am so sorry. I have completely spoiled the whole evening. It was so stupid of me after the lovely time we have had."

Helen did not want to hear any of that and said, "I am so sorry for the terrible life you have had and I am glad that you have told me all about it. It must have taken a whole lot of courage to do so."

Now it was time to go home so Peter asked for the bill. Helen tried insisting that she should pay half of it, but Peter was adamant that it was his pleasure to treat this lovely girl. He had only met her a few days ago but already felt close enough to share with her his difficult early-life story.

On their way home in the taxi, sitting shoulder to shoulder, Peter wondered if he should put his arm around Helen and perhaps kiss her or would that be cheeky as it was their first date? Well Peter did not have to make that decision as Helen took the initiative and planted a great smacker on his lips! Having broken the ice, they were both very happy with their first date and discussed when they might see one another again. Peter said he would not be home until late as his job as a train driver meant that he would be on long-distant duty for most of the week but would be home early on Friday and could see her on Friday night. Helen was delighted with this and suggested that they might go and see a movie somewhere. Peter thought that was a great idea and so they said good night until then.

Helen's mother was just a little anxious until she had heard her come in, then pretended to be doing something in the kitchen. Helen knew, however, that she was just waiting for her to come home. She was delighted and more than a little curious as to how they had got on.

Helen and her mother were very close. She made a cup of tea for Helen and herself and sat down while Helen told her all about the lovely Chinese banquet which they had had and about Peter's mam and himself and the terrible life which they had with his drunken layabout father.

Helen told Andrea how sad it was to sit and listen to Peter describe how his father treated his mam over the years, she recalled how Peter had told her that if he tried to interfere he would be beaten too, so his mam always made sure that he was in bed before his dad came home. However, he was now dead and cremated and could never harm anybody again, so Valerie and Peter were now enjoying life.

Helen told her mother that her next date with Peter would be the next Friday as Peter would be working late for most of the week. They were planning to go and see a movie which she was looking forward to but even more so to seeing Peter as she thought that he was the most wonderful guy she had ever met.

Peter was also thinking the same way and was wishing the week away until Friday. Their visit to the cinema was very enjoyable for them, after which they went for a drink at a nearby pub. They were both tired after a busy week and decided to have an early night and meet again the next night.

Andrea was a little anxious that Helen was very keen on Peter and would like to see and know some more about him before Helen got really serious. So once again she was busy in the kitchen when Helen got in. She asked Helen if she fancied a cup of tea, as she was just doing one for herself, Helen said she would have one so once again the conversation was about Peter and his job with British Rail. She then asked Helen if she thought it would be a good idea to ask Peter if he would like to come and have dinner with them on Saturday evening. Helen was rather surprised at her mother's suggestion but thought it was very nice of her to suggest it and thanked her for it.

She would phone Peter in the morning and ask him what he thought.

Peter was over the moon at what Helen was suggesting and had no hesitation at all, saying he would be delighted to accept Andrea's invitation. Helen also was also very pleased and told Peter she would contact him later on with some details.

Andrea was very excited that Peter would be coming. She was an extremely house-proud woman, so it was all systems go! The house would need to have a complete top and bottom clean. Andrew, Helen's dad, was told to forget about his golf this week as there was so much to be done. He was not overly happy about missing his precious golf but thought it better to do as he was told.

Andrew was then introduced to the vacuum cleaner and given a duster, plus a whole lot of instructions to get on with. Carol was ordered to get all the best tableware and cutlery and make sure that it was all washed and polished.

Then Andrea and Helen sat down to decide the menu and then to go shopping. They decided that a very good joint of topside of beef would be the most appropriate, with Yorkshire puddings and all the trimming. They started off at the butchers which was a lovely family-run business and where Andrea went regularly for her meat. She mentioned to the butcher that she wanted the very best topside as it was a special occasion. They came away with a very good joint and then made their way to the supermarket for the vegetables and all the trimmings. Helen had phoned Peter and told him that her mam was planning to have the meal at around 7 o'clock but if he could come at about 6 and they could all get to know each other.

After the shopping expedition Andrea and Helen made their way home and were very pleased at how Andrew and Carol had performed with their respective tasks. The house was absolutely gleaming, even the tablecloth had been ironed and the table all set with the cutlery which Carol had washed and polished. So far so good. Everything was falling into place very nicely. Andrew had even prepared some lunch for the shoppers, Helen's favourite cheese on toast. So, for all their hard work both Andrew and Carol had amassed a great number of brownie points!

Now Peter was quite excited about going to this meal and wondered what he should take Andrea and Andrew. He settled for a nice bunch of flowers for Andrea and a bottle of decent wine for Andrew.

He was quite aware that he would be under close scrutiny by Helen's parents and probably to a lesser degree by Helen and her younger sister, Carol, so he must be on his very best behaviour and not have too much to drink, especially after what he had told Helen about his father.

So the day went on. Andrea and Helen were busy preparing everything for the dinner at seven. By 5 o'clock everything was ready and looking very good. Then it was time to get dressed. Andrea told Andrew what shirt he should put on. After Helen had got herself dressed and was happy with how she looked, she started to get some drinks organised. She had bought a nice bottle of chardonnay which was in the fridge along with some other bottles of wine, all nicely chilled. She also managed to squeeze in a few bottles of beer she knew her dad liked.

Right on time the doorbell rang, and Peter presented himself, looking very smart indeed. Helen opened the door, giving him a peck on the cheek, and took him into the lounge where the rest of the family were waiting.

Peter offered Andrea the flowers and Andrew the wine. He had also bought a box of chocolates for Helen to share with Carol. Carol was completely charmed. The generous gifts were very gratefully received by all. Helen opened the bottle of Chardonnay and everybody accepted a glass.

Andrea could not spend much time chatting right now, as she was in charge in the kitchen. She wanted to be sure the dinner would be perfect.

Happily Andrew and Peter got on very well, finding that they had a whole lot in common. Initially Peter was not sure how he should address Helen's parents, so to be on the safe side he started formally with "Mr Lawson". Andrew soon put him right, saying, "Don't call me that, Peter. My name is Andrew or Andy if you wish. And my wife's name is Andrea so please call us that."

Helen really wanted to be in the kitchen with her mam, helping with the dinner, but she had told Andrea that she would just stay for a while and see if there were any awkward moments when nobody had anything to say so she could butt in with something and get them going again. But no such quiet moments appeared – there was non-stop chat and especially as Peter was careful to include Carol in everything. Helen then topped up their glasses, including her own and Andrea's, and was delighted with how things were progressing and said she would see how things were getting on in the kitchen.

The dinner was a great success and enjoyed by all. Andrea was pleased with the beef which she had done to perfection – a lovely shade of pink when sliced. Also, all of the vegetables and Yorkshire puds were greatly appreciated as was the homemade apple crumble and custard. After this feast, which lasted about three hours, everybody, including Peter, helped with the washing up which was done very quickly. They then sat around the table again and had some more wine and chatted about everything, except the weather!

Andrea, forever the diplomat, at 11 o'clock told Andrew and Carol it was bedtime. Peter and Helen went back into the lounge and sat on the settee. Peter said it was the best night that he had ever had and that the dinner and conversation was so lovely. He asked Helen to please pass on his comments to Andrea and Andrew. They then settled down for a kiss and cuddle session.

It was still less than a week since Peter had saved Helen from being thrown off the tram because she had forgotten her bag and had no money to pay her fare. Such a lot had happened in that time and, judging by how things were going, it could just be the beginning.

CHAPTER 3

Peter's Approval

Peter was still living at home with his mother. It was now a much happier house. Valerie had made a new life for herself and a whole lot of new friends. She was only 54 years of age and had recently met a chap who was in a very similar situation to hers, except that he had just been divorced from his wife. They had two grown-up children, both of whom had now left home. The divorce came about after he found out that she was having an affair and had been for two years. This chap's name was Martin Brian Jackson.

Martin was two years older than Valerie. They got on very well in the short time they had known one another. However, she was not rushing into a serious relationship this time after her life with Roger. So, at the moment their relationship was purely platonic and would remain so until she got to know much more about Martin and his background. She had told him about her son Peter and how he had looked after her and how he was such a lovely and caring young man, who was almost twenty-one. Martin said he would like to meet him and suggested that he would love to take Valerie and Peter out to dinner one evening. Up to now Valerie had not told Peter about Martin, so she told him that she would think about it and let him know.

Whilst having their evening meal Valerie decided this was a good time to break the news to Peter. Coincidentally, Peter decided that it was time he told his mother about Helen. They were both a little bit on edge as to how to break the ice. Valerie took the plunge. "Peter," she said, "I have something to tell you. In the club, where I go occasionally with my friends Jane and Sandra, I have met a chap who is paying me a lot of attention and who seems quite nice. He is about my age and is such good company. We have chatted at length on a couple of occasions and he has told me quite a bit about his life. He has quite recently been divorced from his wife who he found was having an affair with another man for about two years. They have two grown-up daughters, both of whom have now left home. He has left me in no doubt that he is now trying to get his life back on track and settle down with somebody of a similar age and in a permanent relationship, which means marriage. He told me he lives in a nice house on a good road. The mortgage is almost paid off, plus he has a good job with the local council as a civil engineer. As you know, Peter, I am 54 years of age and it can be a lonely life on my own. However, as you well know after the life that I had with your father, I am very reluctant to get involved with another man so please don't worry, I am not rushing into anything until I am doubly sure."

Valerie went on to tell Peter what she had told Martin of their life, that she was a widow with a son who is almost twenty-one and that her husband died suddenly two years ago but no other details. She added that Martin wanted to meet Peter and was planning to take them both out to dinner.

Peter was delighted that his mother was seriously thinking of getting married again, as at fifty-four years of age she was still quite a young woman. However, was Martin the right man? Possibly, but as mam said, she would have to be sure. He thought it was a very good idea that Martin had suggested an evening out together.

Valerie was very much relieved at having told Peter about Martin and at how he had taken the news and said that she would arrange with Martin when and where.

Peter decided not to tell his mother about Helen just yet as she had enough to think about now. He told Valerie that he would be working late all week and would not be available before Friday so if she could arrange with Martin for then he would be very happy to go along with them.

So Valerie spoke to Martin and everything was arranged for Friday evening at the local Italian restaurant, Da Marios, at 7.30 p.m. Martin was there in good time and was having a glass of wine for himself when Valerie and Peter arrived. The introductions did not take long and then the waiter, Luigi, showed them to their table and took their order for drinks, which both Valerie and Peter were ready for. They were then handed the menu and Martin told them that this was his treat and to order anything they fancied on the menu. Valerie and Peter did not want to order very expensive items and declared that they did not want any starters, but Martin insisted.

Martin knew that he was being scrutinised by Valerie and Peter and likewise Martin was keeping account of what he thought of his two guests.

However, the meal was extremely good and was enjoyed by all three of them. The conversation flowed easily, much to Valerie's relief.

By the time that the meal was over, Martin and Peter were chatting away very comfortably as if they had known one another for years. Peter told him that worked for British Rail as a train guard but that when he turned twenty-one he was going to train to be a train driver. He also told Martin that he left school at sixteen as his parents could not afford to send him to college, so he had no choice but to start work and bring some money home. Valerie watched and listened with great interest and indeed great pleasure at how they were getting on and seemed to be enjoying one another's company. It was now getting late; they had been in there for hours. Peter said he had enjoyed the meal and the company very much and thanked Martin for his generosity.

He then got rather serious and told Martin that, as he was the only offspring of his mam and dad, he felt that he had a great responsibility to look after his mother whom he loved dearly.

He then said, "I don't know if you know, Martin, but my mam does not have many happy memories of her marriage with my dad. From what mam has told me you have had a rather unpleasant end to your marriage. Now you both appear to be of similar age and, if I may say so, both anxious to get your lives back on track. This is something which you are entitled to. I don't wish to appear to be your mentor, because in that regard I am totally out of my depth, however, what I will say is this. Together you make a very handsome couple and I think that I can detect certain chemistry between you. So, my advice to you both is don't rush into anything, get to know one another properly. Go around together, have fun, get together with your friends. Then, and only then, should you both feel happy and secure in one another's company should you think about marriage."

Valerie looked at Martin and they both smiled, then Martin said, "Peter, what you have just said, and the manner in which you have said it, is something which I will never forget. Your advice is something you may hear from somebody double or even treble your age and not from somebody not quite twenty-one years of age. Now if Valerie is happy to follow your advice I certainly am, and I am sure that together we will have some great times."

*

The following day, Peter wanted to meet up with his friends and asked Helen if she would like to contact some of her friends and come along to ten-pin bowling alley where they would all have some fun.

Peter's idea for this was that he and Helen would get to know each other's friends. Helen thought it was a very good idea as she was beginning to feel guilty that she was not keeping in contact as much with her close friends as she should. She had not even seen her best friend Marian for months, although that was because Marian also had a new boyfriend, Jordy, who Helen had yet to meet. So, in all there were twelve, six couples, at the bowling with lots of laughter as well as lots of good humoured criticism at the quality of the bowling! When their session had finished, they all went for a drink and enjoyed a nice couple of hours all getting to know one another. Peter was very happy at how the night turned out and was thanked by all for organising it.

Peter was anxious to establish himself as number one contender for Helen's affections and now embarked on a serious courtship. So, unless he was working late, they would see one another a few times every week either at Helen's house or watching a movie at the Odeon. As the weeks and months went by, their friendship grew and they began to fall very much in love with one another.

They were now both nearing their 21st birthdays as there were only a few days between them, Peter's being first.

They discussed between themselves the idea of having a joint party, thinking it would be the most practical way to celebrate it. They discussed the idea with Helen's parents who thought it was a very good idea if Peter's mother agreed, it would be a great opportunity to meet and to get to know one another.

Valerie was pleased with the idea. She had met Helen on a few occasions and had heard all about Peter and Helen's remarkable first meeting. From what she had seen of Helen, she thought she was a very nice young girl and secretly hoped that Peter and Helen would make their lives together.

With everybody happy about the joint celebrations, Helen and Peter decided on a venue and set the date. Needless to say, the party was a great success, a perfect gathering of friends and families.

CHAPTER 4

Childhood Sweethearts

With Peter's 21st birthday behind him, he was now eligible for his driver training. He approached the training centre to find out what the procedure would be. Unfortunately, the centre was quite a distance away in Manchester which meant that he would not be able to get home every night. For the first four weeks he would have to spend three days at the centre each week, from 9.30 a.m. to 4.30 p.m. each day without ever seeing a train.

First, he was to be taught all about the workings of a railway, including the safety procedures which were paramount and to be observed at all times. Then the signals and signalling which all drivers must be familiar with, plus a number of other matters which a lay person would never know about. At the end of the four weeks the applicants would have to sit an exam to establish if they had taken on-board all which they had been taught. If they had not, they would start all over again for another four weeks, at their own expense; it was vitally important to Peter that he passed first time.

After they had passed, the trainees would be put on an actual passenger train accompanied by a fully qualified driver to observe and appreciate the great responsibility that train drivers had on their shoulders when they drove a high-speed train. Only after two weeks would the trainee be allowed to sit in the driver's seat and actually drive.

At home with his mother, Peter was delighted to see Valerie so happy, he could not remember ever seeing her like this. It seemed like she and Martin really were made for each other. Sometimes on a Friday night, if Peter was not working late, Valerie would have Martin over for dinner and all three of them would sit down together and enjoy a lovely meal over a bottle of wine. This was something which never happened when Roger was alive.

Peter began to think that his mother and Martin were in love with each other. They had been seeing one another for about six months so it was reasonable to think they might now be thinking of getting married in the next year or so. He and Martin had become like father and son with a very comfortable relationship, something he had never had with Roger.

Peter began thinking of himself and Helen. They had now been going out with each other for eight months, Peter was coming near to the end of his train driver training and his finances would be more secure, so there was no reason why they should not be making a long-term plan. Maybe they should now be thinking of making a commitment, getting engaged, hopefully getting married a year after?

Next day was Saturday and an evening together had already been planned. Peter made up his mind, he was going to surprise Helen!

*

In her first year at primary school Helen had developed a crush on a boy called Jordan Howard. Jordan had similar feelings for Helen. They would always be seen together during play time going to and coming from school. They were inseparable – even after they had both left primary school and went to different secondary schools,

Helen to the local comprehensive and Jordan to grammar school.

Neither set of parents encouraged this relationship, which they thought would fade out, especially now they were at different schools. This did not appear to be happening and Jordan's end of year exams were very disappointing. As a result, Jordan's parents forbade him from seeing "that girl Helen" again. She was at a comprehensive school and "exam results were probably not important to her" and certainly would not be going to university as Jordan's parents hoped that he would. So, Jordan reluctantly had to tell Helen that he was not allowed to see her anymore and they would both have to come to terms with that.

They were both very unhappy about what was being imposed on them but felt they could not do anything about it.

It was very hard at first, but weeks and months went by and eventually they began to find other interests to fill in the time.

On the night of the bowling, Helen was surprised to find that her friend Marian's new boyfriend Jordy was none other than Jordan Howard whom she had not seen since she was about fourteen. He was now almost twenty-one. Jordan had grown up to be a good-looking young man. He was at university doing a business degree. They recognised each other immediately but did not say anything about their childhood relationship and pretended they had never met. Helen really wasn't sure why she did that. However, she noticed that Jordan hardly took his eyes off her all night. It made her feel slightly uncomfortable. She was not sure whether she should tell Marian about her long childhood relationship with Jordan, even though it was not a romantic affair. She usually saw Marian a couple of times a week and as far as she knew they did not have any secrets from each other.

She would usually see Marian on a Tuesday evening, sometimes they would just visit either of their houses or occasionally do one another's hair. This particular evening they decided to walk to the local pub and have a drink. After they had got a drink and sat down, Marian remarked to Helen that she looked to be uneasy and was there something troubling her.

Helen said, "Well, yes there is, and I think it's something that you should probably know about. Jordy and I went to the same primary school and, when we were both about eleven, we both seemed to have a crush on each other. We would often walk to and from school together and would carry one another's bags and all those sorts of things. Then when we went to secondary school, I went to Manor and Jordy, who was Jordan then, got into Jesmond Grammar. Even then we kept up our friendship and used to meet and chat and walk around together a lot. This went on until Jordan got his exam results at the end of his first year at Jesmond. His results were very disappointing, and his parents were not happy. They blamed it on the time he spent with me and forbade him from seeing me. There was not any romance in our relationship at the time we parted, though I would say that it was coming, what with teenage hormones and all that."

Marian, who had been going out with Jordy for about six months, was surprised but not upset at what Helen had told her. It was after all a childhood relationship and she just didn't think it mattered in the least to her and Jordy's relationship.

She thanked Helen for being so open and truthful about her and Jordy, she told Helen that she was in love with him and felt that he was very serious about her. She had met his parents and thought that they were quite happy about "their Jordan" and herself seeing one another. She and Helen finished their drinks and made their way home, both feeling happy about their friendship.

CHAPTER 5

Unwanted Attention

Meanwhile, Valerie and Martin's friendship was going from strength to strength. They had been away together for weekends on a couple of occasions. They were very happy with one another's company and found that they had very similar likes and dislikes. They had been seeing each other now for almost a year and were now talking about getting engaged. Both Valerie and Martin had their own houses, so they had to decide where they were going to live. Neither of them had many happy memories of their years in their present houses, especially Valerie, so she suggested, "Why don't we sell both houses and buy one nice house in a good area but not too far away?" She then added, "Martin, if you are happy that we both live in your house I will be happy to do so. Let us think about it for a few days and then decide." Martin did not need to think about it for long. He thought Valerie's idea was good and decided there and then that a new start with a new house was what they should do. When Peter heard about his mam and Martin's plans for their future, he was delighted and thought that everything was being carefully planned and worked out for their lives together.

He also now needed to think about his own future living

accommodation. He did not want to have to share a house with Valerie and Martin after they were married.

One evening, soon after Helen's chat with Marian, she was speechless when she answered the phone to find it was Jordan. She wondered why he would want to speak to her privately. He went on to talk about the ten-pin bowling night, how much he had enjoyed it and especially seeing her again. He told her how much he had missed her and never forgot her. Helen had an idea what Jordan was leading up to. She pressed the recording button on the answerphone machine, to make sure that she would remember everything after the call ended. He then went on to say how lovely she had looked on the night and how it bought back so many memories of their childhood days. Helen was now feeling quite uneasy as she knew what he was coming. When he asked if she would consider having dinner with him one evening she became upset, saying, "Jordan, you have been going out with Marian for about six months. Marian is my best friend. Do you not think that you owe her some loyalty or at least some explanation of what you are planning to do to her? I also think that you may well be aware that Peter and I have long-term plans and will probably be getting engaged shortly."

Jordan then said that he did not have any long-term plans with Marian and was only passing time with her until he met somebody better. Having heard that Helen said, "The answer is NO NO, NO, and please don't ring this number again," and she slammed the phone down. She was glad that she had pressed the record button.

Helen was now very worried about what to do about her friend Marian. Knowing what she now knew about Marian and Jordan's courtship, she played back the recording of the phone call she had just had with Jordan and thought that she must tell Marian what he had said. However, she decided to talk to Peter and see what he would think was best to do. She was seeing him the next day, so she decided to wait until then.

Peter had told Helen that he would like to take her out for a meal as they had not done that for ages. Helen was delighted and was determined that this time she was going to pay for it. She had asked Peter to call for her at her house and they could have a drink and get a taxi from there. She had told her family that when Peter came she wanted to have a few minutes alone with him as there was something she needed to ask him and she would tell them about it another time. When he arrived, she took him into the lounge. After a kiss and a little hug, she told Peter about the phone call which she had the previous evening. Helen had already told Peter about her childhood friendship with Jordan, so she played him the recording of the call for him. Initially Peter was not sure why he was being asked to listen to all of this until Helen said, "I just want you to tell me what you think I should do. Marian is my best friend and confidante. She has been going steady with Jordan for about six months and is in love with him. He now says that he is just passing time with her until somebody else comes along. What should I do? Should I ask her round here and tell her and let her hear that recording? Also, Peter, you heard the answer I gave him about going out with him and never ringing my number ever again. Peter, I need you to tell me what I should do please?"

Peter did not spend long thinking about what Helen should and must do. "As your best friend, Marian is entitled to be told if you know something about her and Jordan that she does not know, and you must tell her as soon as possible."

Helen kissed Peter tenderly, saying, "Thank you, Peter." They spent a very pleasant half hour with her family before taking a taxi to Bibi's Italian restaurant.

When they got to Bibi's they were still early, so they went to the bar and ordered a drink, Peter fancied a beer and Helen had a G and T. The waiter brought the menus for them to have a look at whilst they were having their drinks. Their meal was very enjoyable, and they chatted about Marian and how she would react to what Helen had to tell her, something which she was not looking forward to doing.

They asked the waiter to give them a fifteen-minute break before bringing the dessert. Helen thought that Peter was looking slightly anxious and tense, she had no idea why, but she did not have long to wait. He took her hand and held it very tenderly. "Helen," he said, "you asked me a question earlier this evening, now I am asking you a question. I love you and want to spend the rest of my life with you. Please will you marry me?" Well Helen was so very much taken by surprise. She had hoped to be asked that question sometime soon but certainly not tonight.

She took hold of Peter's hands and looked so lovingly at him and said, "Peter, are you serious?"

"I am very serious, I love you, Helen. Marry me?"

Helen then said, "Peter, yes, yes, yes I will marry you!"

Peter got up and came around to Helen's side of the table and gave her a long and tender kiss, saying, "Thank you, Helen. You have made me so happy."

The couple at the table close by heard all of the proposal and acceptance. They stood up and shouted, "He has just proposed to her and she has said yes so let us give them a big cheer." Well the whole restaurant went wild and came to their table to wish them well. One very kind couple sent them a bottle of Cava and wished them a long and happy life together. It was a lovely beginning to Helen and Peter's betrothal. Helen asked Peter to not tell anybody until she had spoken to Marian about what Jordan had said.

CHAPTER 6

The Jackson Family

Valerie and Martin put their houses on the market and began looking for a suitable house to buy. They fixed a date for their wedding, which was over six months away. Martin was having some problems with his ex-wife and two daughters. He had already paid to his wife what the court had awarded her at their divorce settlement, so she was not entitled to anything from the proceeds of the sale of the house.

His two daughters, Rita and Laura, had left home some years ago. Rita was married and Laura was living with her boyfriend and neither were in any way dependent on their father.

Valerie and Martin agreed that any house which they now buy would be in joint names with equal shares and after their deaths 50% would automatically go to their respective families. All of this would be in their wills when they were married and settled into their new home.

Martin was concerned about his daughters. They appeared to be getting almost hostile towards him since he told them he was selling the house. He asked them both to come and see him one evening to talk things over. "Now Rita and Laura, I would like to explain to you about how life has been for me over the last few years. As you know, we were a very happy family here in this house until something which I do not want to talk about happened. That had a terrible effect on all of us. Our once happy family and home had been torn asunder. You do not have any idea what it has been like for me here over the last few years. The nights I have sat here on my own and cried and pondered over the good times we used to have. Well then, I thought if I don't try and get myself out of this situation, I will go mad. So, I started to go out and hoped that something might happen.

"Last year I started to go to the conservative club and got to know some of the members and found it very easy to get into company there, which was better than sitting at home with nobody to talk to. One evening, when three ladies came in, it was quite busy, which it always is on a Friday and there were not many spare seats. There were a couple of seats near me and we had to do some moving around to get them sitting together and that was partly at the table where I was sitting. They thanked me for being so kind and finding them seats. They asked me if I was a member and I said no but that I had applied to become one. Two of those ladies were wearing wedding rings while the third one was not. They had a couple of drinks and even bought me a drink which I thought was very kind of them. Their names were Valerie, Jane, and Sandra. I was delighted to meet them. I got the feeling that Jane and Sandra, who were the two married ladies and obviously good friends of Valerie's, were trying to get her fixed up. They said they were usually there on Friday nights and would look out for me if I should be there. I thought Valerie was lovely and promised I would be there again.

"So, we parted after saying our goodbyes and, hoping to see them next week, I made my way home with a great feeling of optimism and looking forward to seeing these three ladies next week.

"Friday evening came, and I had by now got my membership

approved. I had taken a little extra time getting ready and made sure I put on a nice shirt and squirted a good show of after shave. The ladies had just come in, so I bought them a drink and sat down. The conversation was rather subdued for a while. The weather was discussed amongst other trivial matters. However, after our tongues had been lubricated the chat began to flow quite effortlessly. Sandra asked what I did for a living, where I lived, did I have a family, and many more things but did not ask if I was married or not. I thought I was being well and truly quizzed and investigated so here goes. I then went on to tell them something about myself. I told them my name and that I was 55 years of age. I said that I had been divorced for over two years and that I had two wonderful daughters who had both left home. I did not go into any details of my divorce.

"Valerie then took over, telling me she was 54 years of age and a widow for over 2 years. She told me she had a son, Peter, aged twenty, who lived with her. She told me she didn't want to go into details about becoming widowed other than to say she did not kill him! That made me laugh. I was very interested in everything Valerie had said and began to chat to her which her two friends helpfully took as a signal to leave us to it.

"That was the beginning of a great friendship which we now have and which we both cherish. So, Rita and Laura, I hope that you understand what it is I am trying to say. Valerie and I have been seeing each other for over a year and we are in love with each other. I have met her son Peter a few times and find him to be a very smart and interesting young man. He has a lovely girlfriend, Helen, and I would very much like it if you would join Valerie, Peter, Helen, and me for a meal to get to know each other.

"One other thing I would like to assure you of is this, the house which we are hoping to buy and make our home after we are married will be in both our names on equal shares and when either of us die our shares will pass on to their family, subject to certain conditions regarding the survivors rights to his or her living accommodation."

Rita and Laura agreed to the meeting, which went extremely well, much to Martin's relief. They all enjoyed each other's company very much and Rita and Laura got on very well with their prospective stepmother.

CHAPTER 7

A Triple Celebration

Helen asked Marian to come to her house for a chat on Thursday evening. She had no idea how she was going to tell her about her phone call from Jordan, but she knew that she must tell her. When Marian came, she took her into the lounge, bringing with her a bottle of wine. After they had a glass of wine and a chat Helen said, "I have something to tell you and I don't know how to start."

Marian said, "Well whatever it is tell me as that is what friends are for."

Helen said, "Ok. Shortly after the time I spoke to you I had a call from your Jordy, all very chatty, he mentioned about the bowling and how much he enjoyed it and also told me about how lovely I looked. Now at that remark I knew what would be next. He said, 'Helen, can I take you out for dinner one evening?' I told him, 'Jordan you are going out with my best friend Marian for the last six months and now you want to take me out, do you think that is fair to her? Also, you must know that Peter and I have long-term plans for the future, so the answer is no, no, no and please don't ring this number again,' and I hung up. Marian, I cannot tell you anymore about what he said, so I have recorded it and I will play it for you."

When Marian heard it, she went pale but could not say a word. Helen put her arms around her and comforted her as best she could and topped up their wine glasses. Marian looked at Helen with tears in her eyes and said, "Helen, I am glad you told me; you are a true friend."

*

As usual, Helen's mother was doing something in the kitchen when she got back from her night out with Peter. Although she had told Peter not to say anything about their engagement until after she had a chat with Marian, she could not hold back from telling her mam when she saw her, so she told Andrea all about how Peter had proposed to her and how she had accepted and the great jubilations in the restaurant which followed when the word went round that Peter had popped the question.

Andrea was delighted at the news and was going to wake Andrew and Carol to tell them, but Helen would not let her, insisting it should wait until morning.

*

On Saturday morning, Valerie was very excited as Martin was picking her up to go to the jeweller to buy an engagement ring. Then, they were going to have a second viewing on a house which they were both very keen on and hoping to agree a deal on today. As yet, they had not agreed any deals on their own two houses but had had lots of viewings. Valerie was hoping to be able to give Peter a deposit to buy a house from the sale of her own house. She had mentioned this to Martin, and he was very happy to go along with the idea. He liked Peter and they got on very well and he was going to ask him to be his best man and very much hoped that he would agree to it.

As Helen had asked Peter not to tell anybody about their engagement, he had not even told his mam. Now she had told

Marian what Jordan had said so he decided it was right that he should at least tell his mam and Martin.

They were so delighted at this happy coincidence, mother and son getting engaged on the same day. This called for a celebration. Valerie decided there and then that she was going to have everybody for dinner the following night; Helen's mam and dad, Carol, and also Martin's two daughters if they wished to come and to bring their partners. It would be a tight squeeze to fit everybody in but this was going to be a night to remember and she needed some help, in fact, she needed a whole lot of help.

First of all, Martin rang Rita and Laura to see if they would come and bring their partners and after some slight persuasions they all agreed they would be delighted. Peter phoned Helen with the same request, including her mam, dad, and Carol. Helen was very happy to confirm that all her family would certainly love to come and that she would be along shortly to help with whatever was needed. Martin decided and indeed insisted that he would look after the wine and help with the shopping. Valerie made out a shopping list which was a major task and she and Martin went to the shops. Peter and Helen got onto dusting and vacuuming and sorting the table out. Trying to fit the required number of seats around the table was a work of art and emergency chairs had to be borrowed from both Martin's and Helen's houses.

On their shopping trip, Valerie and Martin found time to visit the jeweller to buy an engagement ring. Martin had been having a look over the last week at rings so he had a good idea about the type and certainly about the price of the ring that he would like to buy Valerie, so they did not have much time to spend on looking. Valerie was not very fussy as she was so pleased to be getting engaged and they were in and out of the jewellers in a half an hour with a half-carat diamond solitaire, gold ring.

Peter and Helen decided that they could not find time that day to go shopping for a ring so Helen found in her jewellery box a dress ring which would do for now.

Next day, by mid-afternoon, everything had fallen into place; the food was ready for cooking and the house was immaculate. The wine was all in the fridge. Helen said she would go home and get ready and see how the rest of the family were doing. Martin said that he would do likewise and then came with a few chairs which they were short of.

Martin's daughter Rita and her husband Robert, and Laura and her partner Thomas (Tom) were also in the process of getting themselves ready. Laura and Tom had over the last month or so been thinking about getting married and starting a family. So, when they heard about Martin and Valerie and Peter and Helen getting engaged, they thought, well, why not us? Laura thought that it would please her dad greatly if they got married.

So, without telling anybody, they went out and bought an engagement ring.

Valerie's idea for this party was to have everybody there at 6.30 p.m. and have at least one hour for drinks and congratulations and for all to get to know each other. During this hour the oven would be on and the huge leg of lamb which they had bought would be cooking.

Included in the massive amount of wine which Martin had bought were bottles of Cava, most of which were nicely chilled. By 5.30 p.m. Valerie and Peter had their glad rags on and were all ready. Martin had arrived and was looking very dapper and took the chairs which he had brought in and squeezed them in around the table. Helen had also arrived with some cutlery and a few more wine glasses. Peter decided, as he was feeling a little on edge, that it was time perhaps for some pre-dinner bubbly. The others were all in agreement and so the party began.

Then, right on time, Helen's mam, dad, and Carol arrived, followed by Rita and Robert, Laura and Tom. When everybody knew who everybody was and the congratulations had been done, drinks were being served quite generously and conversation was flowing very easily. Tom and Laura asked if they could make an announcement and everybody wondered what this could be. Tom would have liked to have had another drink before saying what he was now going to say. However, he began, "I hope that I am not out of order at this lovely celebration when I tell you that Laura and I have also decided to get engaged and have done so today. If I may be so bold as to say so, now that we are all to be one big happy family, I hope. This must be something of a record, three engagements in one day, and I am so happy to have met you all." This was soon followed by more congratulations from the other two happy couples. The bubbly flowed, toasts were made, and a wonderful and memorable evening had begun.

After all this excitement Valerie had almost forgotten about the meal which they were having until Peter reminded her that the lamb must be done so she dashed to the kitchen just in time.

Helen and Andrea went to help and also Rita and Laura went to lend a hand. By then it was overcrowded in the kitchen and, as the adage goes, too many cooks can spoil the broth, so Rita and Laura promised to do the washing-up instead.

Martin was indeed very happy to hear that Laura and Tom had eventually decided to get married, although deep down he was a little miffed at the timing of the announcement. He had not wanted anything to detract from Valerie and his own celebration. However, he did not let anybody see that he was anything other than delighted.

CHAPTER 8

The Jordan Incident

After Marian had heard from Helen what Jordy had said about her she was shocked and very upset. She had been hoping that he would be proposing marriage at any time now. She tried to console herself by thinking it's better to find out now what he is really like. Deep down though she was heartbroken.

It was time to confront him with her newfound knowledge of his true feelings. So, she got prepared for their next date which was the next day. Marian worked as an administration supervisor at the local council and had made a tape recording of the message, which Helen had made, on her Dictaphone and just to be sure she played it again.

Marian lived with her mother. Her dad had died a few years earlier. She had a brother called Raymond, but he had left home and was living in an apartment which he was renting. He came to see Marian and her mother at least once a week. When Jordy arrived, Marian put on a forced attitude of being friendly and took him into the lounge and got them both a glass of wine. They were both sitting on the settee and Jordan started to sidle along until he was shoulder to shoulder with Marian and tried to kiss her. Marian slightly resisted and moved to the end of the settee and put her wine down on the table. She then looked at Jordan and said, "Jordy, we have been seeing each other now for over six months. Don't you think it is time that we should be thinking of getting engaged? You have told me that you love me, as I have told you, so there is no reason why we should not make a commitment to each other and be thinking of getting married."

By now Jordan was looking rather pale and uncomfortable and was moving away towards the other end of the settee. He said, "Marian why do you want to spoil things? Are we not happy and having a fun time the way we are? Let's leave it like that for now."

Marian then said, "For how long?"

He said, "I do not know for how long, so can we talk about something else?"

Marian reached for her Dictaphone and said, "Would it be something to do with this call which you made to my friend Helen?" and she switched in on loudly. Jordan started to get up as if to leave but Marian pushed him back down on the settee and shrieked at him, "You will sit there and listen to it. You should be very proud of yourself."

He then started to tell her not to have anything more to do with Helen and that she did not know how to tell the truth and that from the age of about 14 he used to have sex with her several times a week. "In fact, loads of the boys at Jesmond Grammar did. She was a total slapper. So she is your friend, is she?"

Marian said, "Yes she is my friend, a very dear friend, and I don't think that she has ever told a lie in her life and when I tell her what you have just said about her don't be surprised if you hear from her. Now, will you please go as it makes me sick looking at you, and I hope that I never see you again." What Jordan did not know was that Marian was recording everything that was said, and Helen would hear it all tomorrow.

When Helen heard the recording of what Jordan had said she was speechless for a time. She then said to Marian, "What should I do? You know that is not true."

Marian said, "I know that it is not true and if I were you I would seriously think about seeing a solicitor as that is a very serious case of defamation of your character, but first you should talk it over with Peter and probably with your parents as well."

Helen thought that was very good advice and said that she would sleep on it or at least try.

Next day was Saturday and, although they had been engaged for a week, they still had not bought the ring and this was the priority for the day. However, Helen decided that before doing anything else she should discuss with Peter the lies Jordan had told Marian about her. Helen phoned Peter asking him to come round as she needed to talk to him. Peter sounded very worried. What could be more important than going to the jewellers and buying their engagement ring? He thought Helen changed her mind, so he dashed over and said, "Helen what is the matter? Please tell me you have not changed your mind."

She said, "It is nothing like that and I am sorry if I made it sound like that. Come in and I will make you a cup of coffee as I also need one. Then I need your advice."

Having got their coffee, Helen told Peter what Marian had told her and recorded what Jordan had said about her. What should she do? Peter thought for a moment but was not sure what she should do. Then he asked if she had told her mam and dad. When she said that she had not he said it would be better if she told them as this was a very serious situation. Jordan was slandering her good name and character and must not get away with it. How many more people had he told this to?

"My advice is that you get your parents in here right now and we can discuss what you should do. My own opinion is that you should see a solicitor and get legal advice on the matter."

When Andrea and Andrew heard what Jordan had said about Helen, they were very upset and very angry. They agreed absolutely with what Peter had said and that it must be done as a matter of urgency.

However, Peter looked at Helen and said, "We have something very important to do today or had you forgotten?" So, Jordan was put on hold for now, but certainly not forgotten.

On their way to the jewellers they were both rather excited about the mission they were on right now. Peter thought back to the tram ride he was on when he first met Helen and to the conductor, who wanted to get her off the tram, and to whom he would be forever grateful. Seemingly, Helen was thinking the same as she said, "Peter I was at this very moment reliving every detail of that tram ride and the Good Samaritan who came to my rescue. That is something which I will never forget, Peter, and I love you so much."

Having got to the jewellers they stood looking at the window display for a few minutes. Helen said, "There is so much to choose from but please, Peter, I don't want you spending a whole lot of money on a ring. Will you promise to let me decide on the price as well as the style?" Having spent quite some time browsing, and with the help of the assistant, they bought the ring, a sapphire and diamond cluster ring, which Helen was very excited about and she slipped it on her finger which she said would remain there to the end of her days.

Having already had the big celebration of the triple engagement party they decided to have a Chinese take-away with Andrea, Andrew, and Carol with a couple of her friends.

So on their way home to Helen's house, with her sparkling new engagement ring, they stopped off at their local Chinese takeaway and ordered loads of their favourite dishes and asked for it to be delivered at 7.30 p.m. Helen insisted on her paying for everything as she told Peter that he had spent enough, she also picked up a few bottles of wine.

When they got home at about 5.30 p.m., Helen, with her lovely new ring, was so happy showing it to her mam and dad and Carol. They all thought that it was beautiful. After they had a quick wash and brush up, they were all ready for a drink, so they set upon the wine which was already chilled at the supermarket. The delivery man with the Chinese was on time with their food and soon they were all settling into a very enjoyable meal.

The Jordan incident was not mentioned while Carol and her two friends were at the table. When they had finished Carol took them into the lounge to watch television.

Andrew spoke first, "Helen, what do you intend to do about, Jordan?"

She said, "I am not sure. What do you and mam think?" Andrew said he did not think that he should be allowed to get away with it as it was a very serious and libellous thing to say about anybody and how many more people had been told this? Andrea was in complete agreement with that and also Peter, so Helen decided that she would enquire about a solicitor who would be interested in such matters.

Next day she asked Mr Miller in the shop if he knew any solicitors and he was most helpful. His niece, Francesca, had recently qualified as a legal assistant and was working for Morris and Co. in town. He said that Francesca would be happy to help and would not charge much. This was a relief to Helen as she had heard that lawyers were very expensive. He passed the phone number on to Helen. She asked her dad if he would be able to come with her if she made the appointment. He said that he would certainly like to be with her and to make the appointment as soon as possible and that he would fit in with whenever it was.

When they got to the offices of Morris and Co., a very impressive glass-fronted building at the Quayside with a marble-tiled reception, they were disappointed to find that Francesca was not taking them up to her office, but instead took them from the lobby to a nearby coffee shop. Helen was relieved that Francesca was a young lass like herself as she thought it would be much easier to explain to a woman than to a man. Francesca asked them to call her Fran. She was very thorough and wanted to know every detail of their relationship such as when it started and how long it went on for, why did it finish, and many more things which Helen found rather embarrassing, especially with her dad being there.

Helen told her about the recording of Jordan's conversation with Marian. Fran was amazed that Marian had recorded it. She asked if Helen had it with her and would she play it for her and could she make a copy.

When Fran had heard it, she said, "Well at least he cannot deny having said it. Now what do you want me to do? Do you want me to sue Jordan for defamation of your good name and character and claim about £20K damages or would you just settle for a written apology plus all expenses? My advice would be that you claim £20K initially, at least it will teach him a lesson and scare him out of his mind."

Helen looked at her dad and said, "What do you think?" He said that she should do what Fran had suggested.

CHAPTER 9

The Legal Letter

By now Peter was a fully trained and trusted member of British Rail's train drivers. He was on his own at the controls of his train and was very happy with his progress since he first started with British Rail six years earlier.

He was now just over 22 years of age and was on a good salary. He had left Valerie and Martin's house and was now renting an apartment not very far from Helen's house.

Valerie, as promised, had given him a generous deposit for him to buy a house. This was from the proceeds of the sale of her old house. He and Helen were now house hunting. They had set a date for their wedding, which was still six months away, and were both now saving every last penny they could. They were in agreement that they would be paying for the wedding. They did not want Andrew and Andrea to be burdened with a large bill as Helen knew that they did not have a lot of money and would almost certainly have to take out a bank loan if they had to pay for the wedding. So, after discussing this with them, Helen and Peter managed to persuade them that this was what they wanted.

The apartment which Peter was renting was on a minimum one-year lease so they did not need to rush into buying a house as there was still nine months left on the lease so they were waiting for the right house to come on the market.

Helen's sister Carol was getting very excited about the thought of being the chief bridesmaid. She, Helen, and their mother were going out on Saturday to try on their dresses which they had been measured up for some weeks earlier. She was now almost 18 and feeling very adult and grown up, especially when she saw herself in this beautiful lilac full-length dress, which was perfect except for some minor alterations. Helen looked absolutely beautiful in her elegant, ivory silk gown and their mother was so proud of them both.

Andrea had not even thought about what she would wear on this special day, so it was time to begin having a look as it would almost certainly take some time to sort that one out. Peter and his best man and Andrew would be wearing top hats and tails which would be hired from the gents' outfitters. Marian had also measured up for a bridesmaid dress but could not be with them on that particular day as she had to go with her mother to see her sister who was poorly and in hospital. She still had plenty of time to go with Helen the week after.

Now Helen had a copy of the letter which Fran had set to Jordan and wondered how he would react to it. She knew that his parents did not have much money and indeed would have struggled to support him through university. She knew that Jordan would not be worried but thought, 'Well anyhow, it is good enough for him after what he said about me, so let him sweat it out for a while.'

Jordan was in fact petrified. *Why did I ever say such things about her? And why did that horrible Marian record what I said? What on earth am I going to do? What am I going to tell my mam and dad?* These were just a few of the questions that Jordan was asking himself after he had read the letter from the big city solicitors, Morris and Co. Now he was in his final year at university, his final exams were only about four months away and he would need to be full time at his studies, but with the millstone around his neck he could not think straight. What was he going to do?

During his time at university he had seen, on many occasions, drugs being sold around the campus and in the bars. He himself had on the odd occasion tried some cocaine but could not afford it very often as it was about £10 for a very small amount. So, Jordan thought if he could get hold of a kilo of the stuff and start to peddle it around the pubs and clubs where he knew it was commonly used, he would make a lot of money quickly. But that amount would cost hundreds of pounds to buy, which he did not have, so he invented a story for his parents, asking for £500. He told them that he had borrowed this money from some of his friends and they were looking for it back. They were not very pleased as they thought the amount of money they gave him each month should be ample to pay his bills and keep him in pocket money without him having to borrow money from his friends.

When they queried this with Jordan, he was not able to give any proper explanation of what he was doing with his money so they thought they should get to the bottom of what was wrong. What did he really want the £500 for? They told him they would not give it to him until he told them the truth.

Eventually Jordan broke down and showed them the letter from Francesca Miller at Morris and Co.

*

Days and weeks were slipping by and the wedding day was fast approaching. Helen and Peter were very much on top of things. The invitations had all been sent out. The reception venue was organised, and the menus and flowers had all been sorted.

Andrea had eventually got her mother-of-the-bride outfit sorted. Valerie also seemed to be all ready and was very much looking forward to the big day.

The only one of Helen's family who appeared to be slightly on edge was Andrew. Helen and Andrea thought they knew why; they had seen him on a few occasions with a pen and a writing pad. It was obviously the father-of-the-bride speech that he was wrestling with, so they did not interfere and left him to sort out.

*

When Jordan's parents had read the letter, well there was pandemonium. Was it true? Could Helen prove that he had said these terrible things about her? When he told them that she had a recording of what he said, all hell broke loose. How could he be so stupid after all his time at university? What were they going to do as a family? They would be destroyed if this should get into the papers.

And when they found out what he had intended to do with the five hundred pounds which he had asked them for they were horrified. To think that he intended to become a drug dealer to make some money very quickly. It was unthinkable. They said that, whatever else happened, that could never be.

*

Valerie and Martin's wedding was lovely although not a very big affair, about 30 people. They had a lovely meal at The Adelphi in Newcastle, following a marriage service at their local church, St Hilda's. Peter was playing the father of the bride part and gave Valerie away. He also gave a short speech after the meal in which he said how happy he was that his mam and Martin had met and had got on so well and looked so happy together.

Having already met Martin's two daughters, Rita and Laura, and their partners, Robert and Tom, at the 'triple engagement party', it was a very easy and relaxed wedding group.

Valerie's two friends, Jane and Sandra, and their two husbands, Bob and William, were all very pleased that this happy occasion had come about from the chance meeting at the Conservative club where they were bunched together at a table with Martin because of a shortage of seats!

The newly-weds were going to Playa de Las Americas in Tenerife for a week on their honeymoon. They had a flight booked, which would be leaving from Newcastle at 6.30 a.m., so with the good wishes of everybody, and plenty of confetti, they left for the airport and the start of their new lives together.

Helen and Peter's wedding day was now almost upon them. Andrew had written his speech and was much more relaxed. Helen and Peter had many friends and family between them; the guest list had snow-balled with much higher numbers than they had initially thought. The hen party and stag party had been and gone and Carol had tried on her bridesmaid dress several times and was anxiously waiting for the time she could wear it for the whole day. The hairdresser was booked to come to their house and do all the bridal party's hair on the morning of the wedding. All of these arrangements had been checked and rechecked, nothing was to be left to chance.

In short, everything was in place for the big day!

CHAPTER 10

Wedding Bells

It was a lovely bright and sunny morning. Peter and his best man were up in good time and enjoyed a hearty breakfast as they wouldn't see any more food again until well into the afternoon. They arrived at the church in good time and Peter checked that his best man, Graham, had the ring and told him to remember which pocket he had it in. The usher then escorted them to their place at the front of the church and left them to wait anxiously.

Meanwhile, the church was now filling up as the guests were filing in. The mother of the bride arrived and was taken to her place by one of the ushers. The organist was now getting his fingers warmed up on the keyboard as he played some light music until he got the signal that the bride had finally arrived … fifteen minutes late!

The bride and her dad waited at the back of the church, ready for the march down the aisle to where the groom and his best man were nervously waiting. But first Marian and Carol, the beautiful bridesmaids, had to make sure the bride's dress and train were perfect. The organist was given the cue to play 'Here Comes the Bride'.

The procession began. To Andrew, the aisle seemed to be a mile long, with the slow pace of the march taking about an hour. However, they reached the end and Andrew handed over the bride to Peter. She looked absolutely stunning and Peter whispered, "Helen, you look gorgeous," and gave her a shy peck on the cheek.

The vicar and his two altar boys were ready and so the marriage ceremony commenced. Graham, the best man, was doing his best to appear calm, which he absolutely was not. He held the ring to be sure he had it to hand when asked for it but just before that he somehow dropped it. The vicar was in mid-sentence when this happened and had to stop while the altar boys tried to find the ring. Fortunately, it had not rolled very far, and they retrieved it. The vicar suggested perhaps that he should hold the ring until it was required. All of this caused quite a giggle in the congregation.

*

Jordan's parents had no idea what to do about the monumental problem which had descended upon them. Their anger had now abated somewhat, and they were no longer so hostile to Jordan since it was not helping to solve anything. They spoke to him and persuaded him to go back to his studies, as it was vital that he did not miss out on his finals.

What should they do? They could not simply ignore it and hope it would go away. Once again, they read the letter from the solicitor which sounded very serious and almost threatening. The demand for £20K was scary as they had very little money and would struggle to find £2K.

They decided to write to the solicitor and say how sorry they were for their son's stupid behaviour but that they were a working-class family and had very little money and it was impossible for them to find that amount or indeed any amount.

Having seen the letter, Francesca wrote to Helen and sent her a copy and asked her what she thought she should do.

At this particular time, Helen had many more things on her mind, her wedding was four days away so she would deal with the Jordan affair after their honeymoon. She phoned Fran to let her know. This would give her more time to think and to consult with Peter and her parents what they thought she should do.

*

The marriage ceremony was complete, including signing the registry documents. The only thing left to do before going to the reception venue was the photographs. This took longer than the marriage ceremony, however this was a very happy occasion, so everybody was on top form and looking forward to the reception and having a few drinks. Valerie and her new husband Martin were both looking absolutely radiant as, of course, were Helen's parents, Andrea and Andrew.

Both bridesmaids, Carol and Marian, were greatly admired by everybody, not least by Graham who had become totally besotted by Marian since meeting her some weeks earlier. Graham was Peter's oldest friend from school. They had been on the rugby team together and, in spite of having seen a lot less of each other since starting work, had always vowed to be each other's best man. Peter was as good as his word and had delighted Graham by asking him to do him the honour. Meanwhile, Carol was being eyed up by one young guest, David, who was a friend of Peter's from work. David had not taken his line of sight off Carol all day.

Rita and Laura, with their two partners, Robert and Tom, appeared to be enjoying themselves and were very amiable with their new stepmother Valerie.

Andrew had arranged with the hotel for him to pay for all the drinks before the meal and paid a good deposit for this. As he was not paying for the meal, he felt that he should pay for something. He also knew that from what he had seen at other weddings when there was very little to drink before the meal and the guests were told to take their seats almost immediately, this often meant the guests were not in a very relaxed mood and the party atmosphere never got going. Also, Andrew himself liked to have a few drinks, especially so as he had to make a speech as father of the bride.

So, when the guests were invited to take their seats, they were all, including Andrew, well in the party mood. Graham was delighted to be seated next to Marian. Both of them were very much in wedding high spirits. They had carried out their roles perfectly, except for the best man dropping the ring during the ceremony! Graham, however, still had the most important part of his job to go – to deliver his best man's speech. He was desperate to pull it off and, of course, impress the lovely Marian.

The meal was of excellent quality and expertly served with an abundance of wine. The father-of-the-bride's speech was wildly applauded. It covered a whole lot of family details, both serious and funny. He spoke of how grateful he was for having such a family, mentioning Andrea, and his two lovely daughters, Helen and Carol. Then, on a rather sad note, about how they were going to miss Helen but that they were so happy to gain a wonderful son-in-law who was such a great person in every possible way. He also added that Peter and Helen would be such a loving and caring couple and would have a great life together.

When Andrew then asked the guests to stand and drink a toast to Helen and Peter, the whole room went into such a long applause that he had to tell them to stop.

Graham's best man's speech was very funny, though with some stories about Peter which Andrew would probably rather not have heard!

After all the formalities were over, and the guests started to move around, Graham and Marian did not move an inch from one another or care to mix with anybody. When the DJ got his music going and the bride and groom took to the floor for the first dance, the chief bridesmaid and best man very soon joined them. Then Carol was on her own at the table but not for long. David, who had been watching her, made his move, darting over to her to ask her to dance. He told her his name was David, a good friend of Peter's, and she said her name was Carol and yes she would dance with him. David was a great dancer and waltzed Carol round the floor very expertly. After the dance was over, he asked if he could get her a drink at the bar and please could he have the next dance after they had a drink. Such was the beginning of the romances for Marian and Graham and also Carol and David – watch this space!

CHAPTER 11

House Hunting

Shortly after their honeymoon in Scotland on the Isle of Skye, Helen and Peter started house hunting. House prices, which had not risen at all for the last five years, were now beginning to fall; it was the perfect time to start looking at what was on offer. Peter had still got about six months left on his lease on the apartment which he and Helen were now sharing.

Peter, thanks to Valerie, had a good deposit to put down on a house. Also, he was by now a fully qualified train driver on a good salary from British Rail. Helen, who had worked in Millers Newsagent since she had left school, was now manageress and was very highly regarded by Mr Miller, or Butch as he was known to his friends. There was a story behind the name which Butch said he would one day tell Helen. Helen had more than doubled the turnover of business over the last two years by introducing many different items of stock such as quality greeting cards and stationery which she knew would sell well in the area. She also, after a lot of persuading, convinced Butch to give the shop a complete makeover and modernisation at no great cost.

Butch was delighted with Helen's initiative, especially when he saw his turnover rapidly increasing. The shop was now a much more pleasant place to work in and Helen felt very proud of what she had achieved, especially when the boss gave her a big increase in salary.

They were now in a good position financially and in a very good bargaining position to buy their first home. They had just bought themselves a little car, a red Ford Escort, which they loved. The Escort enabled them to drive around the area in which they would like to live in and could afford.

Whilst driving around the area on a Saturday afternoon they saw a 'For Sale' sign on a house which was semi-detached on a very nice road, Bluebrook Road in Heaton. They drove past this house several times and wondered should they knock and ask if they might just have a quick look around and find out what the asking price was.

The lady who answered the door was quite friendly and also quite surprised at the request as the agent was supposed to make an appointment to take any prospective buyers to view the property.

However, she thought that this nice-looking young couple would be just the type of people that her neighbours would like to move into the road, so she invited them in. Peter introduced them and explained that they were just married.

*

The inside was like a dream to both of them as they had never seen such a house before. The lady told them that the house had been on the market for some time and they had had to, very reluctantly, drop the price recently as her husband's job had moved to another area and he was already working there so they were eager to sell. The asking price was considerably more than what Peter would like to pay but they both loved this house, which was totally ready to move into.

They told the lady that if she could knock the price down a little more that they would have it and were in a position where they could complete very quickly, probably even within a month. She said she would reduce the price by another £3,000. They said that was great and asked if they could bring their parents to see the house which she agreed to and said they could bring them anytime, so they arranged for the next day.

So, mid-morning on Sunday Helen and Peter, Valerie and Martin, and Andrew and Andrea set off to view the lovely house and were made very welcome by the lady who owned it. Her name was Kathy and her husband's name was Denny, who was home for the weekend but would be going back to his job in Darlington the next day.

The house looked absolutely stunning and both sets of parents were in raptures about it and encouraged Helen and Peter to go ahead and purchase it. Martin said that it was very good value for the asking price as house prices were now on the decline but, no doubt, would begin to rise again in time. This house, in a good area, would increase considerably in value over the next few years and indeed for many years to come.

The deal was done, and Peter and Helen shook hands with Denny and Kathy. The next day both parties advised their solicitors to set the wheels in motion to complete the sale and purchase the house. All went through very smoothly and Helen and Peter were in their lovely new home within six weeks.

*

The romance between Marian and Graham, which began at the wedding of Helen and Peter, was by now a very serious affair and by all appearances they seemed to be very much in love with each other as they were always together. Helen was expecting them to be announcing their engagement at any time and was delighted for her very dear friend Marian. Graham seemed to Helen to be a really nice chap and, of course, he came highly recommended by her dear Peter. He also had quite a good job with an insurance company and had been promoted twice since he started there as a junior office clerk, having left school at eighteen with three good A levels. Like Peter, there was no question of him going to university as his family could not afford to support him over the three or four years in which he would be there. However, he was quite happy with how he was getting on with this large company and was being paid a reasonably good salary so was able to help his parents out by paying them a nominal amount each month for his board. He had built up a nice nest-egg with a building society with which he was hoping to use as a deposit to put down on a house at some time in the future. This would probably not be too far away as the romance with Marian was coming along very nicely and Graham was just waiting for the right moment to ask her to marry him.

*

Helen and Peter were now settled into their lovely new home and they were so proud of it. They had already got to know quite a few of the neighbours, all of whom seemed very happy to have them on Bluebrook Road.

They decided to throw a party and invite all their friends. It was now mid-May and everywhere including the garden was looking great. They settled on the last Saturday in May and started to contact their friends. They first contacted all their parents to make sure that they would be available on that date which happily they were. Graham and Marian were delighted to hear of this party which they assumed would be a very lively affair and were also keen to catch up with a lot of their friends whom they have not seen for months.

Graham wondered if this would be a good time to pop the question to Marian and present her with an engagement ring. He was still undecided.

Helen and Peter were now wondering if they would invite some of the neighbours; however, when they counted up all of their friends, plus their parents, they realised that there would be far too many so they decided not to. The party was a great success and enjoyed by all, especially when Graham, emboldened by a few drinks, decided that it was in fact the perfect time to make an announcement and tell the world about how much he loved Marian. Straight after he got down on one knee and asked her to marry him, using a ring pull as a makeshift ring.

When Marian said yes, the whole house went wild and the party started all over again.

CHAPTER 12

Helen's Happy News

'The Jordan affair', as Helen now referred to it, had been put on hold until after the wedding and now needed to be addressed. Fran wanted instructions as to what Helen wanted to do about it so Helen and Peter had a long chat but without coming to any decision as to what they should do. They asked Andrew and Andrea and Carol round for dinner next evening, telling them that they needed advice as to what they should do about the whole situation.

Helen was of the opinion that Jordan should be taught a lesson. It was a very slanderous statement which he had made about her so why should he get away without being penalised somewhat? She knew that Jordan's parents had very little money and if she pursued the case and took it to court, she had a chance of winning it. Whether she would be awarded £20K which Fran had asked for or not was anybody's guess but, if she won the case, she did not want to put Jordan's parents into the situation whereby they would have to sell their house in order to pay for some stupid thing that their son had got himself into. So, what should she do? It was now decision time.

*

Peter was home early for a change and had just had a shower and got dressed when Helen's parents and Carol arrived. He poured them all a glass of wine while they waited for the dinner to cook and so the debate began as to how they should proceed with the Jordan situation. After they all had another glass of wine and had their say, the consensus was that another letter from the solicitor requesting a positive response to her initial letter would be helpful instead of the negative response pointing out how hard up they were. Fran thought that this was quite a good idea as it would leave Jordan and his family in no doubt that Helen was serious and demanding restitution for the injury caused to her reputation.

On receipt of this letter, Jordan, after discussing it with his parents, decided that they must now see a solicitor and take legal advice on what course of action was available to them. Would the solicitor be willing to take on the case and seek the best and cheapest settlement possible?

Mr and Mrs Howard and Jordan made an appointment with Mr George Humphries of Humphries Solicitors. Mr Humphries was a rather unpleasant character, though on the surface perfectly amiable. His firm was struggling. He was close to retirement and was very bitter about the fact that the practice he had given his life to had not been doing well in recent years. Many of the other law firms in Newcastle were taking cases on a 'no-win-no-fee' basis, since a change in legislation had made that possible, and it seemed very difficult to compete in a single-handed practice like his own. There was no way he could afford to take on any case without an upfront fee from the client.

He knew Tony Morris from University. They had studied law together at Durham. He had always hated him; top of the class, captain of the Rugby First Eleven Team, always going out with the prettiest girls. These days he was increasingly frustrated and envious at how Tony's practice was doing. The office in the Quayside was a gleaming glass-fronted affair, and judging from the car Tony was driving he was clearly raking it in. He had also heard from a colleague about the beautiful house in Gosforth Tony was planning to retire to.

However, when he saw the letter from Francesca Miller of Morris & Co. that the Howards produced the penny dropped when he saw the 'legal assistant' title in the signature. So that's how he's doing so well! Employing paralegals who don't know their arse from their elbow, let alone understand the complexities and subtleties of English Law. As for the so-called case! He nearly burst out laughing. It was lamentable. Imagine thinking that a recording of a guy slagging off his ex-girlfriend was a worthy slander case to pursue in this day and age. It's not as if this Helen whatsername was a celebrity. Even then the case would be very weak and would be laughed out of court. He could not believe that this Francesca Miller girl was not having more close supervision of her work. Well, pay peanuts and you get monkeys. 'I'm not employing any monkeys here,' he thought.

He decided he would go along with it to see how far Morris and Co. would take it and then he would pull out, exposing the shoddy practice and poor client advice that Morris and Co. were peddling. He would report Tony Morris to the Solicitors Regulation Authority for malpractice. He could hardly wait!

If he could also spin a few thousand quid for his time out of this sucker of a family, then so much the better. George was thrilled at the thought and moved now into full on charm-mode.

He told the Howards he would be delighted to take on the case and would look after their interests in the best possible way. There would obviously be costs involved and how much at this stage he had could not say.

Meanwhile, Helen had other things on her mind as she was feeling a bit off for the last few days and wondered why, as she was in very good health and usually full of energy. Next morning, she was not feeling any better and rather nauseous, so she decided to go to the doctors and see what the matter with her was. The doctor examined her and did a few simple tests and asked her if she could produce a urine specimen and gave her the necessary equipment to do so. Having got the specimen, he then dipped it with a plastic stick and exclaimed, "Just as I thought. Mrs Johnson, you are pregnant."

Helen was not sure how to react to the doctor's diagnosis of her complaint. Should she look as if she was shocked or should she look to be delighted? Her first comment was, "Are you sure, doctor?"

The doctor said there was no doubt about it. "Albeit you are in the very early stage of pregnancy so you will now need to register with a Midwife who will look after you all during your gestation period and right through to the birth of your baby."

Peter was on long-distance duty and would not be home until next afternoon. Should she phone the hotel that evening and tell him the news, or would that be too much of a distraction for him in his job as a high-speed train driver? She thought that it would be and decided to wait until he got home the next day. She then thought that she would go round to her family and tell them the news but that would not be fair to Peter as he should be the first to be told.

Next evening, after Peter got home, Helen had a lovely meal prepared for him and was beautifully dressed herself with her hair newly done. She had put a bottle of nice wine in the fridge but would not be having any of it herself. Peter was feeling quite tired as he did not sleep very well at the Travelodge the previous night. However, when he saw Helen all dressed up and saw how the table was set for their evening meal he soon forgot about his tiredness. He had a quick shower and change of clothes and was ready for a glass of wine before his meal. He did wonder if there was something that Helen was celebrating but had no idea what it might be. She gave him a cuddle and a lingering kiss before handing him a glass of wine, and told him to sit down as the dinner was not quite ready. He was still wondering what she was going to tell him. When she sat down beside him, she held his hand and said, "Peter, darling, I have some news," and then stopped for what seemed like ages to Peter and then burst out the news, "I am pregnant! I am going to have a baby; you're going to be a daddy."

Peter was absolutely speechless at what Helen had said. He was so delighted but was not in any way expecting it. He got her in his arms and hugged and kissed her and told her how much he loved her. Then he said, "Why did you not ring me?" Helen told him she was going to but thought it may have been too much of a distraction for him.

Even though Helen did not have any wine, the bottle which she had opened a little earlier did not last Peter very long. He was so excited and would not let Helen do anything during the whole weekend.

Next morning, being Saturday, Helen phoned her mam just to say hello and that they would be in her area sometime during the morning and they would call in for a quick visit if that was ok. Andrea said that would be great and she would have the kettle on. Mam, dad, and Carol were delighted to see Helen and Peter as they had not seen them for about two weeks.

After much hugging and kissing, Peter interrupted and said that Helen had something to tell them.

CHAPTER 13

The Bank Loan

In her mail Helen saw a letter which she knew was from Fran; she opened it excitedly. It contained a copy of a letter which Fran had received from Jordan's solicitor Mr Humphries.

This letter made no mention of any offer of compensation whatsoever and his client was amazed that such a claim had arisen for a casual remark that he had allegedly made but had no recollection of making. However, his client would like to resolve this matter as soon and as amicably as possible and suggested that they should meet and sort the problem out. In her letter Fran told Helen that she was not happy about such a meeting. However, it was up to Helen to decide what to do.

Fran insisted that if the case went to court there was every likelihood that Helen would be awarded substantial damages for the slanderous statement that the defendant had made about her and which was on record. There was no point in him trying to deny having made such a statement. So the ball was in his court and it was up to him and his solicitor to come up with something which could well be the basis for further negotiations.

Helen, after much discussion with Peter and her family, told Fran that she was happy to go along with her advice and see what happened. At the back of her mind she was feeling somewhat sorry for Jordan and his parents, but she still thought that he needed to be taught a lesson.

*

The great news of Helen's pregnancy was the most exciting event in the Lawson family for years. So a celebration was called for. As it was Saturday morning Andrea and Andrew decided that they would organise a party for that evening, but probably not for any great numbers.

Helen said that the only people that she would like to have would be Marian and Graham and, of course, Peter's mother Valerie and Martin. She asked Carol if her romance with David was still going strong and, if so, would they like to share this happy occasion with them. Carol assured Helen that she and David wouldn't miss it. Andrea and Andrew were adamant that Helen was not to get involved in any way preparing for the party as it was for them a great pleasure to do so. She told Helen to contact Marian and Graham and then go to see Valerie and Martin with their good news and also to have everybody there at about 6 p.m.

The party, including the families, numbered ten which Andrea and Andrew found was quite easy to prepare for. Also, it was just right for the table and seating arrangements. The only thing she requested from Helen were a few wine glasses as she could only see about six in her glass cabinet. The party was a lovely and joyous occasion. The wine flowed freely, except for Helen who just had one small glass. There was much toasting to Helen and Peter and so the night passed very quickly.

*

Further correspondence passed between Francesca and George

Humphries, each letter was, to George, hard evidence of very poor supervision of the paralegal and reputationally damaging to Morris and Co. In his letter to Jordan, Mr Humphries pointed out that as things stood at the moment there was no possibility of negotiating a settlement with the claimant. So, his advice was that they should state that if the other party proceed with this false allegation, then the matter would be settled in the court.

Jordan's preferred option was to make an offer of say £5,000 and to plead that he was unable to find any more, as he was still at university and that his parents had little or no money so they would have to try and secure a bank loan or re-mortgage their house which was already at about its limit. Mr Humphries pointed out that he had a very high chance of winning this case and protecting his good name and hence no settlement should be made.

Jordan and his parents were not very happy with Mr Humphries' advice. They were concerned about the publicity of a court case, what if it got in the papers? However, the prospect of winning the case and teaching 'that bloody woman' a lesson was too tempting. So reluctantly they agreed to go along with Mr Humphries' advice.

Mr Humphries had asked them to have money available for a settlement should they lose which he was confident they would not. Humphries made that statement so they would not doubt the case would proceed to court. He could have ended their anxiety with a single sentence, "The claim is without merit." But where would be the fun in that? No, he was going to go as far as he could with this to expose Morris and Co. as the third rate law firm they really were.

Where the Howards were going to find the money, they had no idea, but find it they must. As things stood, Jordan was now really struggling to concentrate on what he must do to pass his final exams which were now only weeks away. His parents were very conscious of this and tried to be as helpful as possible.

They arranged an appointment with their bank manager, Mr Armitage, to whom they explained that, at the moment they did not wish to divulge the reason that they were trying to arrange a bank loan and in time were sure of the amount that they would require. It may well be in the region of £20K.

Mr Armitage was very accommodating and said he would do his best for them. He then wanted to know all about the personal circumstances, such as their house and mortgage commitments, any outstanding loans, any court orders present or pending. He was reasonably satisfied with all of the information which he gleaned from them. He then asked if they would give him their consent to do a credit check on them to which they said that they were quite happy to do. Mr Armitage said that, subject to their credit rating being satisfactory, he would be in a position to advance them their £20k. He was, however, a little concerned that they did not wish to disclose the reason for which they required the money. He assured them that anything which they told him would be treated in very strict confidence and never divulged to anybody else. Having considered his remark, the Howards thought that it was reasonable for the bank to know that the money would be used for. They told him that their son, who was now in his final year at university, had said something about a girl whom he had known since they were children. What he had said was untrue but had been recorded by the person whom he had said it to. Solicitors were now involved, and a claim was being pursued against their son by the girl for damage to her reputation. If this case went to court, and was made public, it would cause much damage to their son's job prospects but it seemed to be their only chance. Mr Armitage professed he was sceptical that the case would be found against them, but he knew George Humphries, who was a lawyer of good reputation in the area, and assumed they were being advised well by him.

Jordan's parents left the bank with the feeling that when the time came, if the court case were to go against them, at least they would be in a position to settle the case. They were not entirely sure how they would repay the bank.

*

After all the celebrations at the news of Helen's pregnancy, it was back to work and routine everyday life. Peter was mostly on long-distance work which meant that he would have to be away at least one night per week and occasionally two nights. On those nights, Helen would sometimes go and stay with her parents and get pampered by her family. Or sometimes Carol would have a sleep over at Helen's house. This was something which both girls loved as they were very close friends and loved one another dearly.

Helen, who by now was fifteen weeks into her pregnancy, was coping very well with no great problems. Butch was very caring and concerned about her and would not let her do anything which he thought might be hazardous for someone in her condition.

Also, he would not let her come in to open the shop in the morning at 7.30 a.m. and insisted that she did not start until 9 a.m. This worked very well as the morning rush would have eased off at 9 a.m. so Butch would then go and have a couple of hours off and have his breakfast and a good rest for a few hours. Helen, in a conversation with Butch, advised him to think about when she would have to have time off before and after the baby was born. She would be off for about six months she told him, one month before and five months after.

She advised him to look out for someone whom they could train to fill in the void for the time she would be off. Helen had, for the last few weeks, been preoccupied with her work, on top of which she had several clinics and midwifery appointments to attend, so the Jordan affair had been very much forgotten about. Then one day in her mail was a rather official looking envelope which she knew must be from Fran. Enclosed with Francesca's letter was a copy of a letter from Jordan's solicitor, Mr George Humphries. Nervously Helen read this letter which stated that his client had not acknowledged that he was wrong in making such a statement which he knew to be true in any case and would not offer anything in settlement. The battle lines were drawn.

Francesca's letter said that she thought the other side were bluffing and that a settlement would come as a court date approached.

Deep down Fran was worried. She had been so confident about this case. She was actually pursuing the case in her own time, trying to make a name for herself in the firm. She hadn't discussed it with her boss Rav Moondi, one of the associates in the practice, but instead was planning to pull off her first case single-handedly. She also wanted to make her Uncle Butch proud and she knew this case was close to his heart. She hadn't thought for a minute it would end up in a hearing. Mr Moondi would have to know about it then and he might be annoyed that she hadn't run it by him already.

She decided to advise Helen to continue with the case and hoped her hunch that the other side would settle closer to the court date would be right.

Helen was now in a real dilemma. If she told Fran to continue with the case there was a realistic chance that she could squeeze a lot of money out of Jordan and his family, which she knew would leave them in a very bad state financially. Did she want to do that? She did not know. Peter would not be home tonight which did not help as she wanted to discuss everything with him before she told her parents. Helen did not get much sleep, or hardly any, as she had so much going on in her mind. She was thinking about Jordan and their primary school days when they were almost inseparable and spent every possible hour together and shared every little detail of news and had their own little secrets.

It was only when they went to secondary school that they began to drift apart somewhat; she to Manor Comp and Jordan to Jesmond Grammar.

She hadn't even known he had been trying to pass his eleven plus. He never admitted to studying and discouraged her from doing any! She had assumed they would both go to Manor. Had he been swotting secretly? Did he want her to go somewhere else so he could ditch her? He had blamed his parents for their split but maybe it was his idea all along? If he had cared about her at all he would have stood up to them. As the years went by and they both grew up, Helen left school at sixteen and started work in the shop. Jordan went on to do his A levels and then to University. It wasn't fair somehow. The more she thought of his abandonment of her in their teens and how badly he had treated her best friend Marian, stringing her along about his intentions and then trying to cheat on her with Helen, the more badly she felt towards him.

Having pondered over all these things during her mostly sleepless night Helen found herself to be more and more of the opinion that she should not let Jordan off the hook very lightly. After all, he would be graduating with a business degree shortly. This would put him in a very different earnings bracket to her who had to leave school at sixteen and seek employment wherever she could find it, doing probably very menial type work. She was determined to pursue the case and make him suffer.

After Peter got home that evening Helen had a nice meal ready for him, after which they both sat down and enjoyed a nice cuddle on the settee. She showed him the letter from Fran together with the rebuttal from Jordan's solicitor.

They chatted for ages about what course of action to take. Helen told Peter all about her mostly sleepless night and having thought about how Jordan had behaved towards both her and Marian that he did not deserve any sympathy, so she was of the mind to instruct

Francesca to carry on with the case or at least until an offer was on the table. Peter said that he agreed with her but that she should talk with her parents and see what they thought. Helen's parents agreed with her decision and so Francesca was told to carry on with the negotiations.

CHAPTER 14

The Photograph

Helen's pregnancy was progressing very well with no great problems. Some of her clothing was getting too tight for her as her baby bump was now beginning to show. Butch was very caring and protective of her. He even got her a nice comfortable chair which fitted neatly behind the counter without being too noticeable. He made sure that she used it whenever possible. Helen was amazed at Butch's caring consideration for her. After all he was a bachelor with no family of his own. Helen thought that he was looking upon her as the daughter which he would love to have had. She even felt a little sorry for him.

Marian and Graham had now set the date for their wedding which was still about a year away. Helen was delighted with the news. Her baby would then be about eight months old and she should by then be back to her regular shape and weight if she worked hard at it after her baby was born. Carol had done her A levels and got her results which were very good – an A and two Bs – and was offered a place at the University of her choice, Bristol, to study English and History of Art. This was a long way from Newcastle which her parents were not very happy about. However, when they thought it over, they did think that it may not be such a bad thing as they were concerned about the romance between Carol and David which had been going on since Helen and Peter's wedding. Carol was only young, and Andrea and Andrew were hoping that with her being away in Bristol for all this time, except for holidays, that the romance would fade away and both her and David would find that there were many other fish in the sea waiting to be caught.

During their many visits to see Valerie and Martin, Helen and Peter were so happy to see the great and loving relationship between them. They both looked fantastically well. They had many friends whom they socialised quite a lot with, including many dinner parties, going dancing, and of course their usual weekly visit to the Conservative club which meant a lot to them because that was where they first met and had many happy memories for both of them.

Peter looked at his mother, who was now so happy and radiant, and could not help thinking when his father Roger was alive and how she looked then – battered and bruised from the drunken behaviour of his tyrant of a father who mercifully had made a very quick exit from their lives just seven years ago, and did not deserve to be very fondly remembered.

*

Helen was due to have her twenty-week scan to see how her baby was coming along. At this scan she would be able to see the baby and even take a photograph of it. She would be asked if she wanted to know the sex of the baby. She had talked this over with Peter on a few occasions and neither of them could decide if they did want to know. Now it was decision time. They decided that they would like to know as it would be much easier for them to prepare for this great event in their lives rather than having to dash around when the baby was born to get either pink or blue little baby clothes.

Well now they knew, and it was going to be pink. The scan

showed a lovely perfect little girl. How delighted and proud Helen felt on her way home from the clinic! She could not tell anybody or show the photograph until she had seen Peter who would not be home until about six. Helen spent most of the afternoon preparing a celebratory dinner for Peter and herself with a bottle of wine nicely chilled for Peter.

In his childhood days, and indeed up to the time when he started to travel on trains as a train guard with British Rail, Peter had never seen any of the county or countryside other than the area in which he was born and brought up in Byker, a working-class area on the edge of the city. There were no facilities or amenities for children to play on, so football was always played on the street which some of the neighbours were not very happy about, especially when a window got broken occasionally.

So when Peter started to travel all over the country on trains, especially when he became a driver, he was amazed to see so much countryside comprising mostly farmland with not a house to be seen for miles and miles, and from the driver's seat at the front of the train he had an uninterrupted view. It was so wonderful to see the farmers at work with all of the great machinery and equipment which they needed to plant and harvest all of the different crops at all of the different seasons of the year. It was just so wonderful to see the amount of work that one person could do because of the equipment which was now available. Peter, since becoming a train driver, learned so much about how and where most of our everyday food came from and the work involved in producing it. He thought that he would have liked and enjoyed being a farmer.

He had recently rekindled his interest in photography. His art teacher at school had taught him how to take and develop his own photos and Peter had found a lovely old Canon SLR camera at a car boot sale. It didn't work but Peter was very good at fixing things. He had to learn as a boy, as his mother didn't have money for repairs and his Dad was useless. He had recently treated himself to a used 135mm lens and was now able to take shots of the farm machinery that fascinated him on his long journeys. He hoped in future to be able publish a collection of these. One day!

On his way home one Friday evening from Southampton to Newcastle, after a very busy week, Peter was beginning to get tired but was nearing the end of his journey with just one more stop before Newcastle and home. It was now almost 8 p.m. as he approached Darlington station which was very quiet and just a few people on the platform as he stopped. Those few people would almost certainly be getting on his train for the short journey to Newcastle.

Whilst waiting for the guard to give him the OK to go, Peter was idly looking around the almost deserted station when he saw two men come out of a waiting room. Each of them was carrying a can of beer. They did not appear to be getting on to his train which Peter thought was just as well as they seemed to be drunk and were arguing with one another. One of them seemed to be vaguely familiar to Peter but from where he was, he couldn't be sure. Having his camera beside him Peter decided to take a shot of them, so he could see the man's face better and see if he would remember who he was. The argument appeared to be getting very heated, they were now facing each other and pointing fingers at each other. Peter was waiting with his camera ready for them both to turn towards him which they did just as he got the signal to go. The photo was a good shot of them and through the telephoto lens Peter recognised exactly who the chap was.

When he got his train safely to Newcastle, Peter was delighted and could not get home quick enough to see Helen, especially since it was also the weekend and he had nothing to do until Monday except to tinker around the house. Maybe he would develop this reel of film?

CHAPTER 15

A Murder Investigation

After a late breakfast on Saturday morning Peter helped Helen to tidy up and vacuumed around the house. Helen was now seven months pregnant so she was getting rather large around the tummy so Peter did not like her doing much housework. After they had done the chores in the house they needed to go and get the weekend shopping from the supermarket. This was the time that they really appreciated their little car as the supermarket was about three miles away. At the newspaper stand in the supermarket Peter noticed a headline in one of the daily papers 'Man Stabbed to Death at Railway Station'. He picked up the paper and read some of the article and soon found out that it was Darlington station and had happened the previous evening at about 9 p.m. There was no doubt in Peter's mind that it must be the same two men whom he saw while he was stopped there last evening. The police were now looking for the murderer who had made his getaway on foot to, where they had no idea, and were appealing for anybody who may have seen anything to contact them immediately. Peter did not know which of the two was stabbed. He had identified the one which he thought looked familiar as somebody who went to Grangethorpe Comp with him. His name was Jake

Steadman. What he remembered about Jake was not very good. He was always in trouble at school, both with the teachers and his classmates. He came from a very poor and downbeat family who lived in a council house which looked very shabby with half of the windows having no curtains. The small garden at the front was piled up with all sorts of rubbish and a whole lot of beer bottles and cans. Poor Jake always looked hungry and would make quick work of his school dinner which was probably the only proper meal he got each day.

Peter had almost forgotten about the two men he had seen at Darlington station the previous evening and had not mentioned it to Helen. Having read the article in the paper he asked her if she would like a coffee and said that they should go to the supermarket cafeteria and have a drink and a few minutes rest. Helen said that she was thinking exactly the same thing. Peter had taken the paper with him and when he got the two coffees he told Helen all about what he had seen at the station in Darlington the previous evening and now the newspaper article which he showed her. Helen was absolutely shocked and wondered if she wanted Peter to get involved by getting in touch with the police. Peter told her that he was duty bound to report to the police what he had seen, even more so because he did not know who stabbed who. As for Jake, whom he had known from his school days, was he the victim or the murderer? He had no idea.

That afternoon he developed the photograph in his cellar dark room and showed Helen. It was a very clear image of Jake Steadman and the other man arguing.

The phone number of the police department which was dealing with the case was in the paper, so Peter phoned and, after explaining what he had seen, was put through to the investigating officer, Detective Inspector Chambers. When he had told the inspector what he had seen at the station on the previous evening, which must have been just minutes before the murder, and that he had a photograph of the men the officer was certainly very interested in Peter and wanted to see and speak to him as soon as possible. Before giving the inspector his personal details, Peter told him that he did not want police cars or vans coming to the house or anybody wearing police uniform. He would prefer to go to the police station and give his statement there if it was not too far away. He explained that his wife was pregnant and getting close to giving birth. The inspector assured Peter that there would not be any police cars or uniformed officers calling to his house as he himself would, if Peter wished, call and take his statement and that he would like to do this as soon as possible. Peter was quite happy with this arrangement and told the officer that he could come whenever it suited him. So, an appointment was made for 4 p.m. that afternoon. The inspector would not divulge over the phone who was the victim. He said that he would tell him when he met him.

So, Peter got ready for what was to be his first interview or indeed first contact whatsoever with a police officer. The inspector arrived at 4 p.m. exactly and introduced himself. His name was Harold Chambers and told Peter and Helen to call him Harry. Helen asked if he would like a cup of tea or coffee to which he said he would love a coffee with one small spoon of sugar. His look and manner gave Peter a much more relaxed feeling than he had since he spoke to the inspector earlier on. This would probably be part of the inspector's training to get the interviewee in a comfortable mood before he got to what was a very important interview in this particular case.

After they all had a cup of coffee, Harry was anxious to get started and asked Peter if he was ready, he opened his briefcase and took out a pad and also a tape recorder. Then, "Can I have your full name, age, date of birth, occupation, marital status? ... Right we have got all of that, so what in your own words, Peter, did you see at Darlington station last evening?" Peter described that as a long-distance train driver he was on his way back to Newcastle from Southampton. Darlington was the last stop for him before his destination. There were not many people on the platform as he approached, probably about eight or ten, all of whom would probably be getting on his train for the last leg of his journey. As he sat in his cab waiting for the signal to go, he had noticed two men coming out of a waiting room, both of whom had a can of beer in their hands and looked as if they were a bit drunk. They appeared to be arguing about something but did not make any attempt to get on his train. One of these chaps looked vaguely familiar to Peter but he could not remember where from, so he took out his camera and, when he got them facing towards him, he took a photo of them. He was thinking that when he had time to look at the photo he would be able to think who this chap was.

Just as he took the photograph, he got the signal to go, so he did not see any more of the two men who were arguing. He had identified the chap whom he thought looked familiar, as a boy he went to school with and who was in the same class. This lad's name was Jake Steadman. Peter then went on to describe Jake and his family background. He then asked the inspector if he could tell him which of the two had been murdered, he was hoping for it not to be Jake. The inspector told him that from the few items of ID they found on the victim it would appear that his name was not Jake Steadman. So, from the information that Peter had just given him, they would be looking for Jake to arrest him on suspicion of murder. He then asked Peter if he could see the photograph of the two men which he had taken. Peter showed him the photo, which was a very good portrait. The inspector told him which of the two the victim was, so Jake Steadman was now definitely their chief suspect.

He told Peter he would take the photo to his control room. He also asked Peter if he knew or could remember Jake's family address. Peter said he could not remember the house number but the road was Blowfell Road on the big council estate in Byker, at the top end of the cul-de-sac, and, if the family were still there, it would be easy to find the number because of the supermarket trolleys and rubbish in the garden.

The photograph, together with the inspector's instructions, were taken to the incident control room and acknowledged by the detective on duty, so the search for Jake began.

CHAPTER 16

A Very Special Delivery

Helen was now within four weeks of her baby's due date. She and Butch had managed to find a lovely lady to take over Helen's duties for the time when she would be off. This lady, whose name was Janet Gardoni, a spinster who had retired a year earlier from her job as a librarian, and was finding that she was getting bored at home so she was delighted to have something to occupy her time, even if it was only for six months. She had come in for a couple of mornings with Helen and soon got to know what her job would entail. Butch was very happy with Janet who was a very smart and conscientious lady. Janet also enjoyed meeting and chatting with the customers who regularly came in for all kinds of quality cards and stationery, which Helen had introduced into the stock.

Helen, on her first morning when she did not have to go to work, thought 'this is great' and turned over in bed and went to sleep for another couple of hours. Peter had taken her a cup of tea before he went to work. When she woke, she was starving and got up and got herself some breakfast. The postman had just dropped some mail through the letter box, so she went and picked it up. Apart from the usual junk mail she found a handwritten letter with a local postmark.

It was a hand-written letter from Jordan, pleading with her not to take the case to court. There was a heartfelt apology for what he had stupidly said about her and for the hurt it had caused her. He went on to say that he had three more weeks before his final exams and he had done very little work on preparing for them as he could not get down to studying and was not getting any proper sleep. He wrote that his parents had arranged a bank loan in an effort to resolve this matter and that this loan was limited to £20K. There would have to be legal fees of both parties. Jordan's parents would almost certainly have to sell their house which was already heavily mortgaged. The outcome of a court action could end up with Jordan's family life destroyed.

"So please, Helen, I am begging you, drop the case. I am talking to the bank manager at the university and I think she will extend my overdraft as I am so close to finals. Together with my savings I can give you £4,000. Please take it. Don't tell the lawyers and we can put this all behind us. I have never stopped caring about you, Helen, and I know what an amazing girl you are. Please, please, accept my humble offer."

After Peter got home and had his dinner Helen showed him the letter which she had received from Jordan. When he had read it through, he said, "Well what are you going to do? It is entirely up to you now. It is a good apology and a decent offer. Yes, Francesca has said if you took the case to court you may be awarded more than the £20K but I would hate for the family to sell their house and be financially ruined. I don't think that you would like to see that happen. I now think that you should talk this over with our parents and find out what they think."

Helen phoned her parents that evening and explained to her dad where she was up to with the Jordan case. She now had an offer of £4K from Jordan plus an apology for what he had said for the hurt he had caused her. Andrew and Andrea were both very much in favour of her accepting the offer and closing down this episode of her life which had caused her a whole lot of worry and pain, especially now as her baby was almost due and would be a very joyful occasion for her and Peter and for all the family.

Helen's first job next morning was to contact Fran and tell her that she was dropping the case. She also thanked Fran for the professional manner in which she had handled the case and that she would let Uncle Butch know, and also write to her boss at Morris and Co. singing her praises. Fran made Helen promise not to do the latter. 'What a modest girl she is!' thought Helen!

At her last appointment with the midwife, which was three weeks before the date for the birth, the midwife explained to Helen what to expect as she came nearer to the big day, explaining she might go into labour anytime now as babies often arrived before their due date. She told Helen to have her bag packed and ready at the first indication that she was going into labour and to come straight to the hospital. After that neither her nor Peter were getting much sleep as any time Helen moved or stirred in the bed Peter would think 'this is it'. Then, one night Helen really did stir and let out a loud cry which she was certain was the cue to go. The drive to the hospital, which was about half an hour away, was not the most comfortable ride that Helen and Peter had. She was sure that the baby was coming at any moment, but she could not ask Peter to stop. However, they managed to get to the hospital. Helen told Peter to run in and get a nurse or somebody to come and get her onto a trolley as she was certain that she could not walk. By the time they got Helen to the delivery room she was ready to give birth to a lovely 8lb baby girl. The midwife was amazed at the speed in which everything had happened. Peter did not know what had hit him. It was now just over two hours since they woke up and here they were looking at a beautiful little baby girl.

It was 4 a.m. and too early in the morning to phone anybody with the great news. The sister-in-charge told Peter that he should now go home as Helen would be going back to the postnatal ward where there was a bed ready for her. He could not go back there as there were other mothers who would be sleeping. He could come back in later at visiting time and take somebody in with him but just one person.

Peter got back home and could not wait to get to bed, but he could not get to sleep as there was so much going on in his mind. As it was Saturday morning, he did not want to phone anybody too early, so he waited until 8 a.m. and then phoned Helen's parents. The phone was answered almost immediately by Andrea. When she heard Peter's voice, she became very excited as she knew it must be about Helen. When Peter told her about everything that had happened in a matter of one hour or two and ended with the arrival of a beautiful baby girl, she was speechless, but so happy.

Peter's next call was to his mother and Martin who were so happy to hear the news after which he then phoned Marian.

After the glad news was circulated to all of their friends, Peter just remembered that he had not had his breakfast. He now started to relax and try to come to terms with the night that he had just had. This was an event greater than anything that had ever happened to Helen and him since they first met and would have a profound effect on them for the rest of their lives. He felt like dancing around the floor. After he had his breakfast, Peter wondered if he should phone Helen on the postnatal ward phone. He thought that he would try and hoped that they would answer.

The wonderful midwife found Helen for him. She was delighted to hear Peter's voice. She told Peter that she was feeling great, and that their lovely baby had slept for hours. "But when she wakes up, she demands attention in a big way!" She had breast fed her twice since and she just took to it so naturally. "So Peter you won't have to get up at night to get a bottle ready! Now I don't think that we ever decided what we should call our baby, Peter, but now it is make-your-mind-up time, so what shall we call her? My own preference is Anna followed by what, I don't know?" Peter said that he liked Anna too and that they should both think about a second name and when he came in at visiting time they should both decide. He told Helen that Andrea wanted to come with him when he came in this afternoon.

"I told her that I thought you would like that so she will be with me when we see you at 2 p.m."

Helen had made a list of things which she needed bringing in both for her and the baby. Peter promised to get what she needed. Though where he would find nipple cream, he had no idea! He said goodbye for now. Peter phoned Andrea and told her that all was well with Helen and the baby and that Helen was looking forward to seeing them at 2 p.m. He asked Andrea if she would please help him sort out the list which Helen had asked for. Disposable knickers, indeed!

CHAPTER 17

Miss Gardoni

Inspector Chambers, in his effort to apprehend and arrest Jake Steadman on suspicion of murder, had dispatched two of this team to what he believed to be Jake's family home in Blowfell Road. They did not have the house number but were told to look for a house at the top of the road with a very untidy garden and windows with no curtains. It did not take them long to pinpoint a house which fitted the description.

After much bell ringing and banging at the door it was opened by a man who did not look very pleased. He looked like he had just got out of bed and had not shaved for days. The pair introduced themselves as DS Sam Mosely and DC Colin Wardle from Darlington police station and showed him their warrant cards. They asked his name which he grudgingly gave as Bert Steadman. They asked if they could come in as they had some questions to ask him. He said, "What are the questions about, and can you not ask them here as the house is in a mess?" They agreed and were actually glad that they did not have to go in as the smell coming from inside was not very pleasant. They asked him if Jake Steadman lived here to which he answered 'no'. They asked him if he knew where he lived to which he answered 'no'. He said that he had left there about two years ago and he had not seen or heard from him since then. He asked the detectives what the inquiry was about and hoped that he was not in any serious trouble to which they told him that they could not tell him that right now and said that if he had any information about his son that it was his duty to tell them or he could be in serious trouble.

After the two detectives got back to headquarters and told Inspector Chambers about their interview with Jake Steadman's father, who insisted that he had not seen or heard from his son for about two years, they did say that they were both of the opinion that despite his appearance and the condition of the house in which he lived that he was telling the truth. So where would they go from there?

They had the photo, which Peter had taken of Jake and the man who was stabbed to death, Inspector Chambers told them to get hold of the local reporter and get it on the front page. A very prominent half-page article about the fatal stabbing at Darlington station two days ago, together with Jake Steadman's photograph, who was the chief suspect in the murder of the victim, Richard Topping, and anybody with any information of the whereabouts of Jake should contact the police immediately on the number given.

By the end of the week there was a very good response from the public. Several sightings of a man resembling the photograph were reported. Most of the responses came from people living in Aston Aycliffe which was not very far from Darlington. The Inspector decided to increase the squad on this case to six, two of which were uniformed officers. The uniformed officers concentrated on the Aston Aycliffe area, and were equipped with copies of Jake Steadman's photograph. The squad of six was then broken down into two sets of three with DS Sam Mosely as the leader of one of the squads and DC Colin Wardle in charge of the other.

They divided the area into two parts, naming all the streets and roads. Each officer was given a list of questions which he was to ask at each house, plus a photograph of Jake Steadman, and so the search began. Within an hour one of the uniformed officers, Constable Jackson, had the surprise of his life. He had knocked at the door of a house on one of the roads which he was allocated to, the door was opened by a young man who seemed very surprised to see a policeman. The policeman introduced himself and explained what his visit was about. He showed the photograph of their chief suspect and said that they had reason to believe that he may live in the area. The man looked at the photo and was rather surprised to see that it was a photo of himself.

He said, "What is the name of this suspect in the photo?"

The policeman said, "It is Jake Steadman."

"I am Jake Steadman and I am very pleased to tell you that I have not committed any crime." Constable Jackson was now in a panic. Here he was face to face with the main suspect in a serious crime, which in this case was murder.

He said, "I must radio my boss who is also on this road looking for you."

Jake said, "Go ahead and radio him and I hope that he has a very good explanation for this." Jackson radioed DC Wardle and told him that he was at number 24 and that he was talking to Jake Steadman and to please come. Wardle could not believe what he was hearing and went to investigate.

"That Plod is probably being taken for a right mug!" he muttered to himself.

*

Peter and Andrea were at the hospital in good time and had to wait some time to be allowed into the maternity ward where Helen and her baby were. Helen was not very happy about how she was looking as she had nothing to wear other than what she came in with last night, her pyjamas and a dressing gown. She had no makeup on, so she was glad to get something nice to change into after she had seen her mother and showed her the lovely baby, Anna. She was feeling fine and was hoping to be allowed home, but the doctor had insisted that she stayed until the next day as her blood pressure was higher than he would have liked. Once they could get that sorted, she could go home.

Visiting time soon went and Helen was now looking so much better after she got herself dressed and put some makeup on. She did get home the next day which she was so happy about. Then Andrea, Carol, and Peter's mother Valerie really pampered Helen and would not let her do anything about the house. They took over the cooking and cleaning for a whole week, by which time Helen was feeling on top form and ready to get back to her usual household chores, including the shopping. The baby, who was now named Anna Louise, was doing very nicely, not too demanding and sleeping well with just two feeds through the night. Helen was absolutely loving motherhood, she felt so blessed.

Andrea had offered to look after Anna when Helen went back to work which she was very grateful for. However, she didn't want to leave Anna for five days and also did not think it would be fair on both of her parents to expect them to do that on a full-time basis as they had their own lives to live. She phoned Butch and Janet to let them know about the baby and how things had worked out for her and Peter. They were both very happy with the news and wasted no time sending cards and congratulations and flowers. Butch told Helen that the shop was running very smoothly and that Janet was absolutely marvellous and so pleasant to work with. Helen was very pleased to hear that Janet was so efficient and that Butch was happy with her so she was now working out a plan which she was going to put to Butch and see what he would think of it. The plan was that if Janet was willing to stay on a part-time basis, they would share the job on terms which would suit them both. It would also mean that Andrea would only have to look after Anna for about three days. She talked this over with Peter before she mentioned it to anybody else to see what he thought.

Peter knew how much Helen enjoyed working in the shop, but had been loving being a new mother even more, so this seemed like the best of both worlds and if everybody was happy with the arrangement it was a very good idea. She phoned Butch next morning at home and had a long and comfortable chat with him, she told him what she had in mind and asked him to think about it before he decided but not to mention it to Janet just yet, until she had spoken to him again.

When she spoke to Butch, he appeared to be very much in favour of Helen's plan. So, they decided to have a meeting, all three of them, Butch, Janet, and herself. They needed to have at least an hour to themselves to discuss how this would work out or if Janet wanted to stay on. They decided to close the shop for one hour, around about mid-morning which was the quietest time of the day. Helen said they should put a notice up in the window to advise customers of the closure and apologise for any inconvenience that this might cause. This closure would be on Wednesday June 18th from 11 a.m. to 12 noon. Helen then told Butch to have a word with Janet, just to give her an idea of what he and Helen were thinking of putting into action. This would give Janet a few days to think if she wanted to be part of it or did she want to finish when Helen came back to work, after all she had retired from a full-time job. Would she want to be committed to a job, albeit a part-time one, on a long-term basis?

The meeting was arranged with all parties now having full knowledge of what the agenda was. June 18th came and at 11 a.m. the doors were locked. Helen had made coffee and had it ready on a little table around which she had sat three chairs. Butch opened the meeting by giving a brief outline of what it was about. He then asked

Janet if she wanted to be part of the team on a part-time basis. The situation had been brought about by Helen's family commitments and having just had baby Anna. Janet said that she was very happy to commit to working with Helen and Butch for a long as they wanted her and was so grateful to them to be given the opportunity to do so. She continued by saying that since she had been part of the small team at Butch's shop, she had been so happy and loved coming to work each morning. She loved meeting and greeting and chatting to many of the people who came into the shop and to be called by her name by many of them. She contrasted this to all the years that she worked at the library and was never called anything but Miss Gardoni.

Helen said that it would suit her to do three and a half days each week and if Janet was willing to do two and a half days then they could sort out who did which days. This could be agreed between them nearer the time as she still had almost three months to go in her maternity leave. Butch was quite happy with this arrangement and the only thing left to sort out was the salaries of each of his two employees. He explained to Janet that Helen had been with him since she left school and put a whole lot of work into making it the thriving little business which it was today. Janet interrupted Butch at this point and said that she did not care about the salary as that was not the reason for coming to work there. She had a good pension and was reasonably comfortable financially and it was for him and Helen to sort out what her salary would be. "And as I have already said. I love working here." After all of that there was nothing else for them to talk about, so the meeting was concluded, the closed sign was reversed, and it was back to business as usual.

CHAPTER 18

Under Arrest

When DC Wardle discovered that one of 'the plods' had indeed found Jake Steadman, he called his boss DS Mosely and told him to come and to see if they had the right man. If so, it would save everybody a whole lot of time and trouble. Mosely wasted no time in getting to where Wardle told him they were. He also took his two assistants with him. Jake Steadman was completely overawed when he saw six men at the door all looking very serious. Detective Mosely then took over. He introduced himself to Jake and explained that as a result of information which they had received concerning the fatal stabbing of a man at Darlington station they needed to take him in for questioning.

Jake protested that he did not stab anybody, but he admitted to being at Darlington station on the day in question and being with the victim and another man whom he had never seen before. The victim, whose name was Richard Topping, was with another man whom he said was a friend of his. His name was Scott Wrigley. Rich had told Jake that he would like to meet him to discuss something and said that the station at Darlington would be an ideal place to meet as there were so many people coming and going at the station they would not attract attention. Rich did not tell Jake that he would have somebody else with him. The reason for this meeting was that Rich was planning to rob the post office in Darlington at 10 a.m. one morning. This was the time when they would have the maximum amount of cash as it was the day when most people collected their pensions.

Mosely told Jake that he did not want to hear any more as he did not believe a word of this made up story and he was now arresting him on suspicion of the murder of Richard Topping. The police officers formed a ring around Jake and Mosely slipped the handcuffs on him. Jake felt like he was in a movie or in some kind of bad dream.

After they took Jake to the police station at Darlington he was asked if he wanted to have a solicitor with him when he was interviewed, Jake said 'yes'. The solicitor was quickly arranged and spent some time with Jake before he was interviewed. Jake protested at the way he was arrested because he had nothing to do with the murder of Richard Topping.

This is what Jake told the investigating officers in his recorded interview with Detective Inspector Chambers and DS Mosely.

He, Rich Topping, and this other guy called Scott Wrigley, whom Jake had never seen before in his life, had been in the waiting room at Darlington station which was empty except for the three of them. Rich had a bag which must have had at least a dozen cans of beer, all of which they had drunk whilst they were in the waiting room. Rich told them of his plan for robbing the post office. First, they had to steal a car which Scott would drive and wait outside the post office. At 9:45 a.m. he and Jake would put on their balaclavas and go in. Rich would have a gun and Jake would have a machete. They would dash up to the counter and demand all of the cash that they had. Rich said that he was not expecting much or any resistance from the two old dears who worked there. Jake would smash the glass partition with the machete. This would scare the two old birds and encourage them to hand over the cash. At this point, Jake had interrupted and said that he did not want to have anything to do with robbing the post office or indeed anywhere else. He then got up to leave and walked out onto the platform, followed by Rich. They were arguing and it was getting very heated at which point Jake told Rich that he would not under any circumstances be part of the robbery. He also said that he had been clean now for three years and was now getting his life back together and that he never wanted to see Rich again and walked out of the station, just as the signal was given to the driver to take the train away. What happened between Rich Topping and Scott Wrigley after that he had no idea. Jake reiterated that he had nothing to do with Rich Topping's murder and suggested that they should now find Scott Wrigley and find out what he had to say for himself.

Jake's solicitor asked DI Chambers what he was going to do as it would appear that his client had not murdered Topping and should now be released. Chambers said he was detaining Steadman pending further enquiries; he would be interviewed again next day. Jake was then asked to give a full description of Wrigley and anything else that he knew about him.

CHAPTER 19

A Sad Day for the Lawsons

When Helen got back home after her meeting with Butch and Janet, she phoned Andrea and asked if she could call and see her for a chat and that she would also take Anna. Andrea was delighted and told her to come right away and that she would have the kettle on. When Helen arrived, Andrea was looking very worried as Andrew had taken a bad turn and was feeling very poorly, which was most unusual for him. He was lying on his bed and did not seem coherent. The right side of his face was drooping down. When Helen saw him, she immediately phoned for an ambulance to have him taken to the hospital as quickly as possible. It did appear that he may have had a stroke, but she could not be sure.

The ambulance arrived within half an hour and the paramedic checked Andrew over before moving him. His blood pressure was very high, and his heartbeat was also very erratic. His diagnosis was that he had a stroke and they needed to get him to Newcastle General as quickly as possible. Helen phoned Carol and told her what had happened and to go to the hospital right away and meet her mam who would go in the ambulance with her dad. She could not go as she had Anna to look after, but she would also go to the hospital when Peter got home which would be about 6 p.m. Luckily, Carol was not very far away and got to the hospital just as the ambulance pulled up. Carol was very shocked to see her dad who was looking very pale and seemed to be unconscious. Her mam was looking very worried and concerned for Andrew, clinging on to him and talking to him even though she knew that he could not hear her.

Helen took Anna home and waited very impatiently for Peter to come home. She could not concentrate on doing anything such as planning a dinner for Peter. He would have to sort something out for himself and look after Anna when he got home as she would go to the hospital as soon as he got back. She could not bear to think that her loving and caring dad might die. He was only 64 years of age and had always looked after himself and kept himself in very good shape. Whatever would her mam and all of them do without him if he died?

Peter did eventually get home and was grabbed hold of by Helen as she told him the news about her dad. When she arrived at the hospital and enquired at the desk about the whereabouts of her dad, she was told that he was in the Stroke Unit. She was informed that she must not go into the unit without first seeing the nurse in charge. However, when she got there she found Andrea and Carol in a waiting room right next to where her dad was being looked after. They were both looking very concerned. Helen hugged both of them and asked if they had heard anything about his condition. Carol told her that the consultant, Dr John Reilly, had just been and said that her dad had had a massive stroke, "a cerebral infarction", and was in a very serious condition. They had given him some kind of clot-busting drug to get the blood supply back to his brain, but it might make things even worse by causing bleeding. The consultant had suggested to them that in the event of a further deterioration, it would not be in his best interests to resuscitate him using CPR. Andrea had agreed, knowing that it was the last thing Andrew would have wanted. They were able to see him; they had just been waiting for Helen.

Andrea, Helen, and Carol tiptoed into the Stroke Unit. Andrew looked as if he was having a very peaceful sleep except that he had a whole lot of wires and tubes attached to him. After a while the nurse who was looking after him whispered to them that she needed to do some observations and tests on Andrew. She told them that they would be able to spend as long as they wanted with him after.

Later that night another nurse told them that Andrew's condition had stabilised a little and they should go home and get some rest. They would need it in the coming days. This was a very sad time for the family, deep down they were thinking that if they left they would never see him alive again. Helen left her phone number at reception with instructions that, in the event of her dad deteriorating, she should be contacted first and so they went home.

Peter and Anna were okay when Helen got home although Anna was ready for her supper which was the first thing Helen had to do while at the same time she told Peter all about her dad and how serious his condition was. Peter said how sorry he was to hear that and told Helen that he had phoned the train driver's department and told them that he would have to have a week off and would not be at work in the morning. Helen was delighted to hear that as she was almost certain that her dad would not survive, in which case she and indeed Andrea and Carol would need Peter's support to come to terms with the fact that they would never again have Andrew there to love and help them with any problems that may trouble them. So, they went to bed and hoped that they might get some sleep.

They did manage to get a few hours' sleep, however, a very sad day lay ahead of the Lawson family. At 7.15 a.m. Helen's phone rang. She knew what the caller would tell her which was that her dad Andrew had passed away. The doctor said he was very sorry, but Andrew had suffered a catastrophic brain haemorrhage and had gone into cardiac arrest. Helen thanked God that Peter was there with her and was now holding her in his strong arms. She could not weep or cry at this time, all that would come later; right now, she had so much to do. But first she had the dreadful news to break to her mam and to Carol.

After she had phoned Andrea and Carol and told them the terrible news, they all had a good cry. Helen told her mam that she would be round to see her as soon as she had fed Anna and got herself dressed. Peter said that there were so many things that needed to be sorted out, such as getting on to an undertaker who would then arrange with the hospital when he could collect the body from their morgue. Peter wondered if there would have to be a postmortem to establish the cause of death as it was so sudden. All this could take a few days before the body would be released to the undertaker to arrange the funeral. Peter knew all of this since his own father's sudden death, so he wanted to be with Andrea, Helen, and Carol to help with the arrangements as they were all very distraught and in shock at this tragic event which had come upon them so suddenly and unexpectedly.

Just as Helen, Peter, and Anna were ready to go to Andrea and Carol's, the postman delivered some mail, most of which was junk. Helen recognised an envelope which she knew was from Jordan. In it, a cheque for £4,000. In different circumstances this would probably be cause to celebrate but today nothing could change the grief and sense of loss which Helen was feeling so she just stuck the cheque back in the envelope and put it in a drawer. When they arrived at her parents' house, which today was not in its usual neat and tidy state, they all hugged and kissed one another and tried to console each other with much weeping and crying. Peter did a quick tidy up in the kitchen and made a pot of tea and made them all sit around the kitchen table and poured everyone a cup of tea. By now everybody was much calmer and started to talk mostly about Andrew and how kind and good natured that he was. All of them had their own memories of what he had done and said.

Peter sat and listened to all of those little accolades and thought how wonderful it must be to have such memories of one's father. What a contrast to his own memories of his father, of whom he did not have one happy memory or one occasion when he'd said or done something kind either to him or his mother. How sad Peter felt after listening to what he had just heard about Andrew, that the only good memory of his dad was the morning that he died.

Now it was time to get down to practical thinking about the funeral arrangements. Peter said that he had made a mental list of things which needed to be sorted out almost immediately, and if they so wished for him to list them for their consideration, he would be happy to do so. Andrea, Helen, and Carol said that they would be very happy for Peter to take over everything because in their frame of mind right now they could not think straight. So, Peter started to outline what needed to be decided right now.

Firstly, did they want Andrew to be buried or cremated? Buried. Second, what type of coffin or casket would they like? A good-quality coffin. Third, did they want Andrew to wear his best suit or to have a shroud? His suit. Fourth, what sort of religious service would they like, if any? Peter himself would like it if they would have a Christian service as a last farewell to Andrew but that was up to the family to decide. A funeral service at St John's church. Fifth, did they have any preference regarding undertakers? No. Sixth, would they like an obituary notice putting in the local paper? Yes. "I will write it," said Helen. Seventh, would they like to have an after-funeral reception and, if so, where? "Yes, you decide where, Peter."

Peter then said that those were the main things which needed to be sorted out and which he would like to get on to as soon as possible. So, having got all that sorted and agreed with the family, Peter said that he would get on with it.

Having spoken to and given instructions to the undertaker, whom he found to be very helpful and thorough, he told Peter that he would take care of everything once he found out if there would be a post-mortem and when that might be done. He gave Peter a list of all the coffins which he usually used, together with the prices, and asked Peter to let him know as soon as possible which one the family would like and also to let him have Andrew's suit and a matching shirt and tie.

They went through the other items which Peter had now written down such as the cemetery, the church, the number of cars required, the obituary notice, the church service, and the venue for the after-funeral reception. The undertaker, whose name was Robert Faulks, told Peter that he was happy to take care of all those details and the only other thing he needed was the wording of the obituary notice which only the family could provide. Then, when he knew which coffin they had opted for, he would email them a detailed list and total cost for everything.

Peter was very happy with Robert's business-like performance and made his way back to Andrea's to discuss it all with the family. It was still only 11.30 a.m. and he had set the wheels in motion for the last journey of Andrew Lawson, a man whom he very much admired and loved. The undertaker contacted the hospital authorities with regards to the death of Andrew Lawson and to find out if there would be a post-mortem and if so when it would be.

The bereavement officer at the General told them that no post-mortem was needed as the diagnosis of stroke had been made on the admission MRI scan. The death had been reported to the coroner, since it was sudden, but the coroner was happy with the diagnosis made by Dr Reilly and so the undertaker could collect the body from the morgue as soon as was convenient.

After this everything fell into place very smoothly and the funeral took place within a week of Andrew's death. It was a sad day for the Lawson family; Andrea, Helen, and Carol, all dressed in black, were all looking very sombre but composed. The church service was quite short but appropriate. Peter had prepared and delivered a great eulogy about Andrew, most of which was serious and rather touching but also included some very funny and good natured little stories about his father-in-law and the good man that he was.

After the service was over Andrew was then taken to his final resting place. Despite the grief which they felt for having to say farewell to the pillar of the family, they were all held together and composed by this giant of a man who had now taken over the role that Andrew had fulfilled for so many years. This young man's name was Peter.

The reception venue was very appropriate for the occasion and with ample refreshments. Even though it was a sad occasion for the family it was so good to see so many friends and acquaintances which they had not seen for ages. So ended the internment of Andrew Lawson.

*

Whatever the grief or sense of loss in the family it was now back to normal life for everybody. Helen, Peter, and Anna were now back to their own house and just picking up on where they were up to before. Helen had almost forgotten about the letter and cheque from Jordan and now needed to discuss with Peter what they should do with this windfall. After she had settled Anna in her cot for her morning sleep, she got the cheque from the drawer and asked Peter to come and sit with her and for them to decide what to do with the money. Peter's first thought and suggestion to Helen was to think of how Andrea's finances were now after she had paid the undertakers for the funeral. He knew that she and Andrew did not have very much money and suggested that Helen should give her mother at least £1000 but that it was her money and she could do whatever she liked with it. Helen grabbed hold of Peter and hugged him and kissed him, saying that she was thinking very much the same, but perhaps not £1000. Peter argued that he thought anything less than £1000 would be inappropriate, especially now as Carol was getting ready to go to university, and her mam would need all the money she could get her hands on. They then talked about their own finances, they both had their own bank accounts and Helen wondered if they should have a joint account. Peter was not sure and said that they should keep things as they are for a while and after Helen had got sorted out with a current account and also got some information on interest rates as she should invest most of that money into a one or two years fixed rate bond where it would earn a decent interest rate. He said that he would look into what rates were available. He explained to Helen that on fixed rate bonds your money was tied up for whatever term you chose. The longer you tied it up for the better interest rate you got.

It was Saturday morning and Helen phoned her mother and Carol just to see if they were alright after the traumatic week which they had just had. Andrea said they were okay and had managed a good night's sleep. Helen asked them to come and have lunch with them on Sunday and that she would come and pick them up. Andrea was delighted as she was glad to get out of the house and wondered if she would ever settle down in this house again. After they had done their weekly shopping at the supermarket, Helen and Peter and of course Anna were having a nice leisurely afternoon. Helen was finding it very hard to concentrate on anything and could not come to terms with the fact that her dad was dead and buried and that she would never see him again. It would have been so nice if he was coming with her mam and Carol for lunch the next day and she could tell him about the cheque from Jordan. Thinking of which, she now thought that she should give something to Carol who was getting ready to start university shortly. She asked Peter what he thought. Peter said that he definitely agreed, and she should give Carol at least £500. So, £2500 of what Jordan had given her was left for her own nest egg. She was very happy with that.

CHAPTER 20

The Manhunt

Jake Steadman was still being held by the police on suspicion of murder but was not charged. Every time he was interviewed, he maintained he was innocent and that when he left the station on the evening in question Richard Topping was alive but not very happy because of what he had just told him. The inspector was now inclined to believe him and would have to either charge him or release him tomorrow. They had already appealed for anyone who had been in Darlington station around the time of the murder to contact them, hoping that somebody may have seen something suspicious. The name Scott Wrigley did show up in their quest to find out something about him. He had been in trouble with the police but only on a minor offence for which he was fined some petty amount at a Darlington court, so he was not on their radar, but they had to find him. Several sightings of Wrigley had been reported to them but no current information of his whereabouts. A number of the sightings which had been reported to them were from an area in South Shields which did not have a good reputation so it would be reasonable to assume that Scott Wrigley could be in such an area. Inspector Chambers then decided to employ the house-to-house inquiry method using the same teams who had been so successful in finding Jake Steadman. All their enquiries on day one drew negative results which Inspector Chambers was disappointed with, but he was determined to push on in an effort to find their prime suspect.

Next day, the team on the house-to-house enquiry resumed their search for Scott Wrigley. DC Wardle was on his third house, he rang the bell, an elderly lady came to the door looking quite frail and worried when she saw this stranger and asked him what he wanted. Wardle could see the concern on her face and in a very reassuring voice introduced himself and showed her his warrant card. He also asked her what her name was which she said was Brenda White but was always called Bren. Wardle then said, "Well Bren I hope that you may be able to help me," and went on to explain about this chap whom he had reason to believe lived in the area and whom he would like to have a chat with. He then showed her the photo of Scott Wrigley. As he showed Bren the photo Wardle was observing her face very closely to see if she showed any signs of recognition of who this photo might be. Bren pursed her lips and said, "You had better come in," and took him into the kitchen where she made straight for the kettle and said, "I need a cup of tea. Would you like one?" Wardle replied that he would. Not another word was spoken until they both had sat down with their tea. Bren then said, "Why do you want to speak to this chap in the photo?" Wardle said that he could not tell her the specific case which they were investigating but it was rather serious, and they needed to speak to him to help with their enquiries and to either eliminate or arrest him. Then Bren said, "Before I tell you anything about this man, I want an assurance that I will not be called as a witness or to give evidence if he should be charged for whatever crime you are investigating."

Wardle assured her that this would not happen and that the chances were that she would never see or hear from him again. Bren opened up and said that she knew where this chap lived and in fact she was a friend of his mother. His name was Scott Wrigley and he always seemed to be in some kind of trouble. "He is involved with a gang from this area who are into drug dealing and many other rackets including shoplifting and burglary. This gang have wreaked havoc in this area over the last three or four years. Many families who can afford to have moved out to other areas because of this gang of criminals. I am scared stiff to open the door to anyone and indeed scared to go to bed at night. Scott's mother knows very well that he is one of this gang but cannot get him to get a job and get away from them, they are a bad influence on him. Her name is Molly Renton now as she remarried, and she is a nice lady. We sometimes visit one another and go to bingo occasionally. Now I will give you her address and please don't tell Molly that it was me who gave it to you. Scott will still be in bed. I don't think you should go there on your own as he is quite a big guy and won't be very happy to see you."

DC Wardle reported back to DS Mosely. He and Mosely then decided what they thought would be the best course of action. So, Wardle took one of the constables with him and went to the address. Mosely and the other officer also went to the street but some distance away from Wrigley's house and waited to see how Wardle was getting on. After he rang the doorbell it was some time before anybody opened the door. The elderly lady looked surprised to see two well-dressed men standing there. She confirmed her name as Molly Renton. Wardle introduced himself and the constable and told her they were investigating a serious crime and were trying to locate a man whom they had reason to believe could help them with their enquiries. He then showed her the photograph. The lady looked very shocked and said, "This is my son. What has he done?"

Wardle said, "We cannot divulge that just now. Does he live here?"

The lady said, "Yes he does, and he is upstairs in bed. Shall I call him?"

Wardle said, "Please do." He then winked at the constable and nodded to him to get the others outside right away. Scott was not very happy at being woken up at this time and demanded to know why. When his mother told him that there were two policemen downstairs who wanted to speak to him he jumped out of bed and told his mother to tell them that they would be down in a few minutes when he'd got dressed and told her to take them into the kitchen and give them a cup of tea.

Scott Wrigley got himself dressed and grabbed a few bits and pieces and stuffed them into a plastic bag. He listened from the top of the stairs to see if they had gone to the kitchen which they had. He then crept downstairs and was just about to open the front door when he was seen by the constable who made a dash to apprehend him but just missed him as he had got through the door and was dashing down the street. But, unfortunately for him, he dashed straight in Mosely and the other officer, who tripped him and had him handcuffed before he knew what was happening to him.

At his interview at the police station Wrigley denied all knowledge of the murder of Richard Topping or even knowing him.

Jake Steadman was still in police custody but had to be either charged with murder or released today as Inspector Chambers could not find any evidence apart from the photograph which Peter had taken of him and Topping at Darlington station to charge him. Before releasing him, Chambers asked Steadman if he would confirm that Wrigley was with him and Topping at their meeting in the waiting room at the station on the day that Topping was murdered. Steadman was reluctant to come face to face with Wrigley, saying he had only met him once and did not like the look of him and said that if he could see Wrigley without him seeing him he would do so. Chambers was happy enough about that and told Steadman to wait just a few minutes while he got it sorted.

Wrigley was brought into an interview room which had one-way glass and was sat across from Wardle and Mosely. Chambers took Steadman into an adjacent room which was looking straight onto Wrigley's face and which Wrigley had no knowledge of. Steadman immediately identified Wrigley as the man who was with Rich Topping on the day when Rich asked to meet him at Darlington station. Chambers reiterated the question, "Was this the man who was with Richard Topping on the day in question?" Steadman answered that there was no doubt whatsoever that this was the man. Chambers then told Steadman that he was free to go and said that he was sorry for having to arrest him but with the photograph which they were given at the time it was reasonable to think that he was the murderer. He then asked Steadman if he had any money to pay for his journey home to which Steadman answered all he had was £3. Chambers took him to the front desk and told the duty sergeant to give Steadman £25 from the safe where they kept some petty cash for incidentals. Jake Steadman was now a free man and vowed never to get involved with anybody or anything which could get him in trouble with the police.

Inspector Chambers went back to the interview room where Wardle and Mosely were still with Wrigley who was denying having been involved in any way. Chambers then told Wrigley that he was charging him with the murder of Richard Topping. He also read him his rights. He told Wrigley that he was to be remanded in custody and would appear at a magistrate's court next morning. Wrigley still maintained that he had never seen Topping and that he was not in Darlington station on the day in question. Wardle then asked him why he attempted to run away when he had called to his home just to ask him to account for his movements on the day that Richard Topping was murdered. Wrigley had no answer to this question.

Chambers wondered if Darlington station had CCTV in operation and sent Mosely to check that out. If they had he was to advise them that the police would want to see the footage of the day when Topping was murdered. He was not sure whether Jake Steadman could be relied on to give evidence in court if he was required to do so, and in which case if the station had footage it would almost certainly show whether Wrigley was there or not as Steadman said that he, Topping, and Wrigley were in the station for almost three hours. Mosely arrived back and was very excited. The station did have CCTV which had been installed just about a month prior to the murder and was very good quality footage. They also handed the tape over to Moseley and asked that it could be returned to them when the police had finished with it.

After Mosely had got the tape up and running, they all sat round and watched it. Mosely knew how to fast forward it or back, so they were soon able to see the period of the day that Topping was murdered and within minutes there were Steadman, Topping, and Wrigley, all with their cans of beer sitting in the waiting room just as Steadman had said. Later on, the tape showed Topping and Steadman outside and they appeared to be arguing over something after which it showed Steadman walking away and out of the station. Then a short time later it showed Wrigley coming out and standing next to Topping. Again, they both appeared to be having a heated argument about something. By this time the station was almost empty as the last train of the day had just left, which was driven by Peter Johnson. Wrigley by this time seemed to be getting more and more aggressive towards Topping and swung a punch at him. Topping in turn punched Wrigley and knocked him to the ground. When he got to his feet Wrigley was then wielding a large knife and appeared to be intent on using it, which he did. With one powerful thrust he plunged the knife into Richard Topping's chest who fell onto the platform and never moved again. At this point Wrigley was seen running out of the station and out of the range of the CCTV cameras. Mosely did a few copies of the station's CCTV tapes and returned the original to the station master at Darlington.

At the magistrate's court hearing on the murder of Richard Topping, Wrigley did not have to plead guilty or not guilty. He was remanded in custody, to appear at the Crown Court at Newcastle when his case was ready for trial.

CHAPTER 21

Carol Leaves Home

It was a Spring Sunday, Peter picked up Andrea and Carol and took them to his house where Helen was preparing lunch. She had put a few bottles of wine in the fridge earlier on, so they were nicely chilled. In an effort to cheer everybody up, including herself, she poured out generous glasses of wine and they all sat down and chatted about many things that had happened over the last couple of weeks. Helen then gave Carol a cheque for £500 and told her about opening a bank account and using the money sparingly. She also suggested to Carol that after she got settled at university, she should look around for a part-time job which would help with her everyday expenses because now that their dad was not there to help her out financially, she should try and support herself.

Carol was delighted with her £500 and also took on board what Helen had said about getting a part-time job when she got to Bristol. The romance between her and David was still on but appeared to have cooled down a little over the last month or two. David was going to Leeds University to do a Geography degree so they would not see much of one another during term time. Andrea and Helen were both pleased that Carol and David seemed to be drifting apart and would almost certainly play the field once they made new friends and settled into living away from home. Carol had already been to Bristol and sorted out her accommodation on campus. She had also met two of the girls that she would be sharing her accommodation with.

Now, the big day had arrived when Carol had to go. It was a sad day for Andrea as she would now be on her own in the house, that was something that she could not bear to think about. However, Andrea, being a very realistic and positive lady, thought that this was something she just had to come to terms with. Helen and Peter did not live very far away and were in touch with her every day. She also had very good and caring neighbours whom she had known for years and were such a tower of strength for her since Andrew died so she thought that this was a challenge which she had to take on.

Peter had worked out that the easiest way to get to Bristol would be by train from Newcastle which would take about four hours with one change on the way. Peter and immediate family travelled free on the railways. So Carol, Andrea, Helen, Peter, and of course, Anna had upgraded their seats to first class for this long trip to Bristol with all the necessary equipment and bedding for Anna who was now nine months old. Extremely comfortable, they enjoyed going through some lovely countryside on a nice sunny morning. After having changed trains along the way they arrived at Bristol at 1 p.m. The return train home was at 5 p.m., so that gave them four hours to get to the university and get Carol installed and sorted out in her new surroundings and hopefully meet her new friends whom she would be sharing her apartment with.

It was a short taxi ride from the train station to the university by which time they were all ready for something to eat. Carol, having been there before, said that there was a cafeteria on campus which was not too far from where her accommodation was but first they would need to go to her room and drop off her luggage. The apartment had four rooms which were almost identical so there was no reason for any of them to be envious of anybody's room being better than their own. Carol had already met three of her would-be flatmates. One of them was called Kate and the other two Sally and Jenny. When they got to the apartment the only one who had arrived was Kate and her parents. Kate was delighted to see Carol and gave her a big hug. The families introduced themselves to each other, all of whom seemed to be very comfortable and probably quite relieved that their daughters were also getting on well with their new friends. They then all decided they were rather hungry and made their way to the cafeteria and shared a table where they enjoyed their tea and sandwich lunch as well as getting to know a lot about one another. After they got back to the apartment the other two had arrived with their parents. Then after all the introductions were over it was time to get to work with all of the parents fussing over where they thought things would be best in their daughters' rooms. This was the beginning of university life at Bristol for Carol, Kate, Jenny, and Sally.

*

After Carol had been settled in at Bristol with her flatmates, Andrea together with Helen, Peter, and Anna made their long journey back to Newcastle by which time they were all ready for bed. Helen insisted that her mother should stay with her and Peter for a few nights until she got used to not having Carol about. This would also give her an opportunity to get acquainted with Anna who was now beginning to take notice of who was who. Helen was due to start work at the shop in a week's time and then Andrea would be looking after Anna three days each week which would keep her busy and also be company for her.

Helen thought that it would be a good idea to go and have a chat with Butch and Janet and agree with Janet which of them worked on which days. Butch and Janet were delighted to see Helen but were disappointed that she had not brought baby Anna with her. After they had chatted about different things and how the shop was doing they then got down to sorting out the work rota which did not take long as Janet was very flexible and said that she thought that Helen would like to have Saturday off to be with Peter, Anna, and also Andrea. Helen was very grateful to Janet for that and thanked her and said that at any time she wanted to have Saturday off all she had to do was just to let her know. So, having sorted out their rota to suit each other, Helen told Butch and Janet that she would be there on Monday and was looking forward to it.

During her chat with Butch and Janet, Helen noticed that Butch appeared to be very well-groomed and very neatly dressed, much better than what Helen could remember about him, also that there was a very definite hint of aftershave and deodorant. She wondered if there was a romance going on between Butch and Janet. She also thought how wonderful it would be if there was and, if so, she would do everything she could to promote it. Janet and Butch were two lovely and caring people who appeared to be of a similar age and neither of whom had many friends or hobbies, Butch's only interest being the shop. Janet seemed to have taken on a new lease of life since she came to work for Butch at the shop and as she herself had said it was wonderful to be called by her name by the regular customers at the shop on a daily basis, and so different from where she had spent 35 years working at the library and where everybody spoke in whispers and where she was always called Miss Gardoni. If only she could relive all those years again, Janet thought to herself, she would not spend them in the library. She was also very relieved that Helen was coming back to work part-time, and they were now sharing the job. How wonderful!

CHAPTER 22

Another Wedding

Marion and Graham's wedding day was now just around the corner, which they were both very excited about. They had checked over the list of dos and don'ts which they had drawn up months ago and all appeared to have been taken care of. Marian had asked her cousin Jessica to be her bridesmaid and Helen to be her Maid of Honour. Graham had his best man, Peter of course, and ushers all organised, the church and the reception venue were all sorted so it was just a matter of waiting for the day.

Andrea had been invited but had declined because of Andrew's recent death, she was not yet ready and without him at her side she was afraid that she may be overcome by her emotions and spoil the whole occasion for everybody. No, she would much prefer to stay at home and look after Anna for the day. This would give Helen a day off from caring for Anna and to enjoy the wedding of her close friend Marian.

Carol's boyfriend David was invited to the wedding but made some excuse that he could not be there which was a big relief for Carol as she was now of the opinion that she would like to end the romance with David so as not to be restricted from seeing anybody she fancied or who might have fancied her. She also thought that David probably was having similar thoughts and would probably like to be a free agent and explore what other fish were in the sea. Carol, with these thoughts in mind, decided to phone David from Bristol to say what was on her mind and thank him for the lovely times which they had enjoyed together, but now that they were so far away from each other at their respective universities it would be better if they both went their separate ways. She decided that a phone call prior to her trip up North for the wedding was the easier way to say this than face-to-face. David sounded relieved. He thanked Carol for the call and said that he understood perfectly how she felt and wished her the very best in her time at university. He also hoped that they would remain good friends and keep in touch with each other. So ended the romance of Carol and David.

The wedding of Marian and Graham was fantastic with about one hundred guests. The church service was lovely, the vicar was a man in his late fifties and very experienced at putting people at ease, especially the bride who was dreading the long walk down the aisle arm-in-arm with her brother Raymond, who was also a bit jittery. However, when they got to the altar the Rev Simon Mather took over and very soon had everybody in the church, including the bride and groom, in a very relaxed mood and enjoying this lovely occasion. The reception venue staff were very experienced in catering for the guests. Adjacent to the breakfast room was a quite large bar area at which Raymond had kindly deposited a substantial sum of money for drinks for everybody prior to the meal being served. So, by the time that they were invited to take their seats for the meal, the guests were all in a very good and relaxed mood. The meal, which was accompanied by an abundance of wine, was most enjoyable. So, the wedding of Marian and Graham went off magnificently and was often spoken of.

After their wedding Marian and Graham were renting an apartment which was quite expensive. They were both determined that they would buy a nice house for themselves as soon as they had saved up enough money for a good deposit on a nice semi-detached house. They worked out what their weekly household bills should be, including gas and electricity. They were both on good salaries and aimed to have a good deposit to buy a home within two years. To achieve this, they would need to be very economical with themselves. No expensive meals out in fancy restaurants or drinking in expensive pubs. They would buy their beers and wines in the supermarket and drink them at home if and when they fancied a drink. Foreign holidays were also blacklisted for the time being. They also worked out a keep-fit programme as they were both putting on a few extra pounds which they did not like. This would start right away, in fact tomorrow morning; for the first two weeks they would jog 1km each morning and gradually build up to 5km. This should keep them in good shape and get rid of any unwanted pounds. At the end of their first year of their saving scheme, Marian and Graham were delighted to see their bank balance had grown and also how fit they both were!

They then decided to start to look around the areas where they would like to live and perhaps view a few houses that may be on the market. They did eventually see a house in Heaton which had just come on the market and looked as if it had just had a makeover. They made an appointment to view it. It was absolutely stunning both inside and outside. The asking price was well over what they could now afford. However, they had learned from Peter how to bag a great deal on a house if you were a first-time buyer. Initially the vendor said that the asking price was reasonable. He had just spent a lot on modernising the house and bringing it to what it now was. They would, however, reduce the price somewhat but certainly not by what Marian and Graham were asking. The estate agent, who wanted a quick sale, advised the prospective buyers that the house was very good value and that they should now offer to split the difference with the vendor and so the deal was done.

Shortly after they moved into their lovely house, Marian found that she was pregnant. This came as something of a shock for her and Graham and certainly was not part of their plans right now. However, they soon came to be over the moon with the fact that they were going to be parents and could not wait to spread the news to their relations and friends. Helen and Peter were delighted to hear from Marian about her pregnancy and invited her and Graham to come over and have dinner with them on Saturday.

CHAPTER 23

The Trial

Inspector Chambers and his team, Detectives Wardle and Mosely, had worked tirelessly to get the trial of Scott Wrigley ready for its hearing at Newcastle Crown Court. They had by now handed all the evidence over to the CPS who were now going through it in great detail to ensure that there were no mistakes of any kind which could give the defence counsel an opportunity to demand that the case be thrown out of court.

The first day of Wrigley's trial was taken up in selecting a jury and getting them sworn in, after which the judge gave a long and detailed account of what their duties as jurors were. On day two he read out the charge against Scott Wrigley and then asked him how he pleaded, to which Wrigley, on the advice of his solicitor, replied, "Not guilty, Your Honour." Wrigley was then told to go into the witness box and made to take the oath to tell the truth and nothing but the truth whilst holding the bible in his right hand. He hesitated for a few seconds before taking the bible as if he was afraid that if he told lies after taking the oath something bad may happen to him. However, he thought that he had nothing to lose so he took the bible and swore to tell the truth and so the trial began.

The barrister for the prosecution, Lawrence Cardwell, did not spend very long with preliminary small talk and was determined to have Wrigley's case ready for the jury to consider by that afternoon. So, he began, "Mr Wrigley, you are being charged with the murder of one Richard Topping at Darlington Station on the day in question. Were you at Darlington station on that day this unfortunate young man was murdered and please remember you are still under oath?" Wrigley began to mumble and cough and shuffle about in the witness box and eventually shouted that he had already answered the question and did not wish to answer it again. At this point Wrigley's solicitor objected to the method of how Cardwell was trying to intimidate his client. This was overruled by the judge. Cardwell then began to search through his bundle of papers and after what felt like fifteen minutes to Wrigley he eventually produced a tape, a copy of which he had already put into the projector and was ready for showing. He explained to the court that this was a valid tape of CCTV footage which was taken on the station's newly installed CCTV system and which the station master had kindly handed over to Inspector Chambers in the course of their investigations into the murder. He then asked for the tape to be switched on for the court to see.

The first five minutes of the tape showed the platform with people coming and going, some getting on and others getting off trains. Then it showed Richard Topping coming out of the waiting room, followed by Jake Steadman, both of whom appeared to be having a very heated argument after which it showed Steadman walk away from Topping and out of the station, just as Steadman had told Inspector Chambers. Then it showed Wrigley coming out of the toilets towards Topping. By this time the station was deserted except for Topping and Wrigley. At this point Cardwell asked for the tape to be stopped and to show a close up of the only two people left on the platform. The enlarged close up of them looked as if they were posing for a photograph. It was a full frontal of both of them. Cardwell then spoke to Wrigley and said, "Well, Mr Wrigley, do you recognise anybody in the picture there?" Wrigley did not answer. Then Cardwell told Wrigley to stand and to face the jury and addressed them, saying, "Members of the jury, please take a good look at the defendant and the picture on the screen and decide if the person on the right of the picture and the defendant standing before you are one and the same. You don't have to say anything at this point, but when all the evidence is heard, and you are charged with delivering a verdict, whether the defendant is guilty or not guilty, it is you that will have to decide." Then Cardwell asked for the tape to be switched back on.

Cardwell, who had seen the tape several times, warned the court that what they were about to see was the gruesome murder of a young man, Mr Richard Topping, and so to be prepared for shock.

The tape rolled on, showing the violent death of Topping at the hands of Wrigley. There was a gasp of horror from the jury and from the entire court. The tape showed Wrigley making a quick exit from the station. Cardwell then addressed the court and said, "Your Lordship and members of the jury, that is the case for the prosecution which proves without any doubt that the defendant Scott Wrigley did murder Richard Topping at Darlington Station." At this point the defence barrister Edward Stanford requested an adjournment for one hour for him to consult with his client. The judge agreed and added that as it was approaching lunchtime that the court would reconvene at 2 p.m.

Stanford thanked the judge and then was taken to a secure room to consult with his client who was brought to him securely handcuffed and with two policemen who were in an adjacent room where they could see but not hear what was being said. "Mr Wrigley, everything you have told me up to now about this case is a pack of lies, it has now been proven beyond any doubt that you murdered Richard Topping. So, the only course of action for you now is to plead guilty as there is nothing that I can do or say in your defence.

Have you got anything to say?"

Wrigley answered, "No."

When the court resumed and the jury were all in place, Mr Stanford was on his feet and said, "Your honour and members of the jury, after consulting with the defendant he has now agreed to alter his plea and plead guilty to the murder of Richard Topping, as charged. I do not wish to put forward any mitigating circumstances, your honour," and then he sat down.

Cardwell then got to his feet, firstly he thanked the defence barrister for his integrity in the matter. He then said, "Your honour, as we now have a guilty plea from the defence counsel, there is nothing more that I wish to say on the matter." The judge then addressed the jury and said, "Members of the jury, thank you for your service here today. You are now stood down from your jury duties. You are welcome to return later this afternoon to hear me pass sentence."

Scott Wrigley was sentenced to life imprisonment with a minimum of 20 years.

CHAPTER 24

Butch's Proposition

Anna was now eight years old and was doing well at primary school. She now had two siblings; Anthony, who was six and also at the same school as Anna, and Andrea, called after her grandma, but whom they called Andi. She was just four. Andrea by now had almost got over the shock of losing her husband and best friend Andrew. Shortly after Andrew's death, one of her friends who was a member of the WI invited her to one of their monthly meetings. She was given a great welcome and asked to sit in and observe what the WI was all about. They were a very active group who got involved in many activities, mostly to do with charitable work and fund-raising for several local charities. The chairlady was a very energetic and active lady who kept them all busy and was very popular with all the members. After the meeting was over, tea and coffee with some little nibbles were available on a help yourself basis. Andrea's friend Judy (Judith) took her around and introduced her to everybody who were all very welcoming towards her and made her feel very comfortable to be in their midst. The chairwoman, Kathy, made a great fuss of Andrea and hoped that she might consider joining them. She did explain that they had a procedure for all would-be members to follow which involved filling in an application form giving some brief details of herself and would need to be seconded by an existing member.

Judy said that she would be more than happy to sign the form, which Kathy then handed to Andrea. Fortunately, there was no problem with Andrea's application for membership of the WI and she was unanimously accepted at the next monthly meeting.

Helen and Peter now both had very busy lives between their jobs and looking after three young children. Peter had been promoted from his job as a full-time train driver to a supervisory role in charge of the drivers' schedules and ensuring that trains were never stopped or late because of drivers not being where they should be at any given time. Helen was now back to working four days per week at the shop which was really booming. Janet and Butch had now been married for almost five years after a courtship of two years which Helen had played a major role in and getting them to set a date for their big day. They were both now very happy and looking years younger than they had before. Helen was Janet's Maid of Honour and Peter was Butch's best man. The wedding was a small affair as neither the bride nor groom had many friends so in total there were only twelve people at the small hotel, The Bluebell, where Butch used to take Janet occasionally for a meal. Helen had talked them into going to the Isle of Man for a long weekend and had booked them into a nice hotel in Douglas. They still talked about the lovely hotel and how they were treated like royalty while they were there.

*

Janet and Butch invited Helen and Peter to come and have dinner with them one evening. Butch had been having thoughts over the last year about retiring. He was now 63 and Janet was 61. Prior to him having met and married Janet he could not bear to think about retirement as the shop was his life. But now, with Janet by his side, he was thinking about how good it would be to travel and have nice holidays abroad and see some places which he had only ever heard of. Janet and he had been thinking that as they were both in good health and were comfortably off, there was no reason that they should not explore some of those places which they read about and seen in the holiday brochures.

All of this they wanted to discuss with Helen and Peter as well as the shop and its future. Butch had thought that it would be ideal to discuss all of this over a nice meal and a few glasses of wine. So, the big night arrived. Helen had got a bunch of flowers and a bottle of wine to take. Both her and Peter had a couple of glasses of wine while waiting for their taxi to arrive. Janet and Butch both looked very nice in their smart casuals, also the little house was shining and very welcoming with a nice smell of something cooking. Butch soon got the wine flowing and looked and acted as if he had drunk a glass or two himself.

Janet had done a very nice hotpot with dumplings and vegetables, followed by home-made apple pie and fresh cream.

Then Butch explained to Helen and Peter that there was something which he would like to talk over with them both, and especially with Helen, whom he said he looked upon as his own daughter. He and Janet had been thinking and looking at their lifestyle and thinking that neither of them had ever travelled anywhere or done anything exciting. They were both now in their sixties and in good health and financially okay so they were thinking that over the next two years they would like to start to take timeout from the shop and have holidays, possibly even foreign trips, just to see if they would like it. Butch also said that he would like to come to some arrangement with Helen about the business as it was his intention, and indeed Janet's, that the shop would be Helen's at some stage.

"We do not need to go into too much detail about that right now, other than for you to think about some part-time staff when Janet and I will be away." He then went on to say that from the first week when Helen came to work in the shop he knew that there was something very special about her and that over the years that she had been with him his life and indeed the profits from the shop had improved year on year. Helen could no longer hold her emotions in check and she went to Butch and threw her arms around him and with the tears streaming down her cheeks she said, "Butch I love you so dearly." She then went to Janet and did likewise to her and said, "You both mean so much to me. Look after each other."

CHAPTER 25

The Millennials

The year is 2008. Anna is now sixteen and has just finished her GCSEs and achieved very good results in all of her nine subjects. She will continue at Jesmond Grammar to do her A levels and wants to go to university to study Engineering, which Helen and Peter are very happy about.

Helen is now fully in charge of the shop; Janet and Butch are getting ready to go on another one of their many holidays, a Mediterranean cruise this time, so Helen needs some part-time staff. Anna is free until September and is looking for some part-time work until then, so Helen asks her if she would like to come and work with her in the shop where she would pay her a reasonable wage. Anna is delighted as she is hoping to have a holiday with a few of her friends so she needs to earn some money for that and to buy some new clothes for sixth form, at last she can ditch that awful grey school uniform!

Last year Butch agreed a deal with Helen about the shop. He told her that he wanted her to have the shop, but that he could not afford to give it to her free of charge. So, he had the business valued by a commercial valuer and offered to sell it to Helen and Peter for 50% of the valuation, recognising all the work she had put in to improving the business over the years. The money was to be paid to him over a seven-year period. He told Helen if she was happy with this arrangement, he would instruct a solicitor to draw up a contract. Butch told Helen to think about it for a week and to talk it over with Peter and if they were both happy about the deal then they should also make an appointment to see a solicitor. Helen was so overawed by Butch's generosity she burst into tears and grabbed Butch, squeezing him tight, exclaiming she had never met anybody like him. Butch was grinning from ear to ear.

Peter was equally amazed by Butch's generosity, his only worry being could Helen pay what was owed to Butch in the seven years which he had asked for. She assured him that the shop was a very profitable little business and that she had even greater plans for it which would make it even more so. She was not yet ready to reveal those plans just yet, even to him. Peter was in suspense.

Anna was now in her third week at the shop and really enjoying herself. She quickly learnt how the shop functioned on a daily basis. The early opening time of 7 a.m. was essential as it was the busiest time, people on their way to work dashing in for newspapers and all sorts of knickknacks. Then at 10 a.m. it eased off for a spell when there was time to have a drink and a rest for a while. Anna's two siblings, Anthony 14 and Andi 12, were now both at Jesmond Grammar and went to their Granny Andrea's house after school. She loved having them for a while each evening and gave them all sorts of treats to eat. She would love to cook them dinner, but Helen would only let her do that occasionally because she wanted to have them at home for their evening meal, which she believed was a time for all the family to be together and to talk about their day. She never allowed any electronic gadgets until they had all finished their dinner and the washing up. Peter was home for dinner most evenings, as he was not driving trains anymore and was now a training officer at GNER.

*

Helen's sister, Carol, was now 34 years of age. She did very well at Bristol University, getting a 2-1 degree in English and Art History. She married David Lomax and they were blessed with two children; Rory, who was 6, and Ruby, aged 4. She'd ended up marrying another David! This was a good source of best-man speech jokes at their wedding.

Carol was an assistant curator at the Newcastle Tate Modern and David was a Creative Project Manager for McArthur Flett, a large city advertising agency. They were living in Whitley Bay. They were very busy, and their marriage had been a very happy one up to now. However, the domestic bliss had just been shattered as Carol had just discovered that David might be having an affair with somebody who worked in his office.

She had seen some suggestive text messages on his phone the previous day and was devastated. She decided to confront him about it after the children were in bed that night. David was usually home at about 6 p.m., but that evening he phoned Carol at 5 p.m. and told her that he was going to be late as something had happened at work which he had to deal with. He told Carol not to bother about his dinner and he would get some fish and chips or something which would do for him the night. Carol replied, "Alright, will you be in the office and what time will you be home?" David hesitated for a second and said he would be in the office and should be home about 10 p.m. but, if he wasn't, that she should go to bed. He then put the phone down. She wondered if she should phone Helen and tell her the situation. She decided not to and to wait until she had it out with David when he eventually got home.

At about 8 p.m. she decided to phone David at the office but withheld her own number. Her call was put on to voicemail which told her that the office was closed until 8 a.m. next morning, but that she could leave a message with her name and number. Carol did not leave her name or any message. At about 10.15 p.m. there was still no sign of David, so Carol decided to go to bed although she knew she would not sleep. Then, at 11.30 p.m., she heard him come in and a few minutes later he was up and in the bedroom. Carol switched on the light and acted as if nothing was wrong. She said, "That was a very long day, David, you must be very tired?" David said that he was tired and started to tell her about what and why he had had to work so late to deal with the problem that had occurred in the afternoon. Carol could definitely smell alcohol on his breath and indeed could see that he had been drinking so she thought it was not the time to confront him about what he was up to but could not help herself and said, "David, tell me the truth, where were you tonight and who were you with? And please don't tell lies as I think that you are having an affair with some trollop called Jade who works in your office."

David turned pale and said, "Who on earth told you something like that?" and started to deny everything.

Carol then sat upright in the bed and shouted, "No lies, I have seen those vile texts on your phone from her! Where were you tonight? I know that you were not in the office and I could smell alcohol off you when you came through that door. Why are you doing this to me and our two lovely children? Please tell me the truth. Are you having an affair? Are you in love with this Jade – whoever she might be? I have always thought that we had such a loving relationship and that we would be together forever. Do your marriage vows mean nothing to you?"

David, upon hearing what Carol had said, started vehemently denying everything, protesting he had been at work. He burst into tears and made as if he was going to hold and hug her, but she pushed him away and said, "David, you will never sleep in my bed again until we get this sorted out. Now go into the spare room and sober up. I don't want to look at you. I want you to have the day off tomorrow and, when the children are gone, we will then discuss the situation rationally and I don't want to hear any more lies."

David started to protest about him having the day off, but Carol did not want to hear. She said, "You can think of a good excuse for having the day off as you are so good at telling lies." She then switched off the light.

Next morning, in front of the children, Carol and David tried to act normally and chatted away with the children, although their thoughts were not very focused on what they were talking about. Whilst Carol was busy getting the children dressed and taking Rory to school and Ruby to nursery, David phoned his office and told them that he would not be in today as he was not feeling well and had a very bad night, all of which was true, but not for the reasons he had said. After she got back from dropping the children off, Carol got two chairs, one on either side of the kitchen table. She sat on one and told David to sit on the other, and then very calmly she said, "David, this is something which I never thought that you and I would have to sit and talk about. We have been married for eight years which for me have been blissfully happy. We have two lovely children and a beautiful home. I worshipped the ground that you walked on and looked forward to seeing you every evening, seeing Rory and Ruby run to the door to hug and kiss you. The number of times which I thanked God for you and our two lovely children. I used to think that life could not be any better and was so confident that you felt the same. David, why? Who is this Jade that you must think is so much better than I am? Is she so much better looking than me? Now I want you to answer all of these questions truthfully and then tell me what your intentions are. Are you having an affair? Do you intend to leave me and the children and set up home with this trollop? If that is your intention, please say so and pack your things and go right now. If that is not your intention you will have a lot of making good to do as I am very deeply hurt, and I don't know if I can forgive you."

David's initial response was to burst into tears. It took several minutes for him to control himself and start to speak rationally. After he had got himself a glass of water and offered Carol one, he said, "Carol, I do not know how I could have been such a stupid idiot to do this to you and our children. I swear nothing has really happened with Jade, just a couple of drunken snogs. We have been out for a drink a couple times, and that is all. I was an idiot just flattered by her attention. I have been so stupid. You are the only people who matter to me and I love you and the children dearly. She is not better than you at anything, and she is not even good looking. She has been hanging onto me in the office for weeks and wanting me to take her out. At the office party last weekend, we had a bit of a kiss, but honestly that is all. She means nothing to me, and I am deeply sorry to have been so stupid. I took her out last night to let her know that she needed to stop messaging me, but somehow we ended up kissing again. Carol, please believe me, I swear and I promise that I will never want to leave you and our children. I now hope and pray that you can find it in your heart to forgive me, please, if you can, Carol. I understand how deeply I have hurt you and as you rightly say that I have some making up to do, but that will not cause me any hardship because the love that I have for you and our two children has no bounds. I am begging you, Carol, that over the coming weeks and months to try to put all this behind you and that in time we may get back to what we were like before this stupid episode, which has now blighted our lives, happened."

Carol, for the first time since they sat down, looked at David. She believed him when he said it had only been a couple of dates and that he hadn't slept with her. David was a terrible liar, in spite of what she had said the previous night. In any case she had now been through all of his emails and texts and there really seemed to be nothing more to it. There were certainly no encouraging messages from David. She even gave him a very faint glimmer of a smile and said, "Would you like a cup of tea?" David said, "Yes please."

After she got the tea and had both sat down, the mood was now slightly more relaxed. Carol reached across the table and got hold of David's hand and held it for a moment without saying anything. Then, out of the blue, she smiled at David and said, "David, I believe you when you say this was nothing more than a silly fling; as you must know, I know about everything that you do and I can read you like a book. You will never get anything past me! I love you so much, but now I do not want to dwell on this cloud which has descended on us for very long, it may very well have taught us both a lesson about what and how much we have to lose. Perhaps we need to spend some time together, just the two of us. It feels like it is just work, kids, sleep, and the same the next day. I believe you when you say that you are really sorry and that it will never happen again. Just give me a few days to get myself together and put all of this behind me and get back to where we were before."

David was about to burst into tears again, but Carol said, "No David. I do not want you to cry anymore. It hurts me to see you like that. Now tell me how you are going to deal with this Jade. She needs to hear that you never want anything to do with her again. You will have to have her moved to the other office. I don't think she will be very pleased. I will leave that for you to sort out and I don't need to know how you do it. Just one other thing, David, on the assumption that your misdemeanour is a one-off and will never be repeated, and the remorse which you have shown for having done it, I will never mention it to anybody, including my own family. They all hold you in such esteem and it would be such a shame to spoil that, David. Let's put it all behind us and get back to our happy family life with Rory and Ruby. I love you so much."

CHAPTER 26

Peter and Jake

Time moves on. Helen and Peter were both very busy in their own jobs. Peter was now exploring the possibilities of going on to a four-day working week. British Rail had been privatised and broken up but Peter worked for one of the biggest national networks – Great North Eastern Railways or GNER. This would take some time to organise as it would mean training somebody right from scratch to do what is a very complicated and responsible job. Helen did not have enough hours in the day to do what she wanted to do in the shop. She had applied for planning permission to extend it and obtain a license to sell alcohol. At the rear of the existing shop there was a sizable back yard which was hardly ever used. The extension which she was planning to build would only take up half the yard and still leave ample space for bins and such like. Helen had an architect draw up plans for the proposed extension. The existing shop was a two-storey building. The upstairs consisted of two small rooms and a very small bathroom. The proposed extension was also two stories. If she obtained building approval, Helen would be able to have a very nice two-bedroom apartment to rent out. All of this now depended on the council's planning department. Helen no longer saw a great deal of

Janet and Butch, as they were more or less retired. She was planning to have them round for dinner some time when they were available for a catch-up.

Peter had now agreed with GNER details for his four-day working week which he could start as soon as arrangements were made for someone to fill in on his missing day.

Anna was now in her final year of university and doing very well with her Mechanical Engineering Degree at Durham University. In her recent exams she had achieved what would be a high 2:1 in her finals. She had begun to believe that a first could well be within her grasp. As well as that she was doing twelve hours per week working for her mother in the shop. She drew just twenty pounds a week of her wages and her mother was saving the remainder for her to have a holiday with her two friends, Lucy and Georgina. They were hoping to go to Barbados in July and began looking out for good offers. Anna asked Helen how much was now in her holiday fund and was delighted to hear that she had fifteen hundred pounds, and rising weekly. She asked Helen if she could have three hundred pounds as she now needed to buy some new clothes for her holiday. Helen said, "Of course you can, and I am going to give you one hundred pounds bonus as well because you have been fantastic for me in the shop." Anthony, Anna's brother, was now 17 and in his first year at sixth form college. He was being urged on and encouraged by Anna and also by his parents who could now comfortably afford to pay for both of them to go to university if they so wished. Andi was almost 15 and preparing for her GSCEs, but at this stage, and like most 15-year-olds, didn't know what she wanted to do.

Peter's mother Valerie and her husband Martin were preparing to celebrate their 20th wedding anniversary which they planned to really splash out on. They were both in really good shape and enjoying a very busy lifestyle in their retirement. Martin often mentioned the advice which Valerie's son Peter gave both of them the first time that they met. What great advice it was coming from a twenty-year-old, what a mature man he was, even at twenty, wise beyond his years. What a wonderful life they'd both had all those years since then.

Helen and Carol's mother Andrea was now getting on in years; well into her mid-seventies but keeping very well and very active. She had lots of friends with whom she socialised quite a lot. It was over twenty years since her husband Andrew passed away. She still missed him and thought about him frequently and pondered over what their life could have been if Andrew was still alive and how proud he would have been to see how well their two daughters had done.

Anna, Lucy, and Georgina had now booked their dream holiday in Barbados and were very excited about it. None of them had ever been on a long-haul flight before. They got a very good deal for a ten-day holiday in a four-star hotel near to Bridgetown in Barbados. They were well lectured by their parents about what they should and should not do; most of all about not drinking too much and also about making sure that they never went out alone.

*

Peter moved on to a four-day week. The chief driver at GNER Newcastle introduced Peter to the man who would be his assistant for four weeks to be trained by Peter on the very complicated and very important role of train scheduling. Peter had never met this chap until he turned up at Peter's workplace one Monday morning. He was a well-dressed and well-groomed man and looked to be a similar age to Peter. He spoke with a rather mild-mannered voice and introduced himself as Jake Steadman. Peter looked and felt rather shocked and said, "Did you say that your name was Jake Steadman?" The chap said, "Yes I am ... Jake Steadman." Peter was now in a real dilemma. Could this be the same Jake Steadman that was in his year at school? Well there was only one way to find out. So, he said, "I am Peter Johnson. I have worked for British Rail for almost twenty-five years. Does my name mean anything to you because I think we both went to Grangethorpe School?" Steadman was now also in a quandary and thought to himself, 'How could this happen to me? This guy knows everything about me and will almost certainly refuse to work with me. Just when I thought that I had got my life back on track it is now going to go to pieces all over again.'

Peter looked at Steadman and held out his hand and said, "Well well, is it not a small world, Jake Steadman? I am so happy to see you. Now we will have a cup of tea and have a good chat." Jake was surprised at the warm welcome which Peter had given him and began to relax somewhat.

Peter made a pot of tea and asked Jake if he took sugar to which he said no. Jake was the first to speak after they had sat down with their tea. Then he said, "What should I call you? Is it sir or Mr Johnson?"

Peter laughed and said, "We do not have any sirs in this place, call me Peter."

Jake then said, "Peter, you know a lot about me and my background and where I came from. My parents, as you well know, were not the most loving people so my childhood days do not hold many happy memories for me and indeed neither do my early adult years."

At this point Peter interjected and said, "Jake, please do not say any more about your background, it is what you are now that really matters. I could tell you about my own background which would surprise you, I may tell you someday, but we will leave all that for now. Tell me how long have you been with GNER and what have you been doing?"

Jake was by now in a rather relaxed frame of mind. He was feeling confident that Peter was not going to spoil anything for him. "I have been with GNER for seven years. I started off as a porter at Darlington station and did about two years at that. I got on very well with the Station Master who was a very nice man, Jack Wallis was his name. He then asked me if I would be interested in becoming a guard on passenger trains and taking responsibility for checking passenger tickets. He assured me that I would not be doing any of these things on my own until I had been trained for at least a month. So, that is what I have been doing for about five years now. I have enjoyed my time working for GNER, it has been the best thing that ever happened to me and has enabled me to get my life on track. I am now married to a fantastic girl called Ginny and we have a lovely baby girl Emily who just turned one. We are saving up to buy our own house and are very happy."

Peter then said, "Jake I am so pleased to hear all that and if there is anything that I can ever do to help you, it will be my pleasure to do so. Now we have some work to do but we must come back to talk about both our backgrounds again. We really do have a lot in common. Just one other thing, Jake, whatever I know about your background will never pass my lips to anybody and I hope that you will do the same for me."

Jake got up and got hold of Peter's hand and shook it and said, "Peter, I am so happy."

They both then got down to work. Peter explained to Jake that when he first started on the job, which he has now been doing for a few years, it all seemed very complicated. But at the end of his first month with the chap who trained him it all simply fell into place quite easily. "So Jake, your first week or so you may sometimes feel frustrated but never mind, I am here to train you and I might add that I am so delighted to have met you again."

CHAPTER 27

Helen's Big Plan

Finally, Helen received her dream letter from the council, telling her that they were happy to grant planning to the shop, so it was now all systems go! She was delighted that Peter was now on a four-day week and was hoping that he would be willing to help out with some of the extra work associated with getting the extension up and running. She had spoken to her bank manager and told him about her plans for expanding the shop and about her plans for a wine shop, for which she has now instructed her solicitor to apply for a licence. Helen and Peter's joint account at their bank was increasing considerably and they were now in a position to pay for the extension and were hoping to set up the wine shop from their own resources. However, the ever-cautious Helen and Peter did not want to leave anything to chance and had arranged with the bank manager an overdraft facility of £5,000 just in case.

Helen decided to ring Janet and Butch and arrange to have them for dinner the following Saturday. They both looked great, very tanned, and much younger looking than they were before they embarked on their new life of retirement and wedded bliss. As usual, Janet brought a lovely bunch of flowers and Butch a bottle of very nice wine. Peter got the party going with a generous glass of wine to everybody and the toast was to Janet and Butch. Anna was helping out preparing the meal, which gave Helen more time with her special guests.

Helen then told Janet about their plans for the paper shop and hopefully for the new wine shop. Peter got out the drawings which the architect had done and explained to Butch what it would all look like when it was finished. Butch was amazed by Helen and Peter's foresight in seeing such potential in his little shop and utilising what he always looked upon as wasted space. He went on to congratulate Helen and to thank her for everything she had done for him and turned his humdrum life into what it now is. He thanked her for bringing Janet into his life; she had also been living a very uneventful life in her early retirement.

What a contrast to their lives now when they never have a dull moment or enough hours in the day. Butch went on to say that within a month of Helen starting at the shop, which now must be all of twenty-five years ago, that he looked upon her as the daughter he never had and had secretly adopted her as such.

Anna had to leave as the meal was almost ready and left Helen to finish it as she was going to meet her friends, Lucy and Georgina.

The dinner was a very happy affair with the wine flowed freely, and there was much reminiscing about some of the various exploits from everybody about days gone by.

Janet thanked Helen and Peter for their lovely hospitality and assured them that it would be reciprocated in the not too distant future. She also congratulated them and wished them every success with their plans for the shop.

*

Helen was anxious to get on with the extension. She contacted the architect who drew up the plans which have been given planning approval. The architect's name was a man called Jason Cardwell. Jason was not surprised but pleased that his plans had been approved. Helen told him that she didn't know any builders and asked if he could recommend a reputable local firm. Jason assured her that he worked with several builders and one in particular that he would recommend. This chap was a small builder who specialised in kitchen extensions and such like. He was a very reputable chap and employed a small team of tradesmen, all of whom have been with him for years. He was very well known in the area and was always kept busy. Jason asked Helen if she would like him to arrange a meeting with this chap and that he himself would like to be there. Helen said that she would certainly like that and also asked Jason if he would act as project manager for the building works. He said that he would be delighted to do so. The builder's name was Joe Brownlow and was trading in the name of Brownlow Builders Ltd. When all three, Helen, Joe, and Jason, had all been introduced to one another Joe said to Helen, "I have been in your shop many times over the years and I must say that I was not expecting a pretty lady like you to be the person I would be dealing with. I was expecting to be dealing with a chap called Butch. Is he not around anymore? I have known Butch for years and I hope that he is alright?"

Helen said, "Thank you very much for your custom over the years, Joe. Butch is fine and having a great life. He is married to a very nice lady called Janet." She then went on to tell both Joe and Jason that she started to work for Butch after she left school and that he was like a father to her, "He was so kind to me and treated me as if I was his daughter. When I got married and was expecting our first child, I told Butch that he would need to find somebody to cover my maternity leave. A retired librarian called Janet Gardoni applied. She was obviously an educated lady who just wanted somebody to chat to. We were very surprised to have such a clever applicant enquiring about the job. We offered her the job. She said yes and so, gentlemen, to make a long story short, Butch fell in love and married

Janet and they are both having a wonderful married life together and now I own the shop!"

Joe and Jason were delighted by this tale of late blossoming love.

Helen was keen to get the conversation onto a business footing. "Now to get down to business. I want to extend it and hope to get a license to sell alcohol and a whole lot of different things. Joe, your architect friend Jason has recommended you as a reputable builder so I would like you to take the details of what needs doing and work out a reasonable price for the complete works. Also, I would like to know how long it will take. I might add that I do intend to get prices from two other builders for the works so keep that in mind."

Joe did a very competitive quotation compared to the other two and also said the duration of the works would not be any longer than twelve weeks, but it may well be less. Helen was really pleased with Joe's quotation and period for completion. She then spoke to Jason and asked him to draw up a contract for both parties to sign and for the work to commence as soon as possible. Helen was very pleased that Joe's quotation was just within what she and Peter had in their joint account as she would not have to use any of her arranged overdraft. There was, however, a lot of work to be done after the building had been completed, such as shelves and counters and such like. This was something which she knew precious little about so she had to work with Jason who knew some shop fitters who could do this type of work.

Joe Brownlow was as good as his word and at the end of week seven the extension was almost complete. Helen was amazed at what the shop would now look like. It was enormous. Also, the upstairs apartment would be perfect when fitted out. She took Peter to see it after they had their evening meal. He was very excited when he saw it and gave Helen a big hug and a kiss and complimented her on her foresight in planning it all.

He was now on his four-day working week and told Helen that he would like to help her in any way that he could so she must tell him whatever it was that she wanted him to do. She told him that as the work was now nearing completion, they must start to think about what stock they would need. She told Peter she would like him to get in touch with some wine wholesalers who would be able to advise him on what would be the most saleable wines and other alcoholic drinks for the neighbourhood, taking into account that it was a working-class area so champagne and very expensive wines would probably not sell too well. She asked Peter to get advice and quotations from three different wholesalers. Peter was delighted with his new role in helping to get this business up and running. He now had come to realise how much work that Helen had put in this venture, so it was now his turn to play his part. It was essential that he got the most competitive prices for whatever stock was required so that the selling prices were also very competitive, especially in her first year of trading.

The wine wholesalers that Peter had contacted for quotations to supply them with wines, spirits, and beers as well as soft drinks, were all very keen to secure the order, including a number of other suppliers who had heard about this new wine bar which was about to open. So, within the week he had quotes from a number of suppliers. He then sat down with Helen to discuss which one they should opt for. They finally decided on one, 'Les Vins Formidables' who, despite the French name, was a Newcastle wine merchant. Peter chose them, not only for the prices which they offered, but on the advice which they gave and their terms for trading. So they got in touch with the manager and asked him to call and see them. By now the builders had finished and the shop-fitters were ready to start with all the shelving, counters, and other fixtures and fittings that would be required.

The rep, Johnny Pearson, turned out to be very knowledgeable in what the shop should look like and advised that display and lighting and branding were vitally important. His advice was very timely as the joiners and electricians were ready to start working on the shelving and electrical wiring. He asked Helen if she would like him to speak to the joiners and electricians. Helen said that would be great as what he was planning was very different to what she and Peter and planned. Whilst he was going into great detail with the tradesmen, Helen got the kettle on and made drinks for everybody. Johnny told Helen that what he was proposing would cost her slightly more than what she was planning but that it would be worth it and would pay for itself in the first year. Also, he was confident that she would be delighted with it when it was up and running.

Well the big day had arrived and it was the official opening of the wine shop, now christened 'Cabernet and Corkscrews'. Johnny had suggested that Friday afternoon would be a good day and time to have the opening and offered to come along and help out. He thought they should have a wine tasting session and that he would supply the wines free of charge. All of this would be paid for by his company and would be set up by one of his staff before the opening. Helen was overawed by what Johnny had in mind and thanked him with a huge hug. She thought how professional he was, which was something that she and Peter were lacking. The member of staff which Johnny had mentioned turned out to be a lovely young lady who turned up with her own van and everything that she needed for her wine tasting.

All of the wines that she had were typical of the wines which Johnny had suggested she should stock and would be reasonably priced and sell well in the area. Her name was Gabriella and she was an expert on wines and could answer any questions which their new customer base might have. After she had set everything up it was soon approaching the grand opening time. Gabriella, who was dressed in jeans and a sweater, asked Helen if there was some place she could change into her, what she called, 'pulling gear'. Helen showed her the small bathroom which she had managed to squeeze into an obscure corner of the extension and was all nicely fitted out.

When Gabriella made her appearance sometime later, she looked completely different. She was dressed in a figure-hugging black dress which was several inches above her knees. She also had a long blonde wig and eyelashes which must be an inch long. Helen and Peter were coming back into the shop just as Gabriella was emerging from the bathroom. They had just gone home to smarten up somewhat for this great event. When Peter saw this lovely young lady he said to Helen, "Who the hell is that?" Helen was also unsure who this lady was and was about to ask her who she was and what she was doing in her shop and then realised it was Gabriella. She looked like she'd just stepped off a catwalk. Gabriella then invited both of them to the wine tasting bar which she had set up earlier; she poured them both a very generous glass of wine from one of the expensive bottles, declining any for herself since she was working. Johnny, the rep, had arrived and he made his way in through the back as there were now quite a number of people waiting outside the front door. He had a small glass of wine and told them that Cabernet and Corkscrews looked 'the business'.

Helen had asked Janet and Butch to come and be special guests. She said that she was expecting quite a number of people at opening time and she would be tied up for an hour or so and that if they came later she should have more time to talk to them. She had booked Anna and Carol to man the tills, one at the wine till and the other at the paper shop till.

As Helen opened the door and saw the number of people outside waiting to come in, she was glad that Johnny was there with his wealth of experience. So, when they were all inside, Johnny got Helen and Peter on either side of him and called for hush for a moment. He introduced Helen and Peter and said how proud and honoured he was to be asked to do this presentation and was thrilled at the number of people who had turned out. He went on to say what a charming couple Helen and Peter were, and that Helen, having worked in this shop since she left school at sixteen, took over from the previous owner Butch, who he was sure that most of the customers knew. He went on, "Helen is the person responsible for introducing Butch to his charming wife Janet; again, I am sure that some of you will know Janet from her many years at the local library. When Helen went off to have a baby along came the lovely Janet to fill in. Neither Janet nor Butch had even been married and had no intentions of ever doing so but found a whole lot of chemistry between them which the lovely Helen encouraged. The rest is history and they were married within a few months and have, ever since, adopted a complete new way of life."

Johnny went on to say that the wine shop with regular tastings and occasional private party hire would be the first of its kind in the area and that he was confident it would add a touch of class to the local community. Just as Johnny was finishing, Butch and Janet were coming through the door, both of them looking very smart and very tanned from a trip to Florida. Helen then took over from Johnny and welcomed her special guests and asked everyone if they would give three cheers for the wonderful Butch and Janet. There was a great burst of applause and hurrays, with many older guests welcoming Butch and Janet back and giving them great hugs.

The grand opening of the wine bar was a great success, especially at the wine tasting bar where Gabriella was kept busy. Her 'pulling dress' and her lovely blonde hair had the men eating out of her hand and she sold lots and lots of wine, all of which kept Anna busy at the till. Out of what they had estimated to be their monthly sales of wines of 500 bottles, plus beers and spirits, they sold almost 300 bottles at the opening event. It was such a good start and very encouraging for Helen and Peter. Johnny also was amazed and delighted at how well the event turned out to be and promised to keep in touch and told them if there was anything he could do for them at any time, all they needed was to ask.

The wine and all of the alcoholic and soft drinks were all doing a steady trade and Helen and Peter were delighted. Their profit margins were excellent and running at 38% so their bank balance was growing very nicely. Peter was concerned that Helen was working too hard and should think about employing a full-time manager. They still had the two-bedroom apartment over the shop which was all ready for fitting out with carpets and furniture.

Helen's sister, Carol, had a flair for interior design so Helen asked her if she would take a look at the apartment and come up with some ideas, but not to be over extravagant with the cost.

Carol was delighted that Helen had asked for her help so they both spent a couple of hours in the apartment one day and agreed everything that would be needed to turn it into what could be classed as a luxury apartment, and would bring in a good monthly rental. Carol shopped around the various furniture warehouses and also bathroom and kitchen shops. Helen had a figure of about £9K in mind to fit out the apartment so she was very pleased when about a week later Carol came to see her and showed her everything that she thought would look nice on her iPhone. Helen was very pleased with what Carol had come up with but was sure that it must be very expensive. When Carol showed the overall cost of everything when fitted, which was just under £6K, Helen was astounded and hugged Carol. She gave her a cheque for the whole amount, told her to order everything as soon as possible and also asked her and David and the children to come and have dinner with them on Saturday.

CHAPTER 28

Jake's Story

Peter's mother Valerie and his stepdad Martin were now getting on in years, although they were keeping very well. It was now near to their silver wedding anniversary. They'd had a wonderful life together over those twenty-five years, with many foreign holidays but also lots of holidays in the UK. They were a very popular couple in the local community, especially in the Conservative Club where they first met when Valerie used to go with her two friends, Jane and Sandra, who were very anxious to get her fixed up with somebody. What a success that had been!

So now they had to get down to arranging their silver anniversary. Valerie and Martin had done a head count of the people that they would like to celebrate their day with. The number was almost one hundred and way more than they could cater for at home. Where better to celebrate this milestone than at the Conservative Club where they first met? It would be much more expensive, but this was a very special day for them, and they were going to enjoy it, whatever the cost, and they thought there would also be a much better atmosphere at the club. So their next job after they had finished their lunch was to drive round to the club and book the function room for their silver wedding celebrations.

*

Peter had almost completed his training of Jake Steadman. Jake proved himself to be a bright chap and grasped things very easily. He still had to pass his exam to prove that he was capable of being left on his own to arrange the schedules. Peter was confident that Jake would pass with flying colours.

In the weeks that they had been working together they had become very fond friends and talked over many things, especially their childhood years and their home life. Neither of them had many happy memories of those years. Peter told Jake about how his father who hardly ever worked and was always demanding money from his mother to go to the pub and get drunk and then come and beat her if his dinner was not ready for him. He went on to say that the only decent thing his father ever did for him and his mother was that he dropped dead on that morning after Peter had given him the option of leaving the family house and never returning.

Jake's parents, who were both dead now, were slightly different. They were both alcoholics. His father was called Bert and his mother was called Barbara. Bert never beat Babs and in their own way they were happy enough. But the state of the house in which they lived left a lot to be desired. Babs never thought about cleaning or about cooking except when she felt hungry. Then, it was mostly takeaways which Jake would have to go for. They had lived in a council estate in Byker, on benefits.

Jake then told Peter how he got into trouble and was arrested on suspicion of murdering the leader of the gang that he used to go around with. At that point Peter stopped Jake and said, "Jake I know all about that case. I also need to tell you that I was the one responsible for having you arrested!" Peter explained how his train was stopped at Darlington station one afternoon and, as he waited for the signal to go, two men came out of the waiting groom onto the platform. Both of them seemed to be in a very aggressive mood. Peter thought that one of those men looked familiar; he had just been given the signal to go on to the last leg of the journey to Newcastle, so he took a photograph of the men and proceeded. He didn't think any more about it until next morning when he looked at the paper and saw the headline. 'Man murdered at Darlington Station'. Peter said, "I looked at the photograph I had taken and was convinced that one of them was you. At that time, I was not aware which of the two got murdered. I knew that the photograph would be vital information for the police in solving this case and that it was my duty to contact them. After I had been interviewed, Detective Inspector Chambers told me that it was not you who had been murdered, so the assumption would then have to be that you were the murderer. At that particular time, I am not sure, Jake, which of the two I would have preferred. I told the detective all that I knew about you, including your address. That really concluded my participation in the case of the murder of Richard Topping but I was both delighted and relieved when the case was finally solved and that you were not the killer, Jake, and that I had not been in the same class with a murderer!"

Peter wondered whether what he had just told Jake was going to affect the good friendship which they had built over the time that they had been working together and was very happy when Jake got hold of him and hugged him and said, "Peter, you are a true friend after what you have just told me. I now know that there are no secrets between us and that you are a man of your word." Peter was so happy that he had told Jake and that he had understood the reasoning behind him alerting the police.

Jake then told Peter how he had met Ginny.

Ginny was a teacher in adult education working for the probation service with the task of trying to train offenders in life skills, enabling them to find paid employment before they got into more serious trouble. She had a very good success rate and got on very well with most of her class. Of course, there were always a few rotten apples that would not reform or be told what to do. After Jake's experience with the police on the murder investigation, he was determined to get himself sorted out and get a job. At his first session with Ginny (or Miss Brett as the class called her) he showed great interest in what she was trying to get through to them, and asked questions about everything which he did not understand. Ginny was pleased to answer Jake's questions and wished that some more of her class would do likewise.

After he had three sessions with her, Jake was Ginny's favourite pupil and she knew that he was determined to turn his life around. This group had two more sessions to go in this particular course, then it was up to each individual to take on board what they had been told or ignore it. At the next session Ginny was trying to find out whether her class had learned anything from what she had been telling them. It did appear that from the answers to her questions that most of them had decided they would like to get away from the useless life which they had led up to now and would try to get a job. Then, one of her class, who never showed much interest in what his teacher was saying, suddenly, on being quizzed by Ginny, turned violent and started swearing and screaming at her. He jumped up and produced a knife and dived for Ginny, knocking her to the floor and plunging the blade into her shoulder. He had lost all control of what he was doing. Jake was the only one of the class to attempt to rescue Ginny. He had nothing to hit him with other than his fist. So, before this madman could strike her again with the knife, Jake landed a full force punch to the side of his head which partly stunned him and knocked the knife out of his hand. Jake kicked the knife away and waited for the madman to partly get up and then landed another killer punch onto his head which left him motionless on the floor.

Jake grabbed the knife in case anybody was tempted to use it. He then grabbed the phone and rang 999. It was answered in seconds and Jake shouted, "Ambulance, urgent!" and gave all the details. Then he looked at Ginny who was bleeding profusely from her shoulder wound. He grabbed a pack of tissues which she had on her desk and took most of them in one hand and held them against the flow of blood that was gushing from her shoulder. The blood continued to seep through the tissues, so Jake did something which he'd seen on TV, on 'Casualty'. He took off his belt and tightened it around the top of Ginny's shoulder to cut off the blood supply. Much to his amazement it worked!

The ambulance and paramedics arrived within twenty minutes, which was a huge relief for both Ginny and Jake. The police then took charge of the madman who was by now coming round from the effects of Jake's second punch. Jake handed the knife to the police sergeant and explained what had just happened. The paramedics were still working on Ginny's shoulder and were anxious to get her to the hospital ASAP. As they were leaving with her on a stretcher, she looked at Jake and whispered, "Thank you. Thank you, Jake."

The local paper had a journalist who was curious to know what had happened when she saw the ambulance and police outside Ginny's office and went to have a look. The police sergeant was delighted to speak to her, her name was Maggie Rainford. She had often spoken to the sergeant on other matters, so they knew one another quite well. He gave Maggie all the details of the stabbing by the madman with the knife and told her that he was one of a group of petty crime offenders who were on a rehabilitation training course. He went on to say that if it was not for the bravery of one of the group, there was every chance that Ginny Brett would have been killed. "This chap's name is Jake Steadman."

Maggie then interviewed Jake and asked him if he would like to have his photograph in the local paper. Jake said that he did not want to. He did not see anything newsworthy in what he had done; he had only done what any decent person would do. Maggie ignored his protests and next day's paper front page was mostly about the hero who saved Ginny from almost certain death at the hands of the knife-wielding madman.

Ginny was making good progress after a surgical procedure to repair the damaged artery in her shoulder, but still had quite a lot of pain. She was also suffering panic attacks at the thought of what might have happened if it was not for the man who had saved her from the psycho. Jake Steadman was a true hero and she was now desperate to see him. She did not have Jake's number, however, she did manage to get an email to him, which he would see the next day on the course where a supply teacher was filling in for her. In the email Ginny told him how much she admired him for his heroism and bravery, also that she would love it if he would come and visit her at the hospital.

Jake felt so happy to think that Miss Brett would want to see him, so, after he had finished for the day, he got himself all dressed up in his best gear and got on the bus to the hospital. Outside the hospital there was a man selling flowers. The only problem was Jake did not have much money and the flowers looked very expensive. The flower man was watching Jake who was now counting what money he had and knew that he was struggling to find sufficient cash for a bunch of flowers. He called Jake over and told him that he would let him have a decent bunch of flowers at half price as they were now coming near to the end of their shelf life. Jake was delighted and thanked the flower man for his generosity.

When Jake approached the enquiry desk at the hospital, he just remembered that he did not know what ward Miss Brett was on. When he asked the receptionist, she knew right away who he had come to see but that the patient's visitors had to be carefully vetted on account of what had happened to her. She asked Jake his name and when he told the receptionist she said, "So you are the brave man who saved the life of this lovely girl? I am so delighted to meet you, Jake." She then called for a porter to come and take Jake to the patient's room.

When she saw who her visitor was, Ginny let out a scream and shouted, "Jake Steadman, my hero! Come here and let me hold your hand." She then began to sob and got hold of Jake's hand and held it for a long moment. Poor Jake felt very awkward and did not know what to say or do, he had never been treated like this by anybody before. However, Ginny, once she had composed herself, soon made Jake feel comfortable and discussed the previous day's events and how near she was to death at the hands of the crazed knifeman and the speedy reaction of the hero of the day, the great Jake Steadman.

By now Ginny was getting tired as she'd not managed to get much sleep the previous night. She asked Jake to pass her handbag and thanked him for the lovely bunch of flowers which he had brought her. She opened her purse and then said, "Jake, now I don't want you to argue about this. I am going to give you this pay-as-you-go phone, which my dad brought in this morning, when I thought I couldn't find mine. I know that you do not have one and also I would really like it if you would come back to see me tomorrow."

Jake was feeling a little uncomfortable about going to see Ginny at the hospital again and risk running into her family or friends. However, when he got there, he was soon cheered up by the welcome that he received from her. Ginny was now sitting out of bed and looking much better. Without getting up she stretched her hand out to Jake who took it and smiled and said, "You look so much better."

She then said, "Mam and dad, this is my hero, Jake Steadman, who saved my life. Jake, this is my mam, Cynthia, and my dad, Jason." They stood up and got hold of Jake and hugged him until he thought they would suffocate him. They thanked him and praised him sincerely for his courage and heroism in saving the life of their only daughter who they loved and treasured above all else. Jason went on to tell Jake that they owed him a huge debt and that they would try to repay at least some of it in the weeks and months ahead.

Jake, who had never thought of what he had done as being anything great and was now almost in tears, told Jason that he did not want anything and was glad to see that Ginny was okay. Jake then tried to return the phone to Ginny, saying it was too generous a gift and totally unnecessary. Ginny butted in and said, "Jake, I want you to have the phone because I want to keep in touch with you and to continue what we were doing before that madman stopped it all. Jake, you were the only one of the group who showed any interest in what I was trying to get through to you. Now I do not want to see that being wasted. From what I know about you, you are anxious to transform your life and get a proper job and earn a living. I am certain that I can help you to achieve this goal. I have quite a number of contacts and I am certain that I can have you in gainful employment very quickly. I am not going to be back in work myself for some time. However, for you, Jake, after I get out of hospital and settled back down at home, I want you to come to my mam and dad's house where we can talk and find out what type of job you might be best suited for. So please, Jake, keep the phone because it will enable us to contact one another when necessary. Also, my dad has given me something else to give to you. It is an envelope with some cash in it, which we all hope that you will accept as a very small portion of what we owe you. If it was not for you my parents would now be arranging my funeral. So please take it and buy yourself some new clothes and whatever else you may need to prepare yourself for this exciting new life which you are about to embark on."

Jake had no idea how to respond to all of this kindness which was being bestowed upon him. When he tried to speak the tears rolled down his cheeks and he could not get a word out. He really wanted to decline the monetary gift, but Ginny's parents insisted and he thought it might be bad manners to decline. Cynthia realised the predicament that poor Jake was in and got up and got a few tissues and wiped the tears from his eyes and cheeks and gave him a hug. Ginny then told Jake she would arrange to meet him once she was home.

*

Over the course of their many chats Peter and Jake realised that, not only had their paths crossed several times in their lives, but also had some uncanny resemblances in how their lives had panned out. Both of them had had difficult upbringings but had improved their lot through hard work and climbing the ranks in British Rail. Through acts of courage and selflessness they had helped people in need; Peter protecting his mother and coming to Helen's rescue on the tram and Jake saving the life of his wife-to-be Ginny. What neither of them knew was that their greatest acts of heroism were ahead of them.

CHAPTER 29

Cabernet and Corkscrews

Cabernet and Corkscrews wine shop was a roaring success. The first month's sales exceeded all of Helen and Peter's expectations. However, Helen was working very hard and needed some help during the week. Peter was still on a four-day week and took the pressure off her at weekends. They still had not got round to sorting out the upstairs apartment. Helen decided to post an advert in the shop window. She had quite a good response to the advert but was not very happy with any of the applicants.

Then, out of the blue one day, a familiar face walked into the shop. Gabriella from the wine merchants walked in and said, "Do you remember me?"

Helen looked at her and said, "Gabriella, of course I remember you. Come in and I will make you a cup of coffee."

Gabriella replied, "That would be lovely, thank you, and please call me Gabs."

After they had their coffee and a catch up, Gabs said, "I was passing, and I saw the notice in the window about the apartment. Is it still for renting out?"

Helen said, "It is. Are you interested in it?"

Gabs said, "I think so. Please can I have a look at it?" Helen took her up and showed her round. The apartment looked fantastic with all of its new carpets and furnishings. Gabs said, "Oh I love it! Please can I have it as it is just what I need? Where I am living now is not very nice, plus we now have new neighbours who always seem to be fighting or playing loud music. so I really need to get away from there. I am also on the lookout for a new job as I am getting bored of what I have been doing for quite a few years."

Helen was very interested when she heard about Gabs looking for a new job. She'd had in mind that she would use the apartment to attract somebody who could be a live-in manager, taking a lot of pressure off her as her life was crazy busy and getting a bit too much. She then said to Gabs, "What sort of job did you have in mind as I am now struggling to cope with this business on my own since opening the wine shop?" Gabs was surprised at what Helen had said. She pondered; *would this be the sort of job I would like? It is only a small business; would I get bored? Is Helen the sort of person I could be comfortable with every day? Is she offering me a job?* "So," she said to Helen, "I am not quite sure but since seeing this apartment, which I love, and what you have just said, Helen, this has made me think. If you were to offer me the job, and we agree terms, I would be living upstairs and working downstairs. It would also save me so much time and money not having to commute to work."

Then it was Helen's turn to speak. "Gabs, all of this has happened quite suddenly so, firstly the apartment, I will take the note off the window and hold it for you for another week for you to think it over. I need to have a chat with my husband Peter about what we should do. Then if we decide that we should take somebody on as a manager we would then want to formally interview you and decide if you were the right person for the job. So why don't we make an appointment for some time next week when Peter will be off. What time would suit you?" Gabs said any time would suit as she would take the day off. So, the appointment was made for Friday at 11.30 a.m.

Helen asked Anna if she could come into the shop for a couple of hours on the Friday while she and Peter interviewed Gabs.

The interview went well. Gabriella ticked most of the boxes. She told Helen and Peter a lot about her nine years with the wine wholesalers. She had a good relationship with all the staff there, including the owners and the managers. She had learned a lot about the wine industry and the variety of wines available. She also said that she was very confident that she could, with her knowledge of wines and with her connections in the industry, make their wine shop a very profitable business. Gabs told them that in the wholesaler's organisation there was a cartel, which kept prices higher than what they needed to be and that, with her knowledge of knowing who was who, she was certain that she could buy wines much cheaper than what they were paying at the moment. She added with a smile, "I should really not be telling you all this, so now you will have to give me the job!"

Helen and Peter were impressed with Gabriella's performance. She had been with her present company for nine years so she must have been honest and reliable and of good character. They then asked her if she would like to leave them for a half hour while they had a chat with each other. Helen said, "Make yourself a cup of coffee and, if you don't mind, I would love one and I am sure that Peter would also like one. You can have a chat with Anna and come back up here in a half hour."

Helen and Peter were both of the opinion that Gabs would make a big difference to their profit margins. However, there were still a number of things to be discussed and agreed before they offered the job. When Gabs, accompanied by Anna, arrived upstairs with the coffee which Helen and Peter were looking forward to, she gave an anxious look at them both.

Anna went back downstairs to look after the shop. Helen, after she had a few sips of her coffee, then said to Gabs, "Peter and I are happy to take you on as manager of the wine shop if we can agree terms, on your salary, your working hours, and on the rent for the apartment. Also, as you know, the wine shop business is mostly done in the evenings so it would not be a 9-5 job. We also have the normal general sales of the shop to think about, all of which are essential to the business, would you be willing to help out with that as and when required?"

Gabs said that she knew she could not stand around in the wine department waiting for somebody to come in for a bottle or two of wine. What she thought was that her working week should not exceed 40 hours, some of which could be evenings up to about 8 p.m. Regarding the early morning starts of 7 a.m., she would not mind doing the odd few mornings but not on a regular basis. She also would prefer not to do any split days such as a few hours in the mornings and again in the evenings so the working hours of each member of staff would need to be sorted out, including Helen and Peter's. Helen thought that this was very wise and would be essential for the smooth running of the business. After much more discussion regarding Gabs' salary and the apartment rental, Helen and Peter were happy to welcome her on board as their business manager.

Once all of these details were sorted out and agreed, the only other question was when she could start. Gabs said that she would like to move into the apartment in a few days' time, but she would like to give a month's notice to her present employer.

CHAPTER 30

Ginny's Plan

After her discharge from hospital Ginny had settled down at home and tried to put everything that had happened in the last week behind her. The one thing that would not go away was Jake and the courage and heroism which he showed, and the total disregard for his own safety. She decided she was going to repay Jake Steadman for what he had done. She called him on his new phone and asked if he was happy with it, to which he said that he was delighted. She then asked if he would come and see her next day and, if so, she would get her dad to pick him up. Jake was a bit reluctant but after some slight persuasion he agreed. Ginny wanted to spend some time alone with him and was keen to get to know him and for Jake to relax and feel at ease in her company.

When Jason arrived with Jake in the car, they both seemed to have got on well and were chatting away. Cynthia gave Jake a hug, as did Ginny. They all sat down in the kitchen and had coffee and biscuits. Then Ginny said, "Right Jake. You come with me." And she led him into the study and sat him down. She said, "Now Jake, please stop calling me Miss Brett, I'm not your teacher anymore, nor ever will be again. I want you to call me Ginny as that is what my friends call me and that is what we are now, aren't we? I want to help you in every way that I can because of what you did for me, Jake. So now, what is my name?"

Jake was now feeling quite relaxed and replied, "Thanks Ginny. I would really like to be your friend".

Ginny told him that she would no longer be working for the probation service. The whole episode had really frightened her. She loved teaching adults and the plan was to get a job in the local further education college, but she was currently taking some time out. What she didn't tell Jake is that she would never be allowed to start a relationship with a student. If she was honest, she always quite fancied Jake, and ever since witnessing his heroics she had begun to develop feelings for him.

Jake decided to tell Ginny of his home life and his parents who did not care whether he went to school or not and the terrible squalor in which they had lived. Ginny was so sorry to hear about Jake's background and gave his hand a pat and said, "Jake, we are going to change all that and give you a much-deserved better lifestyle. Now I am going to suggest to you two things that I would especially like you to do and I will help you with both of them. The first one is to get you a job and get you off benefits. It will also give you a whole lot of pride in yourself. Now, what sort of job would you like? I have contacts with a number of companies who may be willing to take you on. One of the companies that I was thinking of is British Rail. It is a very big organisation and a good company to work for and good scope for promotion for anybody with initiative. Most likely your duties to begin with would be working on the platforms, helping people on and off trains, closing and opening doors and giving the train driver the signal to go. What do you think?"

Jake sounded quite interested but thought he would never get such a job with his background. Ginny said, "Leave that to me and I will see what I can do. The other thing that I mentioned is that after you start work and get settled in, I would like you to think about going to night school two nights a week for a term. I know that this would benefit you enormously. You are a clever young man who has been denied many things in your childhood, including a good education. What do you think?"

Jake was overwhelmed by what he had just heard and wondered if he could handle all of it. "Miss Brett—"

"Stop right there, Jake, what is my name?"

"I am sorry, Ginny," said Jake, smiling, "it won't happen again. I am worried that I will not be able to cope with all that you are planning for me and that I will let you down."

Ginny said, "Jake, trust me, I know that what we have discussed may seem to be beyond you, but I know that you can do it and I will be behind you all the way. Now I am going to phone my contact at Darlington Station and see what we can sort for you. And if she has a vacancy for you, I will take you there myself and introduce you to her."

After she had spoken at length with Jackie, the Station Ground-Staff Supervisor, she said to Jake, "Yes there is a vacancy for you which will be open next week sometime. So, let's have a bit of lunch which my mam has made and after that you can go home and enjoy the weekend and on Monday you can call Jackie to arrange to meet her at Darlington Station."

Jake was now four weeks with British Rail and had done two weeks at his night school class. He had just had his first pay from British Rail and had to open a bank account in order to be able to cash it. Again, Ginny had helped him sort out all of these details. She was very pleased with how he was getting on, in both his job and at night school. She had made a complete recovery from her stabbing ordeal and was starting to think about looking for a new job.

Jake now felt very much at ease in her company and they chatted to each other frequently. He wanted to do something for her in appreciation for all she had done for him and wondered if he should ask to take her out for a meal.

He had never been in a restaurant other than a curry house and did not know what to do or order if he did go but then thought Ginny would take care of everything as she always did. Ginny was surprised and rather delighted when Jake told her that he wanted to do something nice for her. So she told him, "That is very kind of you, Jake," and suggested that they go to her favourite bistro, Caesars, not a very upmarket place but the food was good.

Jake had made a great effort to make himself look his best. He had his hair done nicely and had bought some very smart-looking clothing for the occasion, all of which he could now afford as he was in full-time employment. When Ginny saw him, she exclaimed, "Wow, Jake! You scrub up well." Jake blushed and in return told Ginny that she looked lovely. Ginny then said that they should sit at the bar and have a drink before the meal and said that she would have a gin and tonic and suggested that he have one as well. Jake had never had a gin and tonic before and would have preferred a pint of beer, but Ginny told him that they did not serve pints of beer in the restaurant, though he could have a bottle. So, Jake drank his gin and tonic and then his bottle of beer, after which their table was ready.

Looking at the menu Jake said that he had no idea what to order and was feeling quite hungry. Ginny suggested that for a starter they would both have a prawn cocktail and then Jake should have a rump steak which she knew was good and she would have sea bass. She told Jake that people usually had wine with their dinner, and they should order a bottle. After they had some wine and their starter, Jake was now feeling much at ease and told Ginny that he was so happy that she had come out with him. Ginny also said that she was enjoying herself. She asked Jake if he was happy in his job and what he thought of night school. Jake said he loved his job and was getting on very well with his supervisor. His duties, although he was kept busy, were not very demanding and the time seemed to fly, so yes, he really was quite happy at British Rail. His night school was not as enjoyable and much more demanding but he now realised that it was something that he needed to do and was determined to do. For the first time in his life he realised, from his association with a better class of people, that he was very much out of his depth in their world. He regretted the manner in which he spoke and indeed a number of other things as well.

Ginny was delighted at what Jake had just said, especially about the night school. She knew the Principal of that further education college and had asked them to take special care of Jake. He was working towards gaining his maths and English GCSEs which were essential to get on in his career. She asked Jake if he had any books and what type of books he would like to read and that she would get a few thrillers if she knew what he might like. Jake said that he had only ever read one book and that was a life story of Clint Eastwood which he enjoyed. Ginny said, "That is fine, Jake. I will send you a couple of books tomorrow. Seeing as we have both enjoyed ourselves tonight let's come back here in a month's time when you have read both of them and talk through them. It's a great way to learn; you will get your English GCSE no problem. It will be my treat next time."

By now, having drank most of the bottle of wine, Ginny was getting more and more chatty and said, "Jake, I am very proud of you and if you keep up how you are doing you will have a great future ahead of you, and I am so looking forward to when we meet here in a months' time."

Boosted by what Ginny had said, Jake resolved that he would really do his utmost both at his job and his night school class. He had read the two books, both crime thrillers, which she had so kindly sent to him. By now he had received his second pay cheque and paid it into his bank and had drawn some cash which he needed to pay his rent and every day spends.

The big day for his next meal with Ginny had arrived. Jake had a haircut and bought himself a new shirt and was looking very smart when he met Ginny. He was feeling much more at ease about going to the restaurant this time as well as meeting her. As they made their way to the bar, they complimented each other on how nice they both looked. Jake said he would have a gin and tonic to begin with as Ginny was having one. Ginny detected a marked improvement in Jake's way of speaking. After he had his gin and tonic Jake said, "I am getting to like this. I think I will have another." Ginny agreed and ordered one too.

They chatted away for ages with Jake telling all about his night school and how his teacher was trying to help him to speak better. Their table was now ready, and they were looking at the menu. Jake was much more confident than he was on his first occasion and ordered a chicken risotto. Ginny stayed with the fish but ordered lemon sole. They ordered a bottle of wine and settled into what turned out to be a very enjoyable evening. Ginny said she had lots of books and would like him to read some of them. They would not all be crime thrillers and would broaden his knowledge on many things.

By the time the meal and the bottle of wine were finished they were both looking rather lovingly at one another. Jake reached across the table and took Ginny's hand and held it very tenderly and, looking directly into her eyes, said, "Ginny, I know this sounds mad but I love you."

He had no idea what response he would get and was thrilled when she said, "Thank you Jake. I was thinking very much along those lines myself. But, let us not go too fast and get to know each other much better. You are so kind and caring, Jake. When I told you previously that you had a great future ahead of you this is probably what I had in mind."

On their way home in the taxi they held hands and kissed several times, and made plans to see each other again very soon.

When Jake woke up the next morning, he could not believe what had happened the previous night. Could it be true? It must be a dream. He felt so happy and thought that he now had something to live for. With great enthusiasm he went to work very happy and his boss was delighted with how he carried out his work.

When Ginny told her parents that she was very fond of Jake and even hinted that she might be in love with him they were rather shocked. Cynthia said, "Virginia, how could you? He is from a very low-class family and you are so refined. I know that he saved your life, but you are so unsuited. Why are you always on a rescue mission?"

Ginny said, "It was Jake who rescued me, remember, mam? I know we are from very different backgrounds but now that I have got to know Jake a lot better, I know he is so kind and caring and he is also very bright and is determined to improve his way of life. He is now in full-time employment with British Rail and is going to night classes two evenings a week where he is doing really well, by all accounts. He is a very different person to the Jake that you met a few months ago. He is slowly but surely getting much more confident and comfortable in company. Also don't forget, if it were not for Jake Steadman, I would not be here with you today. I would be in the local cemetery and you would be two very lonely people here, probably looking at photographs of me and saying, 'if only'! I have told Jake that we are not going to rush into anything. We will see how things work out over the coming months. I do know that with Jake's determination to better himself all will be fine."

The courtship of Ginny and Jake progressed quickly. Ginny was delighted with his reports from night school and, when she took him home to her parents for dinner one evening, Cynthia and Jason were amazed at how Jake had improved in all sorts of ways. He was no longer that shy and quiet young ruffian but was now very confident and well-spoken and could hold a conversation with anybody. Also, he was so nicely dressed, well-groomed, and handsome. By the time that dinner was over, both Cynthia and Jason had really taken to Jake and were delighted to see how Ginny and he looked so lovingly at each other.

CHAPTER 31

Gabs' Improvements

Gabs had now moved into the apartment over the wine bar. She really loved it as it was so much better than her old apartment. It also saved her at least two hours per day travelling to and from work. She and Helen were getting on very well and seem to have a lot in common and to chat about. Gabs told Helen that after the early morning busy period, when most people have gone to work, if she wanted to have a couple of hours off that she would look after things. This was something that Helen appreciated very much as she was usually there just before 7 a.m. and the thought of being able to put her feet up for a while was very appealing. She was, however, looking at the old part of the shop which she thought was looking very dated and needed a makeover, but nothing majorly structural. She asked Gabs to have a think about it. Helen was thinking that she would need some additional shelf space as she was often asked for items which she did not stock and it would be good to expand into more lines.

Gabs, having taken stock of the layout, very soon came up with a plan which would give Helen considerably more shelf space. This would involve moving the counter and the till from its present position over to the window. The present counter was quite big and unnecessary. This move would make space for about six meters of extra shelving without causing much upheaval. Helen was delighted with Gabs' suggestion. She had no hesitation in deciding who to approach to do this work, Joe Brownlow, the builder who had done such a great job on the wine bar, would be her man. Joe gave her his quotation for the work and said it would take him three days to do it. Helen loved the new layout and enjoyed moving things about and stocking her additional shelf space.

Gabs was concentrating on how to increase turnover and profits in the wine bar. She shopped around the wine wholesalers to ensure that Helen was buying her wines at the best possible price. The company which she had just left was their present supplier and they had been very competitive up until now. However, she did think that she could squeeze another 5% out of them if she promised to increase the turnover. What she had in mind was that every six or eight weeks she would have a sale, in which she would offer 15% discount to anybody buying six bottles of wine. These sales would be well advertised in the local paper and in flyers which she would have distributed locally.

Before she spoke to Helen about what she had in mind she spoke to Johnny from her old company. Johnny thought that this was a very good idea and that he would be happy to give her the 5% which she had asked for at her first sale. Gabs increased the monthly wine sales by over 100% plus the sales of spirits, beer, and soft drinks by a huge amount. The new shelves Helen had recently fitted and stocked with various types of household goods were almost empty. After Gabs' first sale, when everything had been reckoned up, the profits were considerably higher, and she was very relieved as she had been rather sceptical about the whole idea.

Helen had recently noticed how smoothly business was running and profits were on the positive side month after month. Gabs appeared to be quite happy and was proving herself to be a very business-like lady. Helen also found that she was having more leisure time and was enjoying every moment of it. Peter was still doing his four days per week with GNER and was nearing the end of his time with Jake Steadman, who was now fully capable of working on his own.

So, she thought, why don't we have a holiday? She mentioned this to Peter who thought that it was a great idea and, after they had thought about it for a while, they decided to take Peter's mother and Martin, as well as Anthony and Andi, who were now out of school for the summer holidays.

Helen and Peter were now in a very good financial position thanks to the wine shop and paper shop and the apartment. They had never taken the children abroad and thought that it was time that they got a bit adventurous. They decided to opt for Corfu.

However, Helen realised that the children did not have passports and it would probably take months to get them. Luckily, they had not mentioned the holiday to anybody as yet and decided that they should have a meeting with all concerned to discuss where they should go.

The meeting took place over Sunday lunch at their house and after various options had been discussed it was decided that Colwyn Bay in North Wales was very nice and they should have a week there. Colwyn Bay was situated right in the centre of some lovely resorts on the North Wales coastline so they would be able to explore many of them. Neither was it far to Llandudno or Anglesey, with them having their own transport they could visit any of these places.

CHAPTER 32

Barbados

Anna and her two friends Lucy and Georgina were on the first leg of their journey to Barbados. Their direct flight with Virgin Atlantic was from Manchester. They boarded the coach at Newcastle which would take them straight to Manchester Airport. The journey would take almost three hours after which they would board the plane for their eight-hour flight to Bridgetown in Barbados. They were so excited about this whole venture that they were embarking on and were determined that it would be the first of many foreign holidays together. They had all been lectured to death by their parents regarding how they should behave on this far-away island; don't drink too much, do not get tricked into taking drugs of any kind, always stay together, and never go out alone.

The coach trip to the airport was very pleasant. Everybody on board was in high spirits as they were all flying away to many different destinations. Even the driver was very pleasant and kept them entertained with many stories and jokes about his experiences over many years as a coach driver. They had a fifteen-minute scheduled break at a service station on the M6 which was appreciated by all on board. Their arrival at Manchester airport was right on time.

The little box which the driver had tactically left adjacent to the door was not ignored by many of his passengers.

Having collected their luggage, Anna and her friends made their way to the check-in desks which were very busy. However, they eventually got checked in and they then had to join the long queue for the security check which turned out to be a disaster for both Anna and Lucy. In their hand luggage both of them had various bottles of sunscreen and shampoo and such like; bottles which were well over regulation size and had to be discarded. It took ages to get through security and they'd been hoping to have time to go to the duty-free shop and pick up some cheap drink that they would have in their apartment when they arrived. Unfortunately, they were out of time as their flight was called and they had to get to the departure gate and within a few minutes board the plane.

The Virgin plane was quite comfortable with a decent amount of legroom so, after their early morning start from Newcastle, they were now tired and soon nodded off to sleep and would probably have slept for ages but for the cabin crew who were now serving lunch. However, they did have almost an hour of a snooze and felt much better for it and were really quite ravenous so they tucked in to their lunch. After having missed the duty-free shop at the airport, they were delighted to see the range of duty-free goods which were available on board the flight. Anna and Lucy were also able to replace a little of what had been confiscated from them by the security staff at the airport and decided they would stock up on some gin and vodka for the apartment. By now they were feeling relaxed and enjoying the flight and settled down to watch a movie which was just coming on. The rest of the flight was uneventful and soon passed.

On arrival at Bridgetown their local time was 3 p.m. so they reset their watches which were still showing 8 p.m. Barbados itself is not a very big island so their transfer to their hotel would not take long. Passport control was just a formality as nobody looked at them. Then they just needed to collect their luggage and get onto the bus which would take them to their apartment.

Their apartment was absolutely stunning, with two bedrooms, a comfortable lounge, and a modern kitchen. It was on the first floor of what looked like a very new block. There was a security guard at the main entrance who checked on everybody entering the building to ensure that they were booked in and entitled to enter. After he had checked their tickets, he then showed them how to get to their apartment and gave them their keys. One thing that Anna had already noticed and commented on was that everybody they saw either coming in or going out were all young and of a similar age to themselves which they thought was a very good start to this great adventure which they had embarked on.

After they had explored their apartment, they decided to go out and see if there was a supermarket near at hand. On their way out they asked the security man about the shops. He was very helpful and directed them to the nearest supermarket which was not very far away. They were also on the lookout for a nice restaurant in which to have their evening meal. There was no shortage of eating establishments, clubs, and pubs. This was just the sort of place that they were hoping that it might be. They did a quick shop at the supermarket and made their way back to their apartment and began planning what they would wear for the first night out in Barbados!

It was soon time to get dressed and go out to have something to eat and explore the night life. Whilst doing that, they helped themselves to some large gin and tonics. It was a lovely evening and still quite warm. People were all eating al fresco and the waiters and waitresses were dashing about very busily. They found a restaurant, recommended in their Lonely Planet guidebook, The Bluefin, and asked a waiter if he had any spare tables and were delighted when he said yes. He sat them down at a table for three and handed them the menus. Looking around and hearing people speak they noticed that most people sounded American and also that the majority of those, including the girls, were drinking lager. They all opted for three glasses of lager which came in ice cold glasses and were so refreshing.

Two English girls sitting at a table beside them were anxious to chat and asked if they had just arrived. They introduced themselves as Jenny and Sophie and said they had been there for a few days and were in raptures about everything. They told the newcomers where they thought the best clubs and pubs were, and about some places of interest which they might want to see. Jenny also mentioned that where they were eating right now was one of the better restaurants and mentioned one or two which they should avoid. They all enjoyed the meal which was very freshly cooked food and was very nicely presented.

So, when they had finished and were all leaving together, Anna asked Jenny and Sophie if they could tag along with them to explore the night life. They were delighted to have the trio join them and Jenny said that she and Sophie felt vulnerable with them being just two of them and that they had been approached on a couple of occasions by some unsavoury looking characters who wanted to take them to places. So, the quintet was now established, and they got on really well and there never a dull moment while they were together.

Bridgetown was a regular stop off for all the Caribbean cruise ships. They usually stayed the night there and set off again in the morning. Many of the passengers liked to get off and explore the bars and clubs on these stop-offs so there were usually many different nationalities in the bars and clubs on any given night. The girls found it interesting to see all different types of drinks being ordered and how well the bar staff coped with all different languages.

The bar that Jenny and Sophie took them to, Il Paradiso, was a very pleasant and popular place which was used by the mostly American holidaymakers and was always busy. There was a good DJ on each night who kept it in full swing. The five girls enjoyed the entertainment and each other's company, they got to know each other and were delighted at having met each other. They did, however, agree that they should mostly do their own thing during the day and meet in Il Paradiso in the evening.

Anna, Lucy, and Georgina were delighted with the start of their ten-day holiday in the Caribbean. They had already made new friends and were determined to make it a holiday to remember. After breakfast the next morning they decided to have a day on the beach as the weather was just lovely. On their way to the beach they saw a coach which was picking up a number of tourists and was on its way, touring the island. They asked the driver for details and he said it would be a six-hour trip with stop-offs for snorkelling and exploring the natural beauty of the island. Anna asked the driver if this was a daily trip which he did and he told her it was but that he was full up on this trip, but, if they booked now for tomorrow he would pick them up at this time, right here, tomorrow morning. They asked him how much he charged and were happy with the price, so they decided to book with him and were given tickets for the next day.

Anna and her friends enjoyed a lovely day on the beach on the sunbeds which they had to pay for. After they'd had a couple of hours lazing and reading on the beds, they went for a dip in the sea which was lovely and clear and warm. The three girls swam and snorkelled for hours, after which it was time to look for something to eat. They found a little beach-front bar with plenty of tables outside and ordered cold beers, which again came in lovely chilled glasses and with a few nibbles which they enjoyed. They then went back to their apartment and had another snooze to prepare for the night ahead.

For their evening meal they went to The Bluefin again, where they found Jenny and Sophie who were both hoping that their new-found friends might come in. As they had not already ordered anything, they asked the waiter to find them a table for five which he did. They then ordered their drinks and browsed through the menu and chatted away very happily.

After their meal, which took over two hours, they went for a walk to explore Bridgetown and see what the shops had to offer and were very surprised at how cheap things were compared to home prices. The exchange rate of the pound with the US dollar, which was the accepted Barbados currency, was very favourable so they decided to earmark a day that they would do some shopping. It was now time to make their way to IL Paradiso. As usual the bar was quite busy, but they did just manage to get a table which was just being vacated by another group of seven young people who were heading off somewhere else. Shortly after the girls had settled at their table and were enjoying their drinks and chatting away happily, three handsome-looking young men made their way to the bar and were casually looking around while waiting to be served with their drinks. One of them soon focused his eyes on the table where the quintet of young girls sat, who were already nudging each other about the three young men at the bar. The man's eyes went all around the table and seemed quite interested in what he was seeing. He briefly singled out Anna, both of them locked eyes briefly and exchanged smiles ever so faintly.

After they had got their drinks and were chatting among themselves, the three chaps were getting nearer to the table where the girls were seated. The chap who had smiled at Anna and was now facing the table decided it was time for somebody to break the ice, so he said, "Hello girls. Lovely to hear some English accents, and how are the holidays going?" He was now looking directly at Anna, so she answered and said that they were having a fantastic holiday so far. They'd only been there two days. She then said, "My name is Anna and these are my friends Lucy and Georgina. We are all Geordie girls as you can guess! And these are our new friends Jenny and Sophie from Birmingham. And who might you be?"

He replied, "I'm Simon and these are my friends Toby and Zac.

Please let me get you girls a drink. What would you like?" Anna said there was no need for him to get them a drink, but Simon insisted and called the waiter and ordered two bottles of the local wine, one for the girls and one for him and his friends. He then said, "I see two spare seats, are you keeping them for anybody or would you mind if we get another seat and join you?"

Anna looked at her friends and said, "What do you think?" They all nodded their consent and moved about to make room for the three handsome guys.

When they got all the seats in place and everybody sat down with glasses of wine, which Simon had recommended, they all thought it was a very pleasant drink and Anna thanked Simon for his generosity, which he dismissed and said it was his pleasure and he was very grateful to them to be let join them. He then raised his glass, and everybody did likewise and touched glasses and they all toasted to a great holiday. By now conversation was flowing freely between the group about what they all did. Simon, who was seated next to Anna, said to her, "You seem to be the leader of this group of lovely girls. What brings you to Barbados?" Anna said that she certainly was not the leader. She always wanted to visit the Caribbean and they found this great package deal to Bridgetown and luckily her two best friends were up for it too. They had met the other two last night at The Bluefin restaurant. She went on to tell him they were lovely girls and they'd figured there was safety in numbers!

Whilst Anna and Simon were chatting, the rest of the group were also comparing notes and seemed to be enjoying the company of Toby and Zac, who were both very funny. Toby appeared to be paying a lot of attention to Lucy who he was sitting next to and they both were roaring with laughter at Toby's feeble attempts to do a Geordie accent. Simon and Anna seemed to have forgotten that there was anybody else at the table; they were so taken with one another. Simon told her that he was from London, he was a newly qualified

GP and that he had a flat in Ealing which he shared with Zac. He had two siblings, Steve, who was twenty-one and Debs, seventeen. Both of them lived at home with their parents Eleanor and Charles. The flat in which he lived was a short train ride from his parents' home in Farnham, Slough, and he went for dinner most weeks. His mother Eleanor loved it when he stayed the night and had kept his room for him. Anna told Simon all about her family. At this point the clock seemed to race on. The DJ had finished, and the bar staff were now clearing up. Simon said that we would love to see them again the next night and that he had enjoyed their company. So, they all said goodnight. The girls were excited about the three fabulous guys who joined them at their table, and all agreed that they would be back there the next night. Anna, Lucy, and Georgina said goodnight to Jenny and Sophie and said that they would see them in the restaurant the next night.

CHAPTER 33

An Unexpected Reunion

After a good night's sleep, the three girls were up and showered and had a light breakfast and were ready to go and wait for their tour bus to arrive.

When they got to the coach stop there was nobody else there so they were first in the queue and were hopeful that they would be able to get good seats. They had their tickets ready and were very much looking forward to their trip around the island and especially the reef-snorkelling. After a while there were quite a number of people in the queue. The coach arrived and the driver got out and gave a good cheery 'morning' to everybody. The three girls were first to get on the coach, led by Anna. There were only about fifteen people already on so there was a good choice of seats. Anna suddenly stopped dead. Sitting at the back was Simon, Toby, and Zac! Simon was already on his feet and calling the girls down to the seats which were next to where they were sitting. The girls were flabbergasted. When Simon had everybody seated, he let out a big 'Hurrah!' and told the girls how fantastic it was to have them with them on this trip and went on to say that they had made his day. They had only booked this trip on a whim that morning. Anna, Lucy, and Georgina had rather mixed feelings about this unexpected encounter with the three handsome guys from the previous evening. They certainly were not prepared for seeing them again at this time of the morning, or they would have done their hair and make-up! After the driver had checked everyone onto the coach it was almost full. He took his seat, wished everyone a pleasant trip, and set off.

The driver was very good and described everything and everywhere as they went along and said that their first stop would be at Harrison's Cave which was almost an hour away and that they would spend an hour there which would give them time to have a coffee and explore the underground cavern. The conversation between the girls and Simon and his friends was much more muted than it was the previous night at the bar where they met. However, they all wanted to see the island and so were all looking out of the windows and listening to the driver's commentary on the history of the areas which they were going through.

Simon was thinking more about Anna than the history of the island and thought that they would change the seating after their stop at the cave. His idea was to ensure he was sitting right next to her instead of his friend Zac. Eventually, the driver, who had been talking continually about the areas which they were driving through, said they were now approaching Harrison's Cave, their first stop.

After they had all got off the coach and stretched their legs and looked around, Simon invited the girls and his friends to join him for a coffee. After they got seated in the cafe, Simon asked the girls what they would like and were they hungry. Anna said that they weren't as they had eaten in their apartment and that they would just like a coffee. Simon and his friends said they were all starving as they had not managed to get any breakfast. Simon asked the waiter if they were still serving breakfast and when the waiter said they were the boys ordered three 'Full Americans' and six coffees. Lucy remarked about the coincidence of meeting the boys who they just met the previous night and the conversation flowed easily while they were waiting for the breakfasts. Simon asked about Jenny and Sophie and were told they were having a lazy day on the beach.

Suddenly Zac remarked in his broad Essex accent, "I swear man. No wonder the Americans are so flamin' obese if this is what they have for breakfast!" The three girls creased up with laughter.

After they had their coffee the girls went to the bathroom and left the boys to enjoy their huge breakfasts.

*

On their return to the coach Simon suggested that they should change the seating arrangement for the rest of the trip and said that a more friendly arrangement would be girl-boy. He was walking beside Anna to make sure that she would be his seating partner. So, Lucy was seated with Toby, and Georgina was seated next to Zac. Everyone seemed happy with the plan and the driver started off on the way to Turtle Bay for the snorkelling. Simon told Anna that he thought it was too good to be true when he saw her and her friends get on the coach and hoped that they were not spoiling their sight-seeing trip of the island. Anna assured him that that was not the case and that they were enjoying the company. They chatted away quite comfortably, and the other two couples seemed to be doing likewise, continuous chatter punctuated by shrieks of laughter, based as far as Anna could tell, on mutual micky-taking of each other's accents.

Anna told Simon that this was the first holiday abroad for her and her friends and how worried all their parents were about letting their little girls go to such a far-off place and had warned her not to drink too much and to beware of strange men. At this point she looked directly at Simon and smiled, wanting him to give her some assurance that there was no need to be wary of the three of them. Simon obliged, telling her that even though they had only met the previous night, they were perfectly safe with him and his two friends. They had been on lots foreign holidays before, though this was their first trip to Barbados. He continued chatting about anything and everything, Anna realised she could listen to him all day and just lightly touched his hand saying, "My mam and dad would approve. You are definitely not a strange man!" She told him that she had just finished her third year at Durham University doing Mechanical Engineering and had one more year to do which would be very demanding, but she was determined to do well. Simon chatted about his junior doctor training and current work in a large practice in Ealing.

They arrived at Turtle Bay for the snorkelling and where they would also have a lunch time break. The snorkelling was absolutely stunning; warm crystal-clear water, vibrant coral, friendly feathery fish of every size and colour. Toby claimed to have seen a giant turtle though nobody believed him. Of course, there was the added bonus of being able to check each other out in their swimwear! By now the girls, who had an early breakfast, were feeling hungry and looking forward to getting something to eat. Anna noticed a seafood restaurant with outdoor seating. It was a lovely warm day, 27 degrees, so it was just right for sitting outside, topping up their tans. The three boys were still full from their American breakfasts and so all they wanted was a nice cold beer. Anna insisted on paying for the beer and also the fish and chips for Lucy and Georgina. The fish and chips were lovely but with far too many chips for the girls, so they all finished up sharing with their seating partners. On the final stage of the journey, which was to a monkey sanctuary, the group were now getting tired and felt more like going to sleep than talking to anybody, so it was a rather uneventful but cosy hour. They were back at Bridgetown at 4 p.m. Prior to getting off Simon asked Anna if they would be in Il Paradiso that night, to which she said they definitely would be, and Jenny and Sophie would be with them. They said goodbye to the three boys and made their way back to their apartment to have a couple of hours rest.

That evening, on their way to the restaurant, the three girls wondered if Jenny and Sophie would be envious of them having been out with the three guys all day. However, they had not arranged it like that; it was pure coincidence. Just as they got to The Bluefin, Jenny and Sophie were going in. The waiter took them to a table which was all set out for five. He said that he knew they would be in. He took their drinks order and left them menus. Lucy asked the two what they had done during the day and was pleased to hear that they'd had a very enjoyable day. After a morning on the beach they had got the bus to a place called St Philips which is one of the larger towns on the island with quite a lot going on, including a market where all weird and wonderful things were sold, including some small animals and birds, the likes of which they had never seen before. Then Lucy told them about their day out, meeting up coincidentally with Simon, Toby, and Zac. Jenny and Sophie said that they must have had a great day being out with the three gorgeous guys and were they seeing them tonight? Anna was coy and said that they did not have any definite plans about seeing them, but they might be in the bar tonight.

Another good meal was had, and they went for a walk into Bridgetown to have another look around the shops.

Meanwhile, Simon could not get Anna out of his mind; there was something very special about her. She was very attractive, smart, and very caring. If they should see the girls tonight, he was determined to find out if Anna might be having similar feelings about him.

*

After the girls had another look around the shops, they decided that some of the bargains were too good to miss so tomorrow, whatever else, they were going to do some shopping in Bridgetown. Almost automatically they made their way to the bar and had just got their drinks when the three guys walked in and came straight over to them. The bar was quite busy, and it did not seem that they would get a table so easily tonight.

Toby was getting the drinks for his two friends and himself and thought the girls enjoyed the wine last night so he ordered them a bottle, with one for themselves. Simon was anxious to find a table as he wanted to sit with Anna. He was watching a group of girls and boys who were sitting at a table and appeared to be getting ready to move as they were finishing their drinks. He went over and asked if they were getting ready to go and they said yes, so he called the girls over and had them all seated in a matter of minutes. Anna stayed close to Simon so that when he sat down, she would be next to him. Toby and Zac were also in great demand and had a girl on either side of them. The two bottles of wine were soon finished, and Lucy insisted on getting around of tequila slammers which put a smile on everyone's face!

After a few minutes of discussing the coach trip and tour of the island, Simon wanted to talk about Anna and his feelings for her. Conversation was flowing freely all-round the table, so he said, "Anna. I know this sounds crazy, but I think that I am falling in love with you, even though we only met last night. I think that trip today was meant to be. When I saw you and your friends getting on the coach this morning my heart stopped because, when we left our apartment this morning, we had no intention of doing anything at all. After spending the day sitting beside you, Anna, I am in no doubt that you are a very special girl. Please tell me you feel the same."

Anna, who had been looking straight into Simon's eyes all the time he was talking, got hold of his hand and held it tightly and said, "Simon I have not thought of anything else since last night and when I saw you on the coach this morning. I thought I was going to pass out. I had such a great day. So, where do we go from here?"

Simon said, "We are both in a very awkward situation. You have Lucy and Georgina, plus now Jenny and Sophie. I have Toby and Zac. I know what I would love to do. Let's leave all this lot and get away, just the two of us, somewhere on the island for a couple of days. We have only three more days until I have to go home. I don't want to waste a minute. We can't keep our feelings secret from our friends. So if you don't mind, Anna, I will tell them how we feel about each other and that we want to spend our remaining few days with each other as much as possible and hope that they don't mind us abandoning them!"

After Simon had made this announcement there was great jubilation in the company. Simon's friend Zac said, "What we need is more wine!" He called the waiter and ordered three bottles of prosecco, saying "Let the party commence!" and gave Anna and Simon great big hugs.

Jenny and Sophie were leaving the same day as the boys. Anna, Lucy, and Georgina were not going home for six days so at least the Geordie friends would have some time together, just the three of them.

During their two days on their own, in a thatched beach bungalow right on the beach in Sugar Bay, Simon and Anna had a blissful time. They swam and sunbathed all day, eating local food from the beach bar nearby; much better than all the American food in the big resorts they agreed. Sipping bottles of beer as they watched the sunset, they talked for hours. Simon and Anna had many things to talk about and sort out if they were to have a serious relationship. The biggest problem being the distance between London and Newcastle. They also needed to consider Anna's final exams which she was determined to do well at and get a first if at all possible. Simon's GP work kept him very busy and he didn't have much spare time for travelling to see her in Newcastle. They agreed that they should meet somewhere between London and Newcastle. Birmingham seemed to be about halfway between the two so they agreed to meet there.

Anna said that she was due back at university in early October, but she had a whole lot of work to do before then. She thought the last weekend in September would be ideal for her, so they agreed to meet that weekend. Simon said that he would book somewhere nice and let her know.

The farewells at Bridgetown to Jenny and Sophie from Anna, Lucy, and Georgina were quite emotional as by now all five girls felt as if they had known each other for years. They exchanged numbers and promised to find each other on Facebook and post all the holiday photos.

The farewells to the three handsome London boys was much more protracted, especially between Anna and Simon.

Lucy and Georgina didn't have anything serious going on with Toby and Zac, and in fact already had their sights set on two nice American College boys, who had arrived at the hotel the previous day!

Anna and Simon were clinging on to each other until the taxi arrived to take the guys to the airport, at which point, they parted with a long lingering kiss.

CHAPTER 34

Peter's Daring Rescue

Helen and Peter were counting the days until Anna and her two friends got back from Barbados. They'd had several calls from Anna assuring them that they were all okay and having a great holiday. Helen kept herself busy in the paper shop; Gabs was taking most of the pressure off her in the everyday running of Cabernet & Corkscrew. She had built the business up to what could now be described as a little goldmine. Her regular monthly promotions brought customers from miles away who saw her full-page adverts in the local press. Those adverts were made affordable because of the extra discounts she squeezed out of the wine wholesalers when ordering all the extra wines to meet demand at the monthly tasting promotions.

Helen was in year four of the seven-year payback period, which she had agreed with Butch when she bought the shop. Her monthly payments were minimal compared to the monthly profits from the business. She didn't have any financial problems and she paid Gabs a really good salary. Gabs was very happy, both in her work and her private life. She loved the apartment above the shop, which was so convenient for her, she did not need a car and didn't have to spend hours each week commuting to work.

Helen's mother, Andrea, was getting on in years but had not been very well of late. She seemed to be getting quite forgetful which was worrying Helen, who began wondering about dementia but hoping that was not so.

Gabs was concerned about security at the wine bar, especially when she had her monthly promos as the amount of cash which she took was substantial and she had no security. She asked Helen and, if possible, for Peter to come in for a meeting to discuss the situation. She explained to them why she was so concerned. At her last tasting promo, she observed two particular characters who came into the shop about half an hour before closing time. They wandered around and appeared to be interested in what was happening at the till. They eventually picked up two bottles of cheap wine and as they were making their way towards the queue she approached them and asked if they would mind taking their wine to the other cash desk as they were not in the promotion and needed to be paid for at the other till. They said okay but when they thought that Gabs was not watching them, they put the two bottles down and walked out. Gabs told Helen and Peter that she was almost certain that these two characters were the same two that came into where she worked before, armed with knives, and demanded the cashier open the till and give them everything that was in it. As it happened there was not a great amount of cash in the till, being a wholesale business most things were paid by cheque or credit card. Helen and Peter were worried by what Gabs had just told them and decided they must do something about it immediately.

Gabs told them that in her old company they took on a full-time security guard who was also responsible for patrolling the shop floor which reduced shoplifting significantly, but obviously they were a bigger company and could afford it. This was a different situation and a full-time security guard was not an option. However, Gabs thought that it was mostly at promotion times, when there was a large amount of cash on the premises, that they were most at risk. She said that she would shop around some security companies and see what she could find. She added that the two individuals who robbed her previous establishment had been arrested and charged with aggravated burglary and were sentenced to four years in prison so she thought they must have just got out recently.

Several of the security companies which Gabs contacted were quite interested in calling to see what she had in mind and she asked if they could send a rep round to see her, so she made appointments to see three of them at different times. She thought that if any of them would consider collecting the days' takings at closing time each day that would be best for her, especially with her living on the premises. The first two, although very helpful, did not offer any such services but would send a guard round for two hours before closing time each evening. The third company, who were much more professional, said that they did offer such a service and gave Gabs a written quotation of everything which they would do, even down to putting a large notice on the window saying that no cash was kept on the premises overnight. She thought that the quotation was quite reasonable for what the company was offering to do so she passed everything on to Helen to see what she and Peter thought. She also reiterated her concern about the urgency of the situation.

Both Helen and Peter agreed with Gabs that it was something which should be done as soon as possible. Gab was delighted that Helen and Peter had so easily agreed, it made her feel that she would be so much safer in their apartment at night as there would be no great incentive for robbers to break into the wine shop and her apartment. She thanked them and promised that she would do her best to increase the turnover and the profits to make up for what were now increased overheads.

*

Anna and her two friends were now safely home, much to everybody's pleasure. Helen organised a dinner party to celebrate with the family. Carol, her husband, and family, together with Andrea, were all coming. The fridge was well stocked up with wine and, Anna, looking very tanned, was happily telling all about Barbados and the lovely time which they'd had and the friends which they'd made, Jenny and Sophie from Birmingham and of course the three handsome London boys. She didn't make mention of any romance between her and Simon, that would be for another time when she and her mam would be having a cup of tea and a chat. Anna wanted to know how the wine shop was doing and was concerned to hear about the security problem but pleased to hear about the arrangement to have each days' takings picked up at closing time. Anna was also glad to hear that if she wanted to work about three hours each morning, they would be happy to have her. She said that it would be great as she was skint!

*

Simon, Toby, and Zac had an uneventful flight home from Barbados to Heathrow. They slept most of the way. Fortunately, it was the weekend so none of them had to go to work until Monday. Simon spent most of the weekend at his parents' house. He was in daily contact with his lovely Anna. She had just finished a fabulous dinner which Helen had prepared and had had several glasses of wine when he called her mobile. She excused herself from the table to take the call and went to another room, taking another glass of wine with her. She asked Simon if he had a glass of wine to which he said yes he had, so they both said cheers and chatted away happily for ages. Simon told Anna how much he was missing her and that he loved her. He also said that he had told his mum and dad about the amazing girl he had met in Barbados and showed them her photo and they thought she was stunning. Anna also told Simon how much she loved him and missed not seeing him. She said that as she had only been home for two days, she wanted to get her mam on her own to tell her about this fantastic and gorgeous young GP whom she had met and fallen in love with in the Caribbean.

*

Gabs had now made all the arrangements with the security company to start to collect the daily takings at the first of the month which was almost two weeks away. She was hoping that they could start right away, as she had her end of month promotion coming up. Gabs, in her effort to increase the monthly profits, to compensate for the extra security costs, had now negotiated with the wholesalers for two more wines, which are much more upmarket and expensive than her usual stock. She squeezed the very maximum discount out of them for these wines as she needed to be able to sell them at a very good price.

That week in her advert in the local paper she highlighted what she called her Premier Collection, together with the offer prices. Gabs wondered if she was taking a big risk as even the offer prices on these wines was still quite steep for the area. However, it was too late now to do anything about it so she thought she would just have to wait and see.

By closing time on the first day of the promotion she had sold out of the 150 bottles of her Premier Collection and she had to message the rep to make sure that he stocked her up the next morning with 200 bottles of each. She told Helen about her new initiative and the way the collection had sold out in a matter of hours and how she was hoping for a repeat today. She also mentioned to Helen that she was getting nervous about the amount of cash which she was holding at the moment and which would increase considerably tonight. The security company couldn't start for another two weeks. She asked Helen if she and Peter could come this evening and take all of the cash with them at closing time tonight. Gabs also mentioned that it might be a good idea if they could spend a couple of the busiest hours in the wine shop as there had been quite a number of bottles missing the night before when there were a lot of people in the shop. Helen said that she and Peter would certainly help out in an effort to stop the shoplifting and also take whatever money Gabs was holding. This was a great relief to Gabs as she did not want to be responsible for so much cash. If that night's takings matched the previous evenings that would be a small fortune on the premises.

Helen and Peter, both very casually dressed to look like customers, were on patrol in good time and were very pleased to see how Gabs' promotion was going. Gabs no longer wore her 'pulling gear' for promotions and was dressed in a classier little black dress, but still looked gorgeous. Most people were just picking up two or three bottles of the usual stock and were in and out in a matter of minutes. Others were asking about the premier wines as advertised in the local paper. All of these wines were stored in a display cabinet which was kept locked and only opened when a customer asked to see them. Gabs herself was in charge of the key and was kept very busy. Some customers, drawn in by the amazing promotional prices, brought with them wine carriers and would ask for six bottles and one particular man asked for a whole case.

Peter apprehended a man whom he spotted putting a bottle of wine into an old shopping bag before taking another bottle to the till and paying for it. Peter stopped him as he was going out the door and asked him what he had in the bag and told him to put the bag on the counter and show his receipt. The man tried to run away but Peter grabbed him and put an arm lock on him and held him. By this time Helen had arrived and Peter asked her to take a look inside the bag which the man was holding onto. In it she found two bottles of wine and the receipt for one bottle. Helen told the man that she should call the police and have him arrested for shoplifting; however, she said that on this occasion she would not. She told Peter to release him and she then gave him back his bag with one bottle of wine and told him never to come back into the wine shop again.

It was now coming near to closing time and there were not many customers still in the shop. Gabs was getting ready to start cashing up. Helen was just about to lock the door when two men wearing balaclavas burst in, wielding knives, and pushed Helen towards the till, holding a knife to her neck. One shouted at Gabs to open the till and put the money into a bag which he was holding. Gabs was about to open the till but then she froze as she spotted Peter; the robbers had not seen him because he was bent down sorting out shelves. He was sneaking up behind the thugs with a bottle in his hand. He got within striking distance of the one holding Helen with the knife to her neck and swung the bottle with full force to the side of the thug's head. The knife dropped from his hand and he fell to the floor and stayed there.

When the other robber saw what had happened to his accomplice he lunged at Peter with the knife. Peter, who was by now a three DAN karate master, sidestepped him and grabbed his arm with the knife and swung him round. The knife fell to the floor and Peter kicked it away. He now had the upper hand and could do whatever he liked with this guy. The first thing he did was to grab the balaclava off his head to see what he looked like.

When Gabs saw the thug without his balaclava, she recognised him immediately as one of the two that she had seen some days before in the wine bar, and he was one of the pair who had robbed the wholesalers where she had worked before. The one which Peter had hit with the bottle was now beginning to come to life and was trying to get up. She pulled off his balaclava and recognised him as the accomplice of the one that Peter was holding. Just then the door opened, and four policemen followed by two paramedics walked in. They were in response to an urgent 999 call which Helen had made just a few minutes before.

One of the four policemen was a sergeant who now took control of everything. He told his constables to handcuff the two thugs and told the paramedics to take a look at the one whom Peter hit with the bottle; he did not look very well. The side of his head was blue or six different shades of black and blue and badly swollen. The paramedic said that they must get this guy to the hospital as quickly as possible as, in his opinion, he had a life-threatening head injury. The sergeant agreed and sent one of his constables with the ambulance to the hospital. He then turned to the other thug that Peter was still holding but now was handcuffed and said, "Oh, so we meet again! You must like prison life. Was it not last week that you got out after your four-year stretch?" The sergeant thanked Peter for his bravery in taking on the two villains and said that he would be recommending him for a community bravery award. He also thanked Helen, Gabs, and Stacey, the girl on the paper shop till, for their part in ensuring that these criminals would be going back to prison.

The sergeant told the constables to take the apprehended villains to the police station. He told Peter and the girls that he would need to take statements from them, but it was too late now and that he was sure that they had all had enough for one day. He then said he would come back the following day at a time to suit them.

Helen loaded all the cash into a bag then took Gabs to her apartment to get what she needed for an overnight stay as she was going back with her and Peter for the night or as long as she wanted to stay. Gabs thanked Helen for being so thoughtful, "I really appreciate that and I'm sure I will be ok by tomorrow."

Stacey had just been picked up by her husband and was not due back in work tomorrow. So, with all the cash in a bag, and Gabs with her overnight case, they made their way to Helen and Peter's house. On arrival there Helen sat Gabs down in the lounge and said, "I know it is late, but I am having a drink. Who wants to join me?" Both Gabs and Peter said yes and in a short time the usual two bottles of wine which Helen kept in the fridge had gone. They talked about the eventful night which they had just been through and how different it could have turned out had it not been for the bravery of Peter. Peter did not want to hear any more about that and said that he was glad that he was there and everybody came out of it safely, except for the guy he hit with the bottle who he hoped would be ok. Peter then told Helen that he thought she should shut the shop early the next day. Helen agreed entirely with that idea and Peter said to put a notice in the window saying 'Closed due to unforeseen circumstances.' No doubt the story would make the local press but Peter wanted to avoid any publicity if he possibly could.

CHAPTER 35

Charles's Story

The romance between Anna and Simon was going strong. They called and texted each other all the time. They had just had their romantic weekend in Birmingham which was just wonderful. The Crowne Plaza Hotel, which Simon had booked, was out of this world, the best that either of them had ever stayed in. They talked about a whole lot of things, getting to know everything about each other.

Anna told Simon how she told her mam and dad about this gorgeous guy whom she had met in Barbados and how well they had got on together and were keeping up the relationship, albeit by phone, but that they were planning to meet and have a weekend together. Her dad firstly wanted to know what this gorgeous guy did for a living and was very impressed when she told him that he was a GP.

Anna, who was doing most of the talking, went on to tell Simon that she was starting back at university next month and that this was going to be a very demanding time for her leading up to her finals in May. She asked Simon to be patient with her if she was a bit grouchy with him sometimes as she would probably be feeling tired, but never to forget that she loved him and needed his support. Simon assured her that however grouchy she might sometimes be, he would always be there for her and anything he could do for her would be his pleasure. He went on to say that it was only five years since he was in exactly the same situation leading up to his finals and he had not forgotten what it was like.

The weekend for Anna and Simon was memorable, and if there was any doubt in either of their minds about how they felt about one another any such doubts had now been dispelled. Simon mentioned the probability of them getting together for a couple of days just after Christmas and for Anna to think about it and it was left at that for now.

Simon told Anna all about how he did not always want to be a doctor, but he was good at science at school, and his careers teacher had suggested it. He had easily got the grades he needed to study medicine at Bristol where he'd had an absolute ball and met Toby. Zac was his oldest friend from school. Toby and Simon had worked together as junior doctors in Bristol; long hours and hard work, but lots of laughs. He loved being a doctor and now realised that medicine was the only job for him and felt that it was fate that brought him his perfect career, much like it had brought him Anna.

Anna had been worried that Simon was from a much more wealthy and middle-class background than her own. In fact, Simon's background was not very much different from Anna's. On the second night he told Anna his dad's life story which was very interesting. His grandad, Michael Hallman, was a mechanic and his grandma was a hairdresser. They only had one child, a son whom they called Charles Paul. Charles was a bright boy and managed to get to grammar school. It was his parent's great ambition that Charles would go to university and have a better start in life than what they had. Charles did quite well in his A levels and got into the University of London to do a degree in Electrical Engineering. Three years later he graduated with a 2:1 degree. His parents were so proud of him they even bought him a nice little secondhand car. Charles was delighted. His first job was with an electronic engineering company who made motors for industry and a large proportion of their output was for export to many different countries.

Charles took a very keen interest in how the company operated and took lots of notes on how they made their products, especially the smaller items. He was determined that in the not-too-distant future he would start his own company. It would obviously be in a very small way initially, but who knows, he might one day be in competition with the company he was now working for! Within two years of him joining this company he had been promoted to Assistant Production Manager. This position gave him further insight into manufacturing and indeed into the financial situation of the company. He was surprised to learn that the company was not nearly as prosperous as it had appeared to be.

Charles was intending to spend another two years with the company, to learn everything he could, before striking out on his own. However, in the meantime, he would be a loyal and faithful member of the staff of this company and see if he could do anything to improve their financial situation. In the time that he had been with the company he had built up a good working relationship with everybody and was quite popular with both workers and staff, even the MD Matthew Gatley had taken to Charles and would often have a little chat with him.

The Production Manager, who was Charles's boss, was called Arthur Sharp. He had been with the company for many years and had started on the shop floor and worked himself up to the position he now held. He was a hard worker and always had the interest of the company at heart. He was now in his early sixties and would be retiring when he reached sixty-five.

One day, Arthur was coming down the stairs to the shop floor when he tripped and fell down most of the stairs. He realised that he was unable to stand up and that he had terrible pain in his right hip and lower back. An ambulance was called, and Arthur was taken to hospital where he was diagnosed with a fractured femur and two fractured vertebrae in his lumbar spine. Arthur was told that his injuries were quite serious and that he was unlikely to get back to work within nine months. This was very bad news for the company as he was responsible for overseeing everything that the company produced.

Mr Gatley sent for Charles to come to his office to discuss the situation. He knew that Charles was a very bright young man, but did he have the experience to step into Arthur's shoes?

Charles said that he felt confident that he could take over Arthur's role as Production Manager for the duration of his convalescence and that he would do his utmost to ensure that everything went on as before. Mr Gatley said that he was confident in Charles and wished him luck. He also told Charles that at any time if he was not too sure about something then he should not hesitate to come and ask him what he thought.

In his first week in control of production Charles was happy how things had gone. He did, however, notice that some of the machinery used to break down and might be out of action for a number of hours until the fitters got it going again. All of the machines seemed to be quite old and cumbersome and were getting more and more unreliable. Delivery of some items to parts of Europe were running late as they had not been completed because of machinery failure, all of which was reflecting on Charles's ability to deliver the goods on time. This problem could only be resolved by Mr Gatley and it should have been pointed out to him before now. Charles asked Mr Gatley's secretary, June, if he could have some time with the boss to discuss a rather urgent problem. Mr Gatley readily agreed to the meeting. When he went in Charles was greeted with a nice handshake and asked if he would like a cup of tea.

After they got their tea Gatley said to Charles, "So what is this urgent problem that you wish to discuss with me, Charles, and please call me Matt?" Charles then explained about the production problem which he was experiencing because of machinery failure. Matt was very concerned at what Charles had just said and asked what needed to be done to remedy the situation.

Charles then said, "With the greatest respect, Matt, the problem is with the age of the machinery and its unreliability, and in comparison to modern-day machinery it is inefficient and slow. Also, the number of operatives required to operate these machines is uneconomical, all of which leads to our overheads being much greater than our competitors who have invested in new production methods. This problem is not going to go away and will almost certainly get worse as our tired and old machines get older."

Gatley was shocked and almost speechless at what he had just heard, especially as it had come from the youngest member of staff. Charles, however, pressed on, "Our main problem is that we are falling behind in production and starting to miss out on delivery dates. If this situation is allowed to continue, we are going to lose some of our best clients plus the fact that bad news travels fast and our orders for a lot of what we produce will diminish. Now, my suggestion, for what it is worth, would be that we get several quotations for new machinery. I do appreciate that this will be a very costly operation, which only you can authorise. There is one question which you should consider when deciding whether to spend a whole lot of money modernising your factory, will it reduce your overheads substantially and increase your output?" Charles then added, "Matt, I am sorry to have to give you all of these problems, but I would not be doing my duty as Production Manager if it did not point these things out to you."

Matt stood up and shook hands with Charles and thanked him for what he had said, he then went on to say that he would consider it very carefully.

Next morning, Charles got a message to come to Mr Gatley's office when it was convenient, so he finished what he was involved with and then went to see what Matt had decided. Was he going to get sacked for the impertinence he displayed yesterday in telling the MD of the company how to run his business? He would soon find out. On being shown into the office by June, Charles was pleased to see Matt had a rather welcoming smile on his face and said, "Charles, come in," and shook hands with him. He asked June if she could get them two teas and told her not to put any calls through to him while he was with Charles. He then went on to tell Charles that he had thought a lot about what he had told him yesterday, about the need to modernise the factory and that he totally agreed with him that the factory was now out of date by today's standards and could not keep up with their competitors who had updated their productions methods already.

Charles was delighted at what Matt had just told him and thanked him for the speedy decision.

The newly modernised factory, which had now been up and running for a few months, was fantastically efficient and far more productive. Several of the previous operatives who were near to retirement age were offered generous redundancy packages which they gladly accepted. All delivery dates for finished products were being met and the clients were very satisfied.

Matt got on very well with Charles, who was now the permanent Production Manager since Arthur's injuries proved to be more serious than first thought, and he would not be coming back to work. Charles had been with the company almost three years and still had his ambition of having his own company. He was now 25 years of age and thought that it was time that he did something about it. However, Matt regarded him as the kingpin of the company and as somebody who would always be there. Charles pondered over how he was to break this news to Matt. At one of their many meetings, which were mostly no more than a friendly chat, Charles thought now was as good a time as any to at least mention what his plans were. Matt was really shocked when he heard Charles's plans and practically begged him to reconsider. Charles assured him that he was not giving in his notice to leave the company and that it might be several years before he was in a position to do so.

Matt, who was now almost sixty years of age, wanted to begin to take things easy and delegate some of the workload onto younger shoulders. He decided that Charles's shoulders were just perfect for such a move.

He had no children of his own and had begun to wonder about what he would do with the company. Should he sell it? His wife, Josie, was not in very good health and did not like going on holidays and just liked to do her own thing at home. So, for Matt being at home all day was something that he could not bear to think about; he really needed the company.

Having pondered over all of these things since Charles had told him of his plans for the future, Matt had a brainwave of how he could keep Charles in the company. The next day Matt sent for Charles and, when June had shown him, he found Matt with a big smile on his face. Matt shook hands with Charles and as usual asked for two teas, telling June they should not be disturbed.

He then said, "Charles, I have been thinking long and hard about what you told me of your plans for the future and setting up your own company. I admire you for that and I know that you will be very successful. Now what I am about to propose may help you and make it easy for you to achieve your ambitions. I am willing to offer you a substantial shareholding in this company right now in exchange for a legal agreement that you will commit to staying with this company and share responsibility with me for the everyday running of the company. The substantial shareholding which I am offering you,

Charles, is initially 25% and may be increased as time goes on. I want you to take time to think of what I am offering. If you should agree to accept it there are many details to be sorted out and agreed."

Charles did not need much time to make his mind up about accepting Matt's generous offer and the details were quickly sorted out.

The company was now much more efficient and profitable since the installation of the new machinery. Orders and delivery dates were being met and there was still spare capacity on the shop floor. Charles had instructed the two salesmen to look for new opportunities, which they were now actively pursuing. Matt was very happy and enjoying himself. Most of his work-related problems had gone away and at one of the many conversations he had with Charles he hinted that he was increasing Charles's shareholding to 49%. He wanted to retain control of the company for a little longer but told Charles that as he did not have any family to leave it to, they should now both be thinking of working out a deal that would be amicable for both of them. He also praised Charles for his ingenuity at such a young age in transforming the company.

Charles and his wife Eleanor were now thinking that they should be looking to move to a larger house. They had been married for three years and they both wanted to start a family. Their current house was just on the edge of an industrial estate and was not an area for bringing up children. Charles could now see that his future was secure so they both started looking around better areas. The two areas that they liked best which were about five miles out of Slough were Farnham Royal and Farnham Common. Driving round these areas on a Sunday afternoon they saw a house which was for sale and looked absolutely stunning. They contacted the estate agent, Foxtons, and arranged a viewing, after which they decided it was their dream home. To Eleanor the price was absolutely staggering and out of their range. To Charles, who was more used to dealing and hearing of large amounts of money being discussed, he thought that it was a lot of money but that his prospects at the company were very good. He asked Foxtons if the price was negotiable and, after a positive response, put in an offer which was several thousand pounds below the asking price. Charles said, "We like the house and would love to buy it so we will be on to our building society right away to arrange a mortgage. I am not anticipating any problems and, as first-time buyers with no chain, you should accept this good offer'.'

All went well for Eleanor and Charles and eight weeks after they first saw the house, they moved in.

This was the house where their three children, Simon, Stephen, and Debra, were born and brought up. Steve was now an accountant and worked for a large company and was doing well. His father Charles hoped that he would come and work with him in the company one day. Debs was studying for A levels and wanted to be a vet.

When Mr Gatley reached sixty-four years of age, he decided that it was time to retire and find other interests to occupy his time. He was financially secure even before he worked out a deal with Charles for his shareholding in the company which was 51%. Both he and Charles had agreed that the company accountants would do a valuation of the total value of the company and, after some adjustments for overheads, warranties on machines, which they had sold in the past year but were obliged to maintain to the end of the maintenance period.

Charles had already, with Matt's approval, had long discussions with his bank for the finance for his acquisition of Matt's remaining shares.

They all had a good idea of the figures involved which were substantial. The bank had done their valuation of the company and was happy to finance Charles's acquisition.

So, the big day finally arrived, both sides' solicitors had prepared all the legal documents, then it was time for Matt and Charles to put their signatures on many dotted lines and for the bank to transfer the agreed amount of money over to Matt's account.

All of this had now been done and Charles was the sole owner of the company. He was only six months away from his thirtieth birthday.

*

Anna listened to Simon's retelling of his dad's life story. She was fascinated; in many ways it mirrored her own fathers rise from lowly beginnings to a top role in his field, now Chief Training Officer for GNER, Newcastle; all achieved through hard graft and a strong work ethic.

CHAPTER 36

Christmas

Anna and Simon continued their long-distance relationship and in one of their many calls to one another, Simon asked Anna if she had given any thought to what they mentioned when they met in Birmingham, which he said seemed like years ago. Anna said that she had and that she would really love it if they could get together again for a few days just after Christmas if it could be arranged. Simon was delighted and said that if she was happy with the Crowne Plaza again, he would book it for two nights between Christmas and New Year. Anna said, "Thank you, Simon. I can't wait to see you and I love you."

She then went on to tell him about all the work she had to do in preparation for her final exams which would be in mid-May. She said that she was reasonably happy with the progress and was confident that she would achieve a good result. Graduation day was scheduled for the last week in June at which she hoped that Simon would be there to celebrate with her and to meet her family.

Meanwhile, Cabernet & Corkscrews was going from strength to strength under Gabs' stewardship. It was now known for miles around as being the place to go for great wine – both her usual stock and her Premier Collections of finer wines which she had steadily expanded. Her monthly promotions were famed both for value and quality. She no longer had any problems about having cash on the premises overnight, as the security company had commenced their contract.

Helen and Peter's bank balance was looking healthy enough for them to afford to move house from Longbenton to a better area. That was something Anthony and Andi would love as all of their friends at Jesmond Grammar were from posher areas. Helen didn't not want to go very far from where her mother was as the memory problems had persisted.

They started to drive around the areas where they thought they might like to live in either Jesmond or even Gosforth. On one particular road, which Helen really liked, they saw a 'for sale' sign on a house. It also had a sign saying, 'view by appointment only'. This house appealed to all of them, including Anthony and Andi, so they phoned the agent and made an appointment for the next day. Anna, even though she was really busy, had seen the house on the Internet and loved it and wanted to see this house with them. She was glad to get away from her studies for an hour or two.

They all loved the house, which was a substantial 1930s detached, with bay windows and a double garage. It had been modernised just five years previously and had four bedrooms, two bathrooms, and a secluded south-facing garden at the back. It was situated on a quiet tree-lined road with off-street parking for all the residents. The asking price was more than what they thought it might be, but the agent told them that the owners were getting divorced and wanted a quick sale, so if Helen and Peter were in a position to complete soon, an offer could be made. Peter told the agent that he did not think that it would be a problem and to leave it with him for a few days to get things sorted out.

After they had left the agent, Helen suggested that as they were all together and it was Saturday, she would treat them all to lunch and that they could all give their opinions on the house. The idea of having lunch somewhere nice was approved by all. Peter drove them to the Collingwood Arms, where lunch was being served. They were given a lovely table next to the fireplace and ordered drinks. Helen told Peter that she would drive home and that he could have a drink. Peter was delighted at that and asked for a pint of beer, Anna said that she would like a glass of rose wine and Helen, Anthony, and Andi had cokes.

Just as they were about to order their meals, some familiar faces walked through the door. Marian and Graham and their youngest, Joanna, who was now ten years old, came in. When Helen saw them, she called them over and asked them to join them. The waiter pulled two tables together which was just right for what was now a party of eight. They had not seen one another for ages so they had a whole lot of ground to cover. Helen explained to them their reason for being in this neck of the woods and that they were thinking of moving to a new house and had just viewed one which they all loved. If they could get a mortgage arranged and the price agreed with the estate agent, they would really like to buy it. Marian and Graham thought it would be a very wise move as it was a very good area and house prices were always increasing. After a long and leisurely lunch, at which Peter and Graham had several drinks and Anna also had a few glasses of wine, they said cheerio to each other and promised to keep in touch a lot more.

As Peter had to go to work on the Monday, Helen said that she would go to the Newcastle Building Society or NBS local branch and try to get the ball rolling on arranging a mortgage on what she hoped would be their new home. The mortgage on their present home was almost paid off, plus the fact that they had a substantial deposit to put down on their next house made the NBS manager's decision very easy, provided the valuation of the property was accurate. The manager thanked Helen and told her to go ahead and negotiate the best possible price.

Helen, after her very positive meeting with the building society, knew she was in a strong bargaining position, especially since the owners wanted a very quick sale and they could complete the deal in about six weeks. She phoned the agent and told him that she had arranged all finances and wanted a substantial reduction in the asking price. He told her that he had authority to reduce the price by £8k for a quick sale. Helen told him that it was not enough and that she wanted a £20k reduction. He said that he could not do that but would speak with the owner. The end result was that the original asking price was reduced by £15k. Peter was delighted when he heard what Helen had done. He said that they should have a second viewing of the house and that he would take the following day off so they could have a thoroughly good look around the house. Helen thought that was a very good idea.

The sale went through very smoothly and the Johnson family moved to their beautiful new home on Beechwood Avenue, Jesmond, three months later.

It was mid-December and Anna was very excited about seeing Simon in a few weeks' time. She had had some time off from her studies because of moving house. She loved the new house and was delighted with her bedroom. However, she had to make up for the time which she lost so that at Christmas she could relax and also see Simon, so she was working every hour of the day and well into the night too.

Helen and Peter had invited Andrea, Valerie, and Martin for Sunday lunch. There were still lots of little things about the house that Helen wanted to put her stamp on; some of the light fittings and curtains which the previous owners had left, Helen now thought looked a bit dated. She also didn't like the colour of the worktops in the kitchen. When she talked it over with Peter, he mostly agreed with her but said that it was too near to Christmas to do anything now, so it was left at that for the time being.

She would have liked to have Carol and all of her family for the Sunday lunch but it would be too many for the dining room so she would have to have them again sometime. Andrea's short-term memory was really not very good but hadn't worsened; the doctors didn't think it was dementia. Valerie and Martin were both keeping well but not going on holidays very much nowadays.

Peter picked them all up in his car on the Sunday and took them to the new house for their lunch. They were absolutely thrilled when Helen showed them around and they all wished Helen, Peter, and the family the best of luck in their beautiful new home. Then it was time to get some wine going as lunch would not be ready for some time yet. Helen said to Peter that she would drive them all home so that he could have a drink. She did, however, say that she would have a glass of wine and sit and chat with their visitors for a while. Andrea told Helen that she would have liked to have bought them something for their new home, but she had no idea what to get, so she was giving Helen £100 to get something herself that she would like.

*

Christmas morning dawned in the Johnson household and they were preparing for a magical first festive season in their new home. They all adored Christmas. Helen was determined that it should be a relaxed day. Andrea had come to stay for a few days, or however long she wanted to. Helen set the table in the dining room for breakfast and told everybody to be down no later than 10 a.m. She hadn't prepared a cooked breakfast but there was plenty of orange juice, cereals, and toast.

Andrea was the first to appear at about 9.30 a.m. and Helen gave her a cup of tea while they were waiting for the others to appear.

Everybody was seated by 10 a.m. Helen wanted breakfast to be a nice leisurely affair, not like their everyday breakfasts when they would just grab a slice of toast and a cup of tea while they dashed around getting ready for work or for school. They were all delighted to have Grandma Andrea there and she looked absolutely fabulous in the new outfit that Helen had bought her.

The hour which Helen had allowed for breakfast soon went by, and then, before washing up, they had the present opening with much hugging, kissing, and thanking each other. Now it was time to clean up the dining room and get the table set for their Christmas lunch which Helen had said would be just after the Queen's Christmas broadcast at 3 p.m. With everybody helping out, all was soon shipshape again.

Peter was picking up Valerie and Martin as it was rather a long drive for Martin. They would be getting a taxi back home as everybody would have had a few drinks and would not be able to drive.

Helen and Peter were very happy with their first Christmas in their new home, as were everyone else. The Christmas dinner was lovely and went on for hours, with lots of retelling of family stories and jokes, lots of wine being poured and drank, and songs being sung all around the dining table.

CHAPTER 37

A Surprise Proposal

Christmas was now over, and Anna was on the train to Birmingham for her romantic weekend with Simon. She couldn't wait to see him again as it had been three months since they last saw each other. Anna knew that she and Simon were in a serious relationship. However, there was something which she was pondering over many times while thinking about Simon. She was deeply in love with him and knew in her heart that he was 'the one' but her problem, as she saw it, was the distance between where they lived and the fact that they both come from very loving and close-knit families. For her own part, Anna could not visualise a situation where she would move from Newcastle to London which was nearly 300 miles away. She wondered if Simon was having similar thoughts.

Anna's train arrived at New Street station about a half hour before Simon's train from London was due to arrive. She decided to wait and went to the platform where his train would arrive. When she saw him getting off, she thought he looked even better looking than how she remembered him to be. They kissed and hugged for ages before either of them said a word. Their hotel was only a few minutes' walk away from the station, so they strolled along happily, pulling their lightweight cases behind them. Having checked if they booked a table for dinner and retired to their room where they planned to have an afternoon making up for lost time.

Before starting to get dressed for dinner, Simon phoned room service and ordered a chilled bottle of expensive champagne to be brought to their room as soon as possible. The champagne arrived within a few minutes in a great bucket of ice with two champagne flutes. Their table was booked for 8 p.m. so they still had two hours to drink their bubbly and to get dressed. The waiter uncorked the champagne and then left them to pour their own. After they had gone well down the bottle, they were more inclined to cancel their dinner and stay in the room but decided against it! Their dinner was excellent and accompanied by a nice bottle of Chablis. Conversation during and after the meal, boosted by the champagne and wine, flowed very freely and covered many topics. Anna described the new house that her parents had bought and the lovely Christmas which they all enjoyed there with both her grannies and her grand -stepdad Martin.

Likewise, Simon told Anna all about his Christmas with his mum and dad and two siblings, Steve and Debs. He then went on to talk about work and surprised Anna by saying that he was actually thinking of retraining as a surgeon, in fact as a neurosurgeon. This would involve another seven years back in hospital training, rotating round different hospitals, during which time he would also have to study hard to pass his Royal College of Surgery Fellowship exams.

"There are only three areas in the UK where I could get this training Anna; the one nearest to me is London St Thomas's, another is in Southampton. and the third is in Newcastle. Anna, you and I have a whole lot to talk about whilst we are together here. You know how I feel about you, Anna, I love you so much and you matter more to me than my career. Now to help me decide what I should do, I have something to ask you."

He reached across the table and took Anna's two hands in his and looked her straight in her eyes and in a very tender and loving voice said, "Anna, will you marry me?"

Anna, although she'd had an idea that Simon may well ask her this question at some point, was absolutely stunned. However, and very near to tears, she said, "Yes Simon I will marry you. I love you so much! Whatever you decide to do in your career I will support you in every way that I can."

Simon said, "Thank you, Anna. You have made me the happiest man in the world tonight."

Simon then asked Anna if she would like it if they looked for an engagement ring tomorrow and, if so, it would be his great pleasure to buy her any ring of her choice. She said, "Thank you, Simon, but no thanks. Not just yet. I have still got my final exams in a few months' time and I think that it would be too much of a distraction right now. So, if it is okay with you, what I would really like would be for you to come to my graduation with a ring in your pocket and at the celebrations after the graduation to then give me the ring. What do you think?"

Simon was not too sure and said that it might detract from what the celebration was really about. He was certain she would achieve her goal in her final exams and her graduation symbolised all the years of hard work that she had put into achieving that result. Anna said, "Thank you, Simon. You are so considerate. However, I know that my mam and dad are so looking forward to meeting you and I might add that after everything I have told them about you and the photos they have seen of the two of us together, you can rest assured that you giving me an engagement ring on my graduation day will be the culmination of what will already be a great celebration in our family."

Simon said, "Thank you, Anna, then that's what we'll do. In that case we could still buy the ring tomorrow as we might not get another chance until after your exams and I want you to pick a ring that you really like." Anna thought that was a good idea and so they had some more wine and sat for ages and reminisced about their special time in Barbados.

*

The next morning, after a leisurely breakfast, they took a stroll around the newly refurbished Bullring shopping centre, where many of the top stores were located. Anna told Simon that she did not want him to spend a lot of money on a ring. He said, "Let us first have a look and see what is on offer."

They decided to take a look around Selfridges as they were right beside it. Anna seemed to be more interested in make-up and fashion than anything. However, Simon managed to steer her out of there eventually and headed for the famous Jewellery Quarter. They wandered into a shop and were soon approached by an assistant who wanted to help. They told him they would like to look at some engagement rings. Anna added, "We don't want anything from the high end or the very low end."

The assistant was delighted that Anna had given him that information as he did not want to ask them how much they could afford. He then sat them down on two comfy armchairs at a little table which was covered with some red velvet material. After he had determined what Anna's ring size was, he then opened a display cabinet and took out a tray which had about fifteen rings on it. After she had tried on several rings Anna found one which she liked, a simple, diamond solitaire, set in platinum. She asked Simon what he thought, and he said it was lovely and that if she was happy with it then it was definitely job done!

Anna winked at Simon and then asked the assistant what the price of the ring was and put on a very surprised look when she heard how much. She said, "Sorry, that is much more than we wanted to pay," and started to get up as if she was leaving.

The assistant then said, "Well, just a minute and I will see if the boss can give you a discount." Simon looked totally shocked that Anna, in this top jewellery shop, would even dream of asking for a discount. The assistant was back in a few minutes and said, "Yes the boss told me that I can offer you a 15% discount."

Anna replied, "That is much better. We will have the ring," and she gave Simon a peck on the cheek.

After they had left the shop Simon took Anna's hand and said, "You were just great in there, babe! I would never have thought of asking for a discount in a jewellers, especially not on an engagement ring. The discount will pay our hotel bill. What a smart girl you are."

"I'm a canny Geordie lass, Simon, I get it from me mam!" Anna giggled.

At dinner that evening, Anna looked beautiful. She had spent ages getting ready and Simon had insisted that she wore the engagement ring which she was more than happy to wear. The waiter who served them could not resist mentioning Anna's shiny new ring and congratulated them both on this happy occasion and returned a few moments later with two chilled glasses of prosecco, compliments of the house. What a very exciting day for Anna and Simon, memories of which would remain with them for a very long time.

After they had vacated their room the next morning, they still had some time before going to catch their respective trains home. Anna had now taken off her ring and put it back in the box and given it back to Simon who would officially present her with it on her graduation day.

Whilst sitting in the hotel lounge, Simon said, "Anna we have had a busy but fantastic forty-eight hours and thank you for agreeing to marry me. Now about what you called advancing my career, I have told you that there are only three areas in the country who offer what

I need and one of the three is your hometown, Newcastle. Now if it is ok with you, Anna, I would like to opt for Newcastle. Don't worry that it would be a distraction for you leading up to your final exams because you will have finished by the time I will get there. I will have to apply for a training position in the northern deanery and also give at least three months' notice at work. The practice doesn't know anything about my plans yet and will have to give me a reference for my surgical training programme, so I need to keep them sweet."

Anna was delighted at what Simon had planned and told him that was just perfect. She told him that he would receive a typical Geordie welcome whenever he arrived!

CHAPTER 38

Janet's Hour of Need

Helen had got her new home looking just great and was so happy with it, as were the rest of the family. She mentioned to Peter that they had not seen Janet or Butch for some time and thought that they should invite them for dinner and to see their new house. Peter agreed, as he always enjoyed having them over and they were very good company. Helen phoned their number several times and nobody answered it, so she thought that they were abroad again, so decided to leave it another week and try again.

The dining room, which they rarely used, had been allocated to Anna for her studies for her final exams which were not that far away. This was ideal for Anna as the room was in a quiet part of the house with little or no distractions.

Anna, as much as possible, had put the event of her two busy days in Birmingham with Simon at the back of her mind and was spending about fourteen hours a day in the dining room, studying. She was determined to get a first in her exams and would be disappointed if she did not, especially now that Simon was planning to be a neurosurgeon.

Helen found that she had a lot of spare time to do whatever she liked. Gabs was in charge of the everyday running of the wine shop, which was turning in very healthy monthly profits. The paper shop section was now being run by Stacey who had been promoted.

Gabs' boyfriend Tyler had now moved into the apartment with her and they were planning to get married the following year. Helen was worried that Gabs might want to change jobs when she married and hoped not as she would never find anybody quite like her again.

Helen's phone rang and she was surprised to see that it was an international call. She wondered who it could be. It was a very panicky lady's voice which she immediately recognised as Janet's. After some persuasion to calm down Janet told her that Butch had suffered a heart attack and was in hospital and very seriously ill. She was in a complete panic with no idea what to do. She had nobody else that she could turn to and hoped Helen could help.

Helen eventually found out from Janet that they were in Cala d'Or in Majorca. She knew that she was going to have to go there and help Janet and see what the situation was with Butch. Fortunately, both she and Peter had updated their passports, so she told Janet that she would come to Majorca on the first available flight today if at all possible. She got the address of their hotel, the hospital, and Janet's number. She told Janet she would ring her as soon as she knew anything. She then phoned Peter and told him the situation with Janet and Butch. Peter decided quickly that he should go with Helen which she was very happy about, he told her that he would finish work and come home as soon as he could.

Helen got on the internet and googled 'Majorca flight today.' EasyJet were showing a flight to Palma at 4.30 p.m., so she got on to them to see if it was still available which it was at a very reasonable price, so she booked and paid for herself and Peter on that flight. She now had to sort out with Anna who would now be in charge of the house and her two siblings until she got back, and made sure that she left Anna sufficient money to buy food and whatever else they needed.

Peter had now arrived home and was delighted that Helen had sorted out the flights at 4.30 p.m. which gave them ample time to sort out what they should take to wear even though they had no idea how long they were likely to be there. Helen then phoned Janet and told her that, provided the flight got away on time, then they would be with her at about 8.30 p.m.

Janet was so relieved and so grateful to Helen and Peter for the help they were now showing in her hour of need. She also told Helen that Butch was still very poorly, and the doctors had said that it was very much touch and go if he would recover. Their flight took off almost on time and with hardly any empty seats and landed in Palma on time. They did not have to wait for their luggage to come through as they only had hand luggage, so they were in a taxi and on their way to Janet very soon. Helen phoned Janet to say that they would be with her in about half an hour and asked if they should see her at the hotel or the hospital. Janet said that she was at the hospital and thanked Helen.

It was past visiting time when they arrived at the hospital, so they had to ask permission to be allowed in. When the receptionist heard that Helen and Peter had just flown in from England to see the patient, she was very accommodating and took them to where Butch was. She even organised some tea and biscuits for them and Janet. Helen was deeply shocked when she saw Butch who was just lying there and looked as if he was dead. She bent down and kissed him on his forehead and held his hand and, with tears running down her cheeks, she whispered, "I love you, Butch. Please don't die."

Their tea and biscuits arrived, which they were very thankful for as they'd had very little to eat or drink all day. Janet told them all about Butch's heart attack and how helpless and alone she felt. She thanked Helen and Peter for their kindness and the speed at which they had come to support and help her. She told them that the English consultant who had examined Butch that afternoon had told her that in the next 24 hours Butch could go either way, but he was not at all confident that he would recover. Because of the seriousness of his condition they had put Butch into a single room which was very good. They also told Janet that if she wanted to stay the night, they would put a bed in the room, and she could get some sleep. Helen then told Janet that she would stay with her for the night and that perhaps Peter could go back to the hotel and book a room if there were any available. Peter said, "Why don't we phone the hotel and see if they have a room?"

Helen phoned the hotel and within five minutes she had it all fixed up and so Peter booked a taxi and made his way to the hotel and asked for room service to bring some food to his room.

The second bed for Janet was then delivered to Butch's room, all made up with everything ready to sleep in. Helen insisted that Janet should lay down and try to get few hours' sleep and that she would keep her eyes on Butch who had been her friend and benefactor for many years. Helen found some Nytol tablets in her bag and insisted that Janet take two which would help her get to sleep. After Janet had dozed off, Helen moved her chair nearer to Butch and got hold of one of his hands and gave it a gently squeeze and whispered, "Butch, this is Helen," and just watched him to see if he might have remembered the name. She thought that she saw a very faint smile on his face and again said, "Butch, this is Helen." This time there was a very definite smile on his face and he even tried to open his eyes. Helen held on to his hands and whispered, "Butch, you are going to be okay."

When the night nurse came to check up on how Butch was doing, Helen told her how he had reacted when she told him who she was. The nurse said that was a good sign and said that she would tell the doctor right away. Having examined Butch, the doctor told Helen that there was a very slight improvement in his blood pressure, which was a good sign. He also told Helen to let Butch rest now for a couple of hours, after which she could then talk to him again, telling him who she was. Janet was still asleep which Helen was very happy about, so she settled down on the chair and managed to doze off for about an hour, she felt much better for it. Looking at Butch he appeared to be sleeping very peacefully and, just as she was about to get hold of his hand, he started to move slightly and opened his eyes and looked at Helen for a moment and whispered, "Helen."

She got hold of his two hands and gave him a kiss on his forehead and said, "Butch, you are a marvel. Now you must take it very easy and don't try to do anything. I will call the nurse so she can get the doctor, so for now please just relax."

Helen then pressed the buzzer to call for the nurse who responded immediately and, seeing that Butch was awake, she called the doctor. The doctor was very surprised to see that the patient was now conscious. After he had checked his blood pressure and pulse he told the nurse to give the patient a small sip of water and that he would prescribe him a morphine injection to make him sleep as he did not want him doing anything that could hamper his recovery right now.

Janet had just woken up and, seeing the doctor in the room with Helen, she panicked and got out of the bed and asked the doctor if he was dead. The doctor answered, "No he is not dead, in fact, he is very much alive.'"

After the doctor had left and Butch had fallen into a deep sleep, induced by the morphine, Helen told Janet that the doctor was amazed at how quickly Butch had rallied round from what was a very serious heart condition. It was 3.30 a.m. and Janet had had about five hours sleep and was feeling fine so now it was Helen's turn to go to bed and try to get a few hours.

Peter, after having had a good night's sleep in his lovely hotel room, arrived back at the hospital and was delighted to hear all about Butch's great recovery. He had woken up and was looking much better, however, the doctor advised that he should rest for several more days and told Janet, Helen, and Peter to go back to their hotel for the day and assured them that the patient was doing very well and would be okay.

It was now Tuesday and Butch and Janet's flight home was on Friday. Would he be out of hospital and okay to fly home on that flight? They would just have to wait and see what the doctor would say tomorrow.

The doctor said that Butch was okay to go home, and he was discharging him and that also, in his opinion, he was alright to fly. This was a great relief to Butch and Janet and also to Helen and Peter, although they did not have a flight home booked as they had not known how long they would need to be there if Butch was still poorly in hospital. Fortunately for them, when they phoned the airline there were some seats available on Butch and Janet's flight, so they settled in and enjoyed the couple of days which they had left.

The flight home was uneventful, and they were all very happy to be back home.

Tragically, about a month later, Butch had another heart attack, which this time was fatal. He was 84 years of age.

CHAPTER 39

An Honour for Jake

Jake Steadman is still with GNER. He has had two promotions and is now in a senior position in the company. The night school classes which Ginny got him into, and which he really got to like, have done wonders for him and have changed his whole demeanour. After obtaining good passes in GCSE English and Maths, he went on to take culinary skills and a St John's Ambulance Basic Life Support course, amongst other subjects. His manner of speaking is now so different from how it was when Ginny first met him. Her parents are so proud of him and also think of him as the brave man who saved the life of their only daughter from the madman with the knife. Ginny, Jake, and their daughter Emily are a very happy family who have a very nice home. They have a nice group of friends, whom they meet socially on a regular basis.

Jake was known and respected in the group, not only as the hero who saved Ginny's life, but also for his fantastic cooking. On his culinary skills course he found out that he had a flair for it and became a very popular member of the class which was made up mostly with women. The lady who ran the class was a brilliant chef as well as a very pleasant person who made the class into a very pleasurable hour for all who were involved.

Ginny was amazed at some of the treats that Jake took home from class. She herself being more academic was certainly no Nigella Lawson, but did alright on most things. On seeing some of the lovely recipes that Jake had picked at his cookery class he was soon promoted and encouraged to try them out in the kitchen. He could rustle up a three- or four-course meal with very few ingredients and in quick time.

Ginny and Jake were hosting a dinner party for six of their friends. After much discussion about the menu, they made a shopping list and on Saturday morning, accompanied by their daughter Emily, they went to the supermarket to get everything they needed, including the wine and a bottle of port. Jake told Ginny that if she liked he would cook the meal and prepare everything. She was delighted and said she would get the dining room ready and set the table. The recipe for the meal which Jake was planning was quite simple and would not take very long to cook once everything was prepared. So, after they had a light lunch, they both set about doing what they had to do. They could have done with a much bigger fridge to keep all the different ingredients cool, including the wine. However, Jake managed to fit in all that needed to be kept chilled. He then sorted out all the cooking utensils which he would need.

By mid-afternoon they had got everything looking shipshape so they decided to have a good chill out before having to get dressed for dinner and the arrival of their guests.

The guests were three couples, with four of them working in Ginny's department. They all knew the history of how she came to be married to Jake, who after all used to be a petty criminal, but of course was now a reformed and law-abiding citizen.

The other couple, who were called James and Cheryl Hartley, came into Jake and Ginny's life on an occasion many years earlier when they were having a weekend break in a lovely hotel in York.

On the Saturday morning Ginny, Jake, and Emily were having a swim in the hotel pool, as were a few other people. After having done about ten lengths of the pool Jake had enough and told Ginny that he would get out but that she and Emily could stay in as long as they liked as they were enjoying it. Ginny, who was not a very good swimmer, just liked to splash about mostly in the shallow end and was chatting to another lady who had a little daughter who was of a similar age to Emily, both of whom were having a great time together. The other little girl was called Florence, but her parents called her Flossie. Ginny and Flossie's mother, Cheryl, were now sitting on the side and just paddling their feet in the water. They had momentarily forgotten about the two girls. Flossie, who was not a very good swimmer, had followed Emily into the deep end and panicked when she could not feel the bottom. Emily had now swum to where her mam and Flossie's mam were sitting. When Cheryl saw Emily but could not see Flossie she said, "Where is Flossie?" and screamed out her name several times without getting any response. Jake, who had just dried himself off and was putting on a robe, heard this lady's screams and looked into the pool which was by now almost deserted.

He saw immediately what the panic was all about, at the bottom of the deep end he saw a little girl lying motionless. Throwing his robe off he dived into where the little girl was lying, grabbed hold of her, and got her up to the side of the pool. He then turned her over and got down and started to give her mouth to mouth resuscitation. Five rescue breaths, just as he had learned in his St John's Ambulance course. After the third really good breath Jake thought that he detected some slight sign of movement in the little girl. He checked for a pulse in her neck but could feel none. He knew he would have to begin cardiac massage. He had only ever done it on a dummy in class which was adult size and the idea of doing it on this tiny little girl terrified him. However, he knew that it was the only chance to save her life, so he pushed the heel of his hand into the centre of her chest repeatedly, counting to 15, and then gave another two breaths, covering her mouth and nose with his. He continued to work in this manner while presumably those around him summoned help; he was completely unaware of it, focusing only on bringing this girl back to life.

All this time, which seemed like hours to all who were watching, but in reality was less than a few minutes, Flossie took a breath. She coughed and water spilled out from her lungs. Jake placed her in the recovery position. She became pink. It seemed utterly miraculous. Just then the paramedics came running to the pool. Jake told them ever so quietly what he had done and then stepped back into the crowd which had now gathered. The paramedic applied an oxygen mask and examined Flossie who was breathing rapidly. He said they would take her to York Hospital where she would be well looked after and probably kept in for a day or two.

Whilst the paramedics were getting the little girl on to a stretcher a man whom Jake had never seen got hold of his hand and said, "Thank you! I am Flossie's father; you have just saved her life. We have to go with her now to the hospital, but you will be hearing from us. My name is James, James Hartley."

Jake looked at Ginny and Emily and said, "Let's go right now, I am so ready for my breakfast." Whilst waiting for their breakfast to arrive, Ginny got hold of Jake's two hands and held them tightly and said, "Jake Steadman, you are my hero and my husband and I love you so much." Emily then put her arms around Jake's neck and kissed him and said, "Thank you, Daddy, for saving Flossie's life. You are a superhero!"

Just as they finished their breakfast, a reporter and cameraman from the local paper arrived. They wanted to interview the hero who had saved the life of the little girl who had so nearly drowned in the pool. Jake told them in no uncertain terms that he did not want to be interviewed or photographed. All he had to say was that he was so happy that the little girl had made a full recovery and he wished her and her family all the best.

As they were about to sit down for dinner that evening, they were approached by Flossie's father James who assured them that Flossie was very well but that the doctor at the hospital had insisted on keeping her in for the night just to make sure that was okay. Cheryl was staying in hospital with her.

He pleaded with Jake and Ginny to join him for dinner which they did. James told them, "Jake Steadman, we will be forever grateful to you for what you did for Flossie this morning. I wish there was a way in which we could repay you for your deed of great heroism in bringing our little girl back to life."

Then Jake said, "Thank you, James, for those kind words but that is the only reward that I require. I am so happy that Flossie is okay, and I hope her little chest is not too badly bruised after the CPR. One thing though I will be eternally grateful for are the night school classes which Ginny encouraged me to go to. The basic life support class being just one of the several classes which I have attended and, thank the Lord, has this morning enabled me to save the life of your little girl."

James had tears in his eyes and thanked Jake again. In the course of the meal they found out a whole lot about each other. He and Cheryl lived in Sunderland, not a million miles from the Steadman's.

Ginny, Jake, and Emily were leaving the following morning, so they exchanged contact details and promised to keep in touch with each other, which they did and became staunch friends.

*

Their dinner guests were due to arrive in less than an hour. Jake opened a bottle of wine and poured two glasses, one for Ginny and one for himself, just enough time for them to get into a party mood. Jake's menu was very much appreciated and applauded and with the wine being generously poured, the evening was a very pleasant occasion. Emily and Flossie were now both in their early teens and had become very close friends.

The other two couples were called Muriel and Chris Longton and Frances and Joe Burton. There was much discourse during and after their excellent meal and many topics were discussed. Joe Burton was a solicitor dealing mainly with family law and in particular with children from deprived backgrounds who had been abused or neglected. His wife, Frances, was a magistrate who often had to deal with cases brought by her husband Joe. This did not in any way interfere with how she dealt with a case, even if her husband was the prosecuting solicitor. Now Frances brought up the subject of magistrates in general terms, and the fact that there was now almost a shortage of such and that she would like to see more people applying to get on the bench. "I have in mind someone that I know would make an excellent magistrate and deserves nothing less. The person I am thinking about is none other than our host here tonight, Jake. I am well aware that you did not have an ideal start in life, but you have more than repaid your debt to society, not least with your good deeds. We have here two people whom you have snatched back from death's door, one of whom is your lovely wife and in more recent times the lovely Flossie. Now, Jake, please let me put your name forward for this honour which you are well entitled to have."

Jake was absolutely astounded that anybody could even think of such a thing and was speechless for a moment. He looked at Ginny and asked her what she thought. Ginny replied that she thought he would be an outstanding magistrate, but it was entirely up to him. Jake said that with his criminal record he did not think that he would be accepted for such an honour.

Frances went on to tell Jake that his record would be disclosed in the application which she would submit to the Justice Department, together with details of how the applicant had turned his life full circle and was now an upstanding family man and pillar of the community, whom she had known for a number of years. She went on to say that she hoped that all of her friends there that night would support the application.

Frances's application, which was supported by all of her friends, for Jake to be enrolled as a magistrate was met with very mixed comments at the Justice Department. However, Frances, who was a senior magistrate, had made such a strong case for Jake to be sworn in as a magistrate that they agreed to at least interview him.

Jake was accompanied by Joe Barton at his interview. However, even without Joe, Jake made a great impression on the interview panel. They thanked Jake for his well-intentioned application and that they would let him know within a week if he was successful or not.

Jake's application was successful, and he now deals with many cases which are very similar to those he himself used to commit!

CHAPTER 40

Anna's Success

Anna had finished her exams and was waiting very anxiously for her results. She was fairly confident that she had done well but it was a case of wait and see; there was nothing else that she could do now.

She was now working at the wine shop as Gabs was having a well-earned two-week holiday and had gone to Tenerife with her boyfriend Tyler. Stacey, who was part-time at the shop, was doing the early morning shift so Anna or her mother Helen did not have to be up very early.

Simon was now almost ready to move to Newcastle to begin his surgical training and asked Anna to look for a nice flat for him, somewhere which should be convenient for her to come and visit him occasionally. Anna did not need to be told that as she knew that she would visit Simon more than occasionally!

Her hours at the shop were mounting up and she was amassing a lot of money which she was hoping would be used for a holiday with Simon soon after her graduation. After viewing several flats, all of which were not to her liking, she found one which she thought would be ideal for Simon near the Quayside. It was convenient for both the Freeman Hospital and for her. She told the landlord who the flat would be for and that it would be a one-year lease initially. She photographed the flat both outside and inside and sent the photos off to Simon who came back to her right away, replying, "It looks fantastic. I will send a deposit."

Anna's job at Cabernet & Corkscrews was just what she needed right now to keep her mind occupied. She was anxious about her exam results and also anxious, although very excited, about Simon's arrival in Geordie land.

The waiting was over, and the big day arrived when the exam results were out. Anna nervously read her results and subtly punched the air with a silent Yesss! She had got her first. She sat down and read them again to make sure and then she burst into tears. All of her fellow graduates were there to pick up their results, most of whom were jubilant and hugging one another. Others were looking gloomily at their results. One girl wailing, "My parents will go mad. I have only got a 2:2."

Anna did not mention to anybody that she had got a first until one of her many friends asked her how she had done. When she told her, the girl shouted for all to hear, "Anna got a first!"

She was hugged and kissed and congratulated by so many of her friends, but she felt sorry for those who did not do so well. She then phoned her mam who was anxiously waiting for the news. Anna was just able to whisper, "Mam, I got a first. I will be home in about an hour," and then put the phone down. Helen was glad that Anna had ended the conversation after she told her she had got a first as she was also in tears and unable to speak. Now she must organise a celebration for this evening just for the family and perhaps her mam, Andrea.

After telling her mam, Anna's next call was to Simon. His phone was on voicemail, so she simply said, "Babe, I got my first, I love you. I can't wait to see you."

On her way home Simon called her and said how delighted he was at her achievement and how lucky he was to have such a clever and lovely girl who had agreed to be his wife.

When Anna got home, Helen hugged and kissed her for ages and told her how proud she was of having such a clever daughter. After lunch they both went shopping for what Helen said she needed for a celebratory family dinner.

Anna's graduation was now only two weeks away and she had just had a message from Simon saying that he would be moving to Newcastle the week prior to her graduation which was just perfect. She asked her parents if they would like her to bring Simon home to have dinner with them on the day that he arrived. Helen said that she was thinking very much the same thing, and that they were all looking forward to meeting this mystery guy that they had heard so much about. After all, he was hundreds of miles away from home and in this strange place where the only person he would know was Anna. She said, "Yes pet, you must bring him here for dinner and a taste of our Geordie hospitality!"

Anna was really ecstatic about everything, her exam results, her wonderful family, Simon's arrival in five days' time. Life does not get better than this, she thought to herself. Now she needed to go and see the landlord of Simon's flat and hopefully get a key as she wanted to make sure that everything was okay. The flat looked stunning and she was confident that Simon would like it. She inspected the kitchen, which was small but had got everything in it. She decided to stock it up with food. On the morning he arrived, Anna was at the station in good time to meet him. Simon got off the train and before he could put his luggage down, she got hold of him and gave him a great smacker of a kiss.

Simon was over the moon with the flat and said that it was much better than the one which he had in Ealing and considerably cheaper. Anna made them both a coffee after which they tried out the bed for suitability. Anna took Simon for a stroll around the town and Quayside which, while obviously not nearly as big as London, was nevertheless very impressive.

"I always thought it was grim up North," Simon quipped, and Anna poked him in the ribs jovially. She pointed out the hospital and the University where he would be spending a lot of his time.

After they had lunch in a nice little bistro, Anna told Simon that he should go back to the apartment and have a good rest as he had a busy night ahead of him and she would pick him up at 6 p.m. She then went home where her mam and dad, Andi and Anthony, were all busy getting the house shipshape in preparation for Simon.

Helen insisted that Anna should now go and have a couple of hours rest as there was nothing more to be done until evening. Anna was delighted at what her mam had said and lay down but could not get to sleep as she had so many things on her mind. However, she did manage a little rest after which she had a quick shower and got dressed into her best jeans and a sparkly top. When she got to Simon's flat, just after 6 p.m., he was all dressed in smart casuals. Anna did not want any kisses or cuddles as she had spent ages putting on her make-up and did not want it all over Simon. Anna noticed an empty wine glass in the sink and thought that he must have done some pre-loading. She smiled to herself and thought why not?

Helen, who had been watching out for the arrival of Anna and Simon, missed them as they drove onto the drive. Anna had a key for the front door and so they just walked in and shouted, "Mam, we're here!" There was a scramble from the lounge to the hall which Helen, who was looking lovely, won followed by Peter, Andi, and Anthony.

The warmth of the welcome which Simon got left him in no doubt whatsoever that Geordies were very special people, and within half an hour he felt as though he was already a member of the lovely Johnson family.

The meal which Helen had prepared was delicious and the whole evening was a very enjoyable occasion with no awkward silences. Young Andi was clearly besotted with Simon and they all chatted away happily, helped on by a steady flow of wine from Gabs' Premier Collections. Simon knew that, so far, he had only said hello to Anthony who was sitting directly opposite him so he was next on his list to have a chat with. "So, Anthony, how's it going mate?"

Anthony, who was only 17 and was not allowed any wine but could have a few beers, was delighted that Simon had at last paid him some attention. He told Simon that he would be doing his A levels this year and that he was doing Maths, English, and Economics. Simon was impressed and encouraged Anthony to work hard at his studies and that it would all be worthwhile in the end. They talked about football; Anthony, of course, supported Newcastle who unfortunately, were not doing very well at the moment. Simon said that he was a lifelong Chelsea fan but did not go to watch them very often anymore.

Now Simon turned to his hosts, Helen and Peter. He thanked them for the delicious dinner which he had enjoyed very much. He congratulated them on their beautiful home and their lovely family. He thanked them for agreeing to let Anna go on holiday to Barbados, even though it was the last few days of his holiday before they bumped into one another. "She is a remarkable and amazing person and I congratulate her and you on her great achievement in her exams. I am so looking forward to her graduation next week."

Peter thanked Simon for his kind words and said that they too were very proud of Anna and so looking forward to her big day.

CHAPTER 41

Graduation Day

Anna's post-graduation celebration was being held at The Vermont, a trendy boutique hotel which was not very far from the university. This prompted Anna to ask Simon if he would like to ask his parents and two siblings to come and meet her and her family. They could not come to the graduation ceremony as numbers were being limited to family members only. Simon was delighted at Anna's suggestion and said that he would ring them in the morning and see if they fancied a weekend in Newcastle. After all, that was where he was going to spend the next four or five years or maybe the rest of this life. Eleanor and Charles were delighted at Simon's invitation and said they would almost certainly be able to persuade Debra and Stephen to come and meet this young lady, whom they had heard so much about, and to see where their big brother would be living for the next five years or more. They also mentioned that Stephen would probably want to drive and show off his new Range Rover.

Simon, having got confirmation from his mother that they were all excited about coming to Newcastle and meeting Anna and her family, booked them all into The Vermont. He also booked himself in as he wanted to be with his family for the time in which they would be in Newcastle.

Well the big day which Anna had for so long been dreaming about had arrived. Despite all the excitement in the Johnson household, Helen insisted that they all have a good breakfast. The graduates all had to be in position at the university by 11 a.m. The ceremony was due to start at 11.30 a.m. Anna looked beautiful in her new scarlet dress, which her mother had bought her, so all she had to do was slip on her robes and mortar board. Helen and Peter were so proud of their lovely Anna.

The graduation ceremony was a tremendous affair. Seeing all the young Engineering graduates, all dressed up in their gowns and mortarboards, looking so smart though probably a little nervous and over-awed by the magnificence of this occasion, was very special. Then, the ceremony began, and the graduates were called by their name to be presented with their diplomas and congratulated by the Vice Chancellor. The applause was almost non-stop as the names were called in quick succession. The graduates who had gained firsts were called last; there were not very many. Anna was last-but-one to be called and her eyes were searching for her family and Simon. She spotted them and heard the rapturous applause they were giving her. She locked eyes with Simon and in a split second she gave him a smile, miming, "Thank you."

The graduation ceremony was over, and the many photographs were taken. Anna and her group were on their way to the hotel, looking forward to getting to the bar. Helen ordered a gin and tonic, which prompted the others to do likewise, except Anthony who asked if he could have a beer.

Simon's family had not arrived yet but were not too far away as Charles had just phoned Simon with their ETA which was less than an hour away – just enough time for another quick drink and a bathroom trip.

Helen organised a buffet lunch, after which she thought that they would go home for a few hours and leave Simon with his family to settle into their rooms. Dinner was booked for 7.30 p.m. Just then Simon jumped up and ran to meet his family who had just come through the door.

Introductions did not take very long and Peter ordered drinks for everybody, including himself. Anna was chatting very comfortably with Eleanor, her future mother-in-law. Andi and Debs, who were of the same age, were getting along like a house on fire. Poor Anthony who did not have anybody round about his age thought that his best bet was with the men and hoped that he might get some more beer! Peter and Charles were discussing the distance between Slough and Newcastle and how long it took Stephen to do the journey. The lunch buffet was now being served and they were really ready for something to eat. The buffet was very good with a great selection of cold meats and salads and chips, which was just what they all needed after an early start.

So, the first meeting of the Johnsons and the Hallmans was a very happy and enjoyable occasion.

The Johnsons got up to leave, saying bye for now. Helen told them that their table was booked for 7.30 p.m. but she thought that they should meet at 6.30 p.m. for drinks. Her suggestion brought nods of approval from everybody. Before they parted Anna gave Simon a peck on the cheek and whispered, "Don't forget you know what!"

It was around 6.25 p.m. and Simon and Stephen were the first to come down. They were sharing a room so they thought they should go and get a head start on the others. On the way down Simon confided in Stephen that he was going to ask Anna to marry him and give her an engagement ring that night. He had an idea she was not going to say no.

When they got to the bar Simon said, "This is my round, Bro, will you have a gin and tonic?"

Stephen replied, "Yes, a large one please."

Simon said, "Me too." He also told the barman to have a few bottles of champagne ready.

Right on cue, and within two minutes of each other, the Johnson and the Hallman families arrived all looking very smart. Anna, however, really stood out. She looked stunning in a blue strapless dress and went straight to Simon who kissed her very tenderly on her lips.

The champagne started to flow, as did the conversation. This was just the perfect gathering of both families for what was Anna's big day. Simon took Anna aside and asked if she thought that he should propose before the dinner or wait until after. Anna said, "Now is as good a time as any, babe, go for it!"

Simon made sure that everybody had champagne and filled his own glass and he then asked for a bit of hush as he had something very important to do.

He then got down on one knee and got hold of Anna by her hand and said, "Anna, my darling, Anna. Will you make me the happiest man alive and marry me?"

Between joyful sobs Anna replied, "Yes, yes, yes! I will!"

He then placed the perfectly fitting ring on her left ring finger, whispering, "Thank you, Anna, I love you."

Both families erupted with excitement, hugging, kissing, and congratulating the lovely couple and each other. This was the culmination of a day in Anna's life which she would never forget, and the celebration went on well into the night, cementing the bonds between the Johnson and Hallman families, which would last forever.

THE END

ABOUT THE AUTHOR

P.J. Lowry was born in Ireland in the 1930s.

Leaving school at 14 and making his life in England from the age of 18, there was never much time for reading or books until after his retirement 20 years ago.

In 2019 he wrote his first book, his autobiography; although not published, it was produced and printed for his friends and family and was enjoyed by many.

Humble Heroes is his first novel.

Printed in Great Britain
by Amazon

59690160R00145